A Garden

OF

Glass

Blades

A Novel

M. A. Morales

All rights are held by the author

Cover designed by Miblart

Title page images by Canva

Written by M.A. Morales

Copyright © 2023 by Michelle Morales

The uploading and distribution of this book without the permission of the author is theft. Please contact the author with any inquiries as to the use of the author's intellectual property.

First Edition: December 2023

ISBNs:

979-8-9871958-6-4 (paperback)

979-8-9871958-7-1 (ebook)

For more content by this author, go to:

elleoaks.com

Send inquiries to author at

Gmail: mamoraleswrites@gmail.com

Or contact via form on elleoaks.com

Chapter One

The bronze sun rises on another day, by the grace of the gods. The soldier looks over the cliff ledge at the community of huts below. Concrete structures with no more than rusty sheets of metal for roofs. The humble living of the farmer.

The mountain village springs to life before the rays of sunshine caress the lands of their peaceful valley. He removes his map from the pocket of his overcoat. Not needing directions, for only one road leads to the village from the north, but to check that this village is the one. The last phase of his journey. The final destination. He marked off the names of the villages he passed through until he arrived here. The winding path through the mountains will lead him there. The tales and accounts of the townspeople along his way assured him in this village, Hoja Rosa, he would find who he searches for. This is the village, the home, to the warrior of the glass sword.

Ilian extinguishes the fire and rolls up his blankets, tying every last utensil and belonging to the saddle of his majestic brown and white horse. He finishes the final knot of the lasso and takes a deep breath. The day heats at a rapid pace with the harsh summer sun. Ilian makes his way down the dirt path.

Dust flies up from the road as the wind sweeps through the land. The dry earth of the valley cries for rainfall, the sight of which will not be seen until winter arrives if the gods choose not to send the blessing. The people of the valley worship different gods than those of the city. Some say for this reason the farmers live in poverty. Their prayers arrive at no more than an ethereal wall, not entering the ears of the gods. Ilian, a faithful servant to the divine Governor of Micacao, wishes those he meets will understand the error of their ways. The compassion he demonstrates to these unknowing sinners will grant him mercy and grace. The gods may forgive the villagers' ignorance. And perhaps the farmers and laborers will understand it is by their own fault, and not the government, for the poverty-stricken villages and inabilities to find opportunity for growth and progress.

Many a man, woman, and child walk past the soldier. He smiles in greeting, in return they give no more than grimaces accompanied by the seldom glare. They travel to their plots of land carrying machetes, baskets, sacks, and pots of food. Some women of the valley drape their babies to their backs, all those able needed for the harvest. Their feet drag uphill as another day of harvest steals from their energy. Their sunken in eyes and sun spotted faces prove these laborers dedicate themselves to hard work despite the empty table they meet at the end of each day.

Houses appear every now and again along the path. He arrives closer to civilization. Ilian observes with stolid face the squalid conditions. Tattered clothes dry on the canopies of bushes and saplings. Maize and bananas hang from wooden support beams, meant to prevent the metal roof from folding in on itself. Two young children play with sticks in the dirt. When their eyes meet the soldier, they drop their toys and run through the hanging blanket acting as a door. Ilian frowns, sympathy growing in his heart.

A stray wolf, rib cage protruding from its form with an outline pushing against the flesh, passes in search of food for its young. The soldier continues forward. His eyes wander the village in his curiosity. Born and raised in the city, he never strayed beyond its wall despite his occupation. As a soldier, guarding the Governor served as his primary duty. Until now.

Ilian enters the town center. Several teen boys sitting on concrete steps leading from a house smirk at the soldier, whispering their taunts and spitting in his direction. Ilian turns away and ignores it, not wishing for an altercation. Plastic bags and food scraps fill the sides of the streets. The lingering smells of fresh chicharrones, sweet bread, and burning trash piles hit in a distorting mixture. The houses do not appear richer but for the cooking pots with flowers planted within on the roofs. A second level constructed of wood, similar to those houses found outside of the capital, sit atop the concrete base. Ilian passes into the store with the structure as such. Though no more than one's house converted to sell goods, the owners make a sufficient living off these wages alone.

"Good day," he greets, the middle-aged woman bowing her head in respect of his class. "I'll take a jar of milk, bar soap, half a kilo of rice, and cinnamon, if you will."

The shopkeeper rises from her stool to search the shelves of her store for the items on his list. Every few seconds, she glances in his direction, either to check that he does not steal or in worry of his silent judgments of her humble establishment. One by one she places the items on the wooden countertop the local carpenter constructed for her. Ilian licks his lips in thinking about his sweet treat of rice and milk. He has eaten nothing but stale tortillas and beans for days. His sweet tooth calls to him for attention, desiring the only treat he can recall with the little he has tied to his horse.

Ilian withdraws a gold piece from his pocket and the shopkeeper's eyes bulge at the sight. He gives the piece to her. She stares in confusion, not having the means to give him change. The woman knows her humble store and any savings she possesses would not be sufficient.

"The change is yours," Ilian says with a smile. The shopkeeper bows her head in thanks. The soldier turns to leave but then stops himself. "Do you know anything of the warrior with the glass sword?"

The shopkeeper slips the gold piece into her brassiere and nods.

"Can you tell me about her?"

The shopkeeper hesitates. Ilian sighs. He puts his hand into his pocket, withdrawing another gold piece. Ilian slides the coin across the countertop. The shopkeeper looks into his eyes, wondering if she is meant to grab it. Her hand slides toward it, Ilian withdrawing his own, knowing she's accepted the bribe.

"Her name is Cordaya," the woman says as she examines her second gold piece. She rolls it around in her hands in the joy which the money will bring her family. "She's the laborer, though more so the adopted child, of Ernesto and Nelida Morez. Take the road that leads further down the mountain. They live around the first curve. A large bougainvillea bush near the steps to their porch."

"Thank y-"

"Good luck catchin' her. She's probably working."

"Yes. Thank you for your assistance," Ilian bows and exits the store. He ties the bag to his horse, and they continue down the path.

The litter filling the road grows scant the further they travel from the busy town center. The houses lack the improvement. Wooden shutters hang limp from the windowsills. Tarps with coffee beans drying in the sun occupy one side of the road, the dust from the dry season and passerby like a fine powder on top. Ilian notices a pack of stray wolves approach. They glare and growl at the soldier, no more than intimidation in their territory. The soldier pays no attention, despite clutching the saber at his side should he need it.

Ahead, he notices the bougainvillea bush in full bloom, its salmon flowers adding a pleasant scent to the air and refreshing color to the community of unpainted, aged houses. Ilian observes the supposed home of the warrior. No sign of prestige nor honor visible on the stained concrete walls or the pile of lumber scattered out front. Ilian gazes at the house, wondering if this is truly his final destination.

Not that he expected to find a castle or palace constructed of diamonds or gold in rural Micacao. However, he did expect more of a famed warrior. The stories and legends the other villagers told of mentioned she may be the child of god and man. The daughter of a demi-goddess of war with mortal man. The soldier shook his head at the ridiculous thought. The warrior, this Cordaya, may be strong, but she is mortal. This house, with its lack of riches and pride suggest just that.

Ilian approaches the house and knocks on the cerulean, metal door. No answer. As mentioned by the shopkeeper, all residents went to work. He knocks again with the same result. Ilian sits on the concrete block acting as a step to the porch, wondering what his next move will be. He notices an older woman walking down the street with a basket of cabbages on her head. He rushes to her aid.

"Allow me to assist, mam," Ilian says as he lifts the basket from the woman's head, the wicker scraping his chest as he struggles to hold on. The basket slips in his grip, wondering if he'll make it to the woman's residence. He wonders how the woman managed to make it from town, if not further, without the weight crushing her thin neck. Some from the city spoke of the village people's incredible strength, though Ilian mistook their jests of invisible muscles as no more than slurs. Ilian peers at the white-haired woman, with a small frame and wrists so thin he knew they would not take much to break. The origin of her strength within the shell.

"Thank you, kind gentleman," she responds with a frail voice. She offers a smile. Empty spaces exist where teeth rotted had fallen out. The soldier returns the smile with gritted teeth and clenched jaw, his fingers going numb. "Right there on the porch is fine," she says, pointing to the house of the warrior.

Ilian releases a breath of relief, the distance not near as far as he expected to travel. He drops the basket on the porch, hearing a crack of the wicker underneath. A cabbage hops the edge, but the soldier catches it before it touches the ground. He puts his hands on his hips and takes deep breaths, attempting to calm his heart. He fans at his face, refusing to remove his indigo uniform jacket, made of a thick cotton which causes him to sweat, believing it indecent to undress before the elderly woman. The uniform was not only a show of status but of loyalty to the Governor. Ilian takes a seat next to the older woman.

"Do you live here?" he asks, hoping he had found a resident of the house.

"No, no. This is my youngest sister's house," she replies, coughing up phlegm with her response. Ilian looks away, ashamed to think that many of the trained soldiers, younger and in better health than the woman, could not compete in terms of stamina. "I'm droppin' off a couple of heads for her. Can you believe they're charging fifteen copper each? They say the heat. Ay, this summer's been a hot one. Hot, hot, hot every day."

"Yes, I can imagine. The rays feel harsh here in the valley."

"They say the forest spirits are punishing us. The priests call us to take to the land, care for our crops and the forests. I see youngins like you throwing trash all over the place. Just remember to do your part. We all have to."

"Yes, mam. The act of littering is uncivilized."

Her smile drops and she gazes at him with his response. She examines his uniform and looks toward the road. Ilian bites his lip in irritation at his formalities, understanding his vocabulary and higher-class grant to him a greater vision of the world. But he must limit his intellect if he wishes to bond with the villagers, their education stunted in comparison to his own, which causes pity to course through him.

"Mam. Would you tell me of the young lady who lives with your sister?"

"Their worker? You talk about Cordaya?"

"Yes, mam. Who is she? Where did she come from?"

"Yes," the woman starts, staring at the clear sky. She licks her cracked lips and swallows the saliva build up in her mouth. "Cordaya... She's a quiet one. Barely eats. Work, work, work. Say she's the fastest there is. I don't doubt it. She can fill a basket of coffee beans in an hour my sister tells me."

"And what of her fighting? Does she train here?"

"No, no. We do not permit violence here in the town. She has the blessings of the Gods to protect our people."

"Is she human?"

"Excuse me?"

A series of loud screams fill the air. People run down the street from the town center, panic worn on their faces. They grasp the hands of their children and seek shelter. Smoke rises. Ilian stands and squints, trying to see what could be happening. The older woman uses Ilian's leg to pull herself up. She abandons her basket of cabbages and takes off. Ilian watches after her, confused by the chaos. He grabs the arm of a young boy running past, stopping him in his tracks.

"Why do you run?"

"The bad men are here. They're destroying the stores and houses. Killing all in sight. Let go of me," the boy speaks at a rapid pace and attempts to shake Ilian's hand free from his arm.

"What of the town's armies? Where are those set to protect the town?"

"You soldiers really are stupid."

He breaks of Ilian's grasp and darts down the road. The soldier throws on his jacket, removes his saber from its holster, and jogs uphill. A group of women in long skirts and sandals stumble as they run, their shrill screams burning into Ilian's mind. A barbarian chases after them and grows nearer every second. Ilian delivers his prayers to the gods and intervenes.

"Stop right there, brute," he commands, holding his blade in front of him as a threat if the barbarian refuses to listen. The barbarian slows to a stop and unsheathes his own weapon. A straight blade made of steel. Their weapons glimmer in the sunlight, the harsh heat only adding to Ilian's irritation.

"I see. The gov'nor's sent his dogs to deal with us. Well, we'll show 'im."

"I demand you and your people to stop terrorizing these citizens."

"You think we take orders from dogs. I'll stick you like the gallos."

The barbarian swings his blade back and forth in intimidation. Ilian notices a sliver of extra shine where the blade meets the guard.

"Alexandrite in the blade... only one nation I know of does that..." Ilian mumbles, staring in confusion. As the barbarian suggests, their tribes work alone, bands of thieves marauding small towns and villages. But their weapons suggest otherwise.

"Who sent you?" Ilian asks. The question bursts with the strength of a command that comes with consequences if unanswered.

"We ain't nobody's dogs. I'll show you."

The barbarian charges the soldier. Ilian strikes the blade with his own, dodging the attack. He kicks at the barbarian, clad in thick leather for protection, making contact with his core and pushing him back. The barbarian rises and commits to another charge. He slices through the air with his blade, glaring into the eyes of the soldier. Ilian holds his saber in front of him and takes a deep breath, focusing his energy and strength into his counterattack. The barbarian swings at his head. Ilian slices and ducks, cutting the wrists of the barbarian. The enemy drops his sword and screams in pain. Ilian delivers a swift act of mercy into the barbarian's gut. His enemy falls to the dry earth, saturating it with his own blood. Ilian gazes upon his opponent.

The yells of the villagers ring out in the center above. Black smoke clouds the sun. Ilian dashes to the scene, uncertain of the probability of his victory given he is only one soldier amongst many barbarians.

He slows to a creeping step when he enters the town center. Houses burn. Blankets torn down from their position in the windows and doors lay in shreds in the streets. Shattered glass litters the roads. Children cry in the alleyways, not knowing when they will meet their fate. Ilian sees the bloodied corpse of the shopkeeper in the doorway to her store. He offers a prayer that she may be forgiven.

"Hey! It's the governor's dog!" a barbarian yells to his comrades.

A group of three march up the street. Leading the way is a brute dressed in fine, sturdy leather with a sigil burnt into the chest piece. An eagle. They flash their blades, made with the same alexandrite sliver as the other. This proves to Ilian the piece had not been stolen but gifted.

"The gov is sending his dogs to protect the people now, is he? Since when did he care 'bout the country folk?" the leader jests.

Ilian wishes to defend the governor but does not wish to admit that his role is not to protect the people but as a messenger. He thinks through a response, not wishing to stain the blessed name of the governor.

"Our governor does what he can to protect the people of his lands," Ilian states.

As the words pass his lips, he second guesses them. Before today, he would have proudly declared to all the nations this exact statement. But as Ilian gazes upon the destruction, the pillaging of the innocent and razing of their town, he wonders. Where were the soldiers to protect these people? It pained him to look upon the sight.

"Oh, right. That's why they're living in cracked, old shacks. These people ain't even worth our time. How much you think we gain from towns like these, huh? Barely even to make a living, I'll tell you that much. Good thing we like our jobs."

The group bellows at this last line. Their laughs ring through the empty town, echoing in Ilian's skull. He glares at the barbarians, gripping his sword in ferocity. Their leader notices his aggression and decides to force him to action.

"Is the dog angry? Let's teach him who the real masters are."

They step forward, but one freezes in his tracks. With a groan of pain, all turn to see a blade protruding from his abdomen, blood trickling from his mouth and wound. The blade draws back and the barbarian collapses. Behind him stands a woman with copper skin and hair darker than obsidian pulled back from her face. Her eyes form no more than slits as she glares at the barbarians, knowing of the destruction they've caused.

"The warrior of the glass sword..." Ilian whispers, looking upon her in awe.

The leader of the barbarians flashes his sword at her, passing it from hand to hand in his confidence. The warrior does not move her eyes from his form. They blaze like the lava in the chamber of a volcano, intense and bright. Her sword reflects the sunlight, gazing upon her all the more difficult. The blade, clear as a crystal in color, drips blood from its smooth edge, drinking the liquid to satisfy its thirst. A sword bestowed upon her from the gods.

"A young miss like you should've run away with the rest of 'em. No? But now you've killed one of my own. No mercy for you, eh."

The barbarian lunges at her with his sword. She swings her own, pushing his away. Her breathing is controlled, releasing an exhale upon the strike, inhaling deeply moments before. They circle one another. The barbarian slices at her. She ducks and swipes at his feet with her leg. He falls to the ground, and she pierces the blade through his skull. Ilian's jaw drops. Her facial expression remains unchanged. Serious yet determined. She does not find joy in the task, but she performs her duty nonetheless.

The last standing barbarians sneak to close in from different sides to strike. Ilian jumps into the fray. The barbarian behind swings down to slash the skull of the warrior, but Ilian's blade intercepts the attack. He grabs the collar of the brute's shirt and pulls him back. The barbarian spits his curse to the ground and lunges at the soldier. They exchange throws, blade crashing blade, the metallic collisions ringing through the air. Their battle calls more barbarians to the scene.

The warrior with the glass sword wastes no time. She dodges the attack of the brute in front of her, slashing his chest as she slides past. Her eyes focus on her next opponent. She runs forward, lips sealed and sword steadied. Ilian cannot help but glance amidst his own battle, the glare of the crystal sword in the sunlight blinding.

The oncoming barbarians attempt to shield their eyes from the glare, knowing if they lose track of the warrior it could be their end. But she understands it is their end, glare or not. Not even the rain would drown the fire burning in her soul. Resolve ignites her spirit, the gods granting her the strength she needs.

Ilian returns his eyes in time to leap back from an attack. The tip of his opponent's blade punishing his lack of focus. Ilian grabs his side, knowing the injury to be minimal, but the blood screams as it escapes without care. Ilian grimaces while dodging another attack. The soldier tightens his grip and slices the air and into the shoulder of the barbarian. A scream of pain mixed with his battle cry, the barbarian throws his body weight at the soldier.

"You dog!"

Ilian gives pause, waiting for the perfect opportunity. Mid leap, the barbarian will not be able to change direction. The soldier waits. Every millisecond counts. When the clock strikes, Ilian releases his force upon the barbarian. He brings his fists together and smashes the head of his enemy with the pommel of his saber. The barbarian hits the ground and Ilian delivers a swift death.

The warrior with the glass sword stands like a statue amidst the fallen brutes. The ground around her puddles with the blood of her enemies. Her sword shines brighter than before, despite its position in her shadow. She stands, paralyzed, not a cut nor scrape upon her flesh. Flawless but for her raw fingers from picking coffee beans earlier. The sweat trails down her forehead.

She sheaths her sword and unwraps the bundle of fabric she had tied around her midsection. It cascades into a long piece of fabric, decorated with the image of yellow lilies. She wraps it about herself, transforming the fabric into a full-length skirt which hides the brown tights underneath. She gazes at the barbarians a final time and continues her trek through the village to help and defend those of her town.

Ilian watches as she leaves, not knowing what to do. He does not wish to approach her, for her senses may still be heightened after the battle. But he does not wish that she gets away. His loyalty to the governor comes first, and he chases after her.

"Cordaya, wait!" he yells after her. She turns back with wide eyes, wondering how he knew her name. Her pace quickens. She rounds the corner down a side street, and he manages to grab a hold of her arm. Her eyes meet his. He clenches his jaw, the fury in her expression casting fear within him. She yanks her arm from his grasp but remains in the same position, staring at the soldier in contempt.

"I've been searching for you. The warrior of the glass sword. I've come from the capital to take you to the Governor. He requests your presence."

"I decline the offer."

Her words, though mumbled, are stark and straight forward. She turns her back and begins to walk away when Ilian calls after her.

"It's not an invitation, fair warrior. The Governor requests your presence. It's a formal command, if you will."

"And I decline," she answers with her back to him. She marches forward, scanning the streets for any other malicious presences.

The soldier, frozen to his place, can do no more than peer after her. Confusion circles about his head. He thought denying a request from the Governor to be impossible. The mere significance of His Grace's name should spark action and inspiration into even the weakest and most fragile of souls. And yet the warrior walks on, insulting the capital that protects them.

Ilian shakes his head. He cannot return to the capital without her. A strategy is necessary. Ilian takes a knee and prays, knowing the gods will provide him the answer.

Chapter Two

I lian struts downhill to the house. He notices some of his bags missing from the saddle of his horse. He swallows a curse and glances down the road, wondering if the uncivilized thieves had gotten far. His stomach growls in complaint of the sweet treat that may never arrive.

With a sigh, he loosens the knot of his satchel and withdraws mixed grain bread and a sealed bowl of isich baked beans with onion. Not the food he is accustomed to, considered the poor man's meal in the city. But it was all the family at the last home he stayed at had to offer for his journey. The people, although living with the bare minimum they could afford, offered all Ilian would need to feel comfortable. No hotel in the city acted as hospitable. Ilian left his tip, after their many refusals but acceptance through grace. Ilian takes a seat on the porch and eats his lunch.

He notices an older couple, bandannas covering their head from the harsh rays and bags and pots in hand. Sweat drips down their faces, dirt covers their hands. The man squints his eyes at the soldier on the steps, tightening the grip of his machete. Ilian rises. He gazes at the house and then at the couple, realizing this must be their residence. He brushes the breadcrumbs from his uniform and returns the empty bowl to his satchel, licking his teeth beneath closed lips to remove any food caught in the crevices.

"Hello, fine citizens," Ilian flashes his charming smile and slightly moves his chest so the sun reflects from his pin, drawing attention to his status. "Are you the Morezes?"

"That is correct," the man replies with a dry throat, his tone low and calm. "Who are you? Tax collector? Census taker? Or has the governor decided our village deserves protecting now?"

"I am-"

"We don't need your kind around here."

"Ernesto, be kind," his wife whispers as she whacks his arm with the back of her hand. "He's sweating to death, blood on his jacket, and no doubt needs a drink of fresh water." Her voice raises to speak to the soldier. "Come on inside. Excuse our messy house. It's not like those you're used to, I suppose."

Ilian gulps, wondering of her husband's reaction. But he walks past Ilian and unlocks the door, motioning for the soldier to go in. Ilian bows his head in thanks and enters their humble homestead.

The floor, made of a slab of concrete, glistens with the faded bulb hanging from above. Small insects fly about, sacks of vegetables and crates of fruit on the floor against the wall. Ilian looks around for the gas stove and cooler box, unable to spot them. Nelida Morez enters through the corridor from another section of the house. She approaches an H-shape structure of concrete blocks with a thin sheet of metal on top. She places lumber in the top hole and ignites it with a piece of sapwood. As the metal heats, she dips a cup into a tall pot of water and brings it to the soldier.

"Take a seat and rest yourself," the woman says as she pulls out an old wooden chair at the table.

Ilian slips off his uniform jacket, unable to bear the heat any longer, places it on the back of the chair, and sits down, his eyes curiously observing the space. He watches as Nelida opens the door to the hutch and removes a covered bucket. She places it next to her stove and removes the lid, placing it nearby. She rolls the dough into a ball and then presses down. Her hands, experienced in the craft, make a perfect circle, which she places on the heated metal to cook the tortillas. Nelida notices Ilian's smile.

"Do you know who left the cabbages on the porch?"

"Yes, mam. Your sister. She ran when the brutes began their attack."

"She'll be back then. Ernesto! Bring the cabbages inside!"

Ilian takes a sip of his water, not knowing how to fill the silence. He hopes the warrior will return. The sooner he gets her to the capital, the better standings he'll be at with the Governor.

"Where are you from?"

"I come from the capital. The Governor sent me on a mission."

"The capital, huh?" Nelida giggles. "Sure is different here than in your capital. Us poor people must be an eyesore."

"No, mam. It fills me with pity and compassion, surely. But I would never think to insult your class of people."

"Our class? Hmm." Nelida glances at the soldier before moving her eyes back to the tortillas, flipping them by hand as they cook.

"Is this the first attack to hit this village?"

"They've tried before. But it appears these barbarians were clever. Managed to destroy houses and kill in the town center."

"And this village has no alarms? No trained officers? No armory of weapons in emergency?"

Nelida giggles and shakes her head. Ilian bites his lip, not wishing to insult her jests of his rational thoughts. The entire situation lingers in a place foreign to the soldier. Despite living in the same nation, their living conditions and protections differ unimaginably. Opposite ends of the spectrum. Did the gods punish as so? It all appeared... unfair.

"When did you meet Cordaya?"

Nelida's face rises, an expression of shock upon it. Her eyes turn to no more than slits as she tries to read Ilian. The purpose of his supposed mission hazes the air.

"Well," Nelida Morez licks her lips and wipes the sweat from her forehead, the heat from the stove brushing her bronze skin. "She was very young when she knocked on our door asking for work. Maybe four years old. Alone. Her hair was messy, and her clothes were many sizes too big. But her skin was flawless. We asked where her parents were. She didn't know. All she knew was that she wanted to work. So, we did just that. We gave her a place to stay and food to eat. She never left. She's like the child we always wanted but never could have. She was our gift from the gods."

Ilian averts his eyes, not wishing to talk religion at the moment. He thinks about her words, the circumstances of Cordaya's origins. Not even the warrior knew of her parents or birthplace. It's no wonder legend forms about her deeds and life.

Ernesto Morez enters through the door and sets the basket of cabbages on top of a sack of potatoes. Newly showered and bare chested, Ernesto accepts the drink his wife prepares for him and takes a seat.

"So, soldier, eh? What is a soldier like you doing in these parts?"

"I'm on a mission from the Governor, sir."

"That pin there means you're a palace guard, doesn't it? Why would he send a guard as a messenger?"

"I suppose the Governor trusted in me, sir."

"What brought you to my house, soldier?"

"Ernesto-"

"I have a right to know-"

"Yes, you do. I came here to find Cordaya. Story has spread of her abilities. She's the warrior of the glass sword. As so they speak of her in all parts. The Governor wishes to meet with her."

"I've known Cordaya a long time," Ernesto says with a smirk on his face. "I can assure you, she has no interest in meeting your governor."

"It is not an invitation," Ilian responds, his hands clenching into fists, his teeth gritting. "It is my duty as a member of the Governor's guard to fulfill any requests he has. I am to take Cordaya to him. Whether she wishes so or not."

Nelida wears an expression of concern, but Ernesto's shows his amusement.

"Right. Well... good luck with that."

Ernesto walks out the door to the porch. Ilian hears the footsteps of another and a mumbling of voices. Cordaya enters, her eyes like daggers piercing through Ilian's spirit. She looks to Nelida, speaking through no more than brain waves to check if she is okay. Nelida offers a gentle smile and continues baking tortillas.

Ilian stares at the table. All his efforts brought him here, right to her house. He had defeated hundreds of intruders, divulged the plans of countless assassins, yet he could not develop a strategy on how to lead the warrior to the governor. He rests his elbows on the table and places his head within them.

Nelida places a plate of rice, beans, and fresh tortillas in front of the soldier.

"Eat up. You look starved."

"Thank you, mam."

Ilian places his hands together and prays to the grace and mercy of the gods before accepting the food. His snack earlier did not but subdue his hunger which found its way to the surface again. He stares at his food, plotting in his head how best to complete his mission. The idea strikes him, though he is unsure it will work.

"Excuse me, Mrs. Nelida?"

"Yes?"

She sets another plate on the table across from his. Cordaya walks in and kneels at her chair. Ilian watches as she prays, mesmerized by her focus and commitment. The warrior rises with a glance in his direction before taking her seat. She shoves handfuls of rice and bean into her mouth, her tortilla her utensil. Ilian looks away, not wishing for his thoughts to insult the warrior if she really has been chosen by the gods.

"Yes, soldier?" Nelida Morez asks, pulling him to attention.

"Yes, Mrs. Morez. Might I ask the favor of renting a space to stay in your homestead whilst I am here in the village. I will pay."

Cordaya freezes, her ears attentive, listening for Nelida's answer. Nelida peers at Cordaya and then at the door her husband left through earlier. With mouth open, she searches for her answer.

"And I'll work for free."

Ilian glances at Cordaya who closes her eyes, knowing the answer Nelida should and will give.

"I'm sure we can find space for you," Nelida answers with an endearing smile. She understands his motives but chooses to trust that the soldier will learn. In his adaptation to their poor village, she hopes his eyes will open to a whole new world. A lesson he can take back to his governor.

"Thank you, mam. And you may address me by my name. Ilian."

"Well, Ilian. Make yourself right at home."

Cordaya rolls her eyes. She uses her tortilla to scrape the last pieces of rice and bean and carries her empty bowl away to wash it. Ilian stares after her.

He cannot explain how she fascinates him so, but when in his presence, he can't help but look at her. Though no goddess of vanity, she possesses a strength and power unknown to any mortal. Ilian wonders of the circumstances of her birth, of her parents, of when she learned she had a gift.

Ernesto Morez walks through the door and takes a seat.

"My love, we need to clear the old storeroom for our new guest," Nelida says with a tilt of the head at Ilian. Ernesto does not appear surprised, rather waves his hand to let her know he'll get to it. "And he'll be joining us tomorrow. Maybe he can collect the lumber while Cordaya and I clean the coffee beans."

With slanted eyes, Ernesto observes the soldier.

"You're a fit boy, aren't you?"

"First in my physical training class. That is why I'm a personal guard of the Governor."

"Then you'll have no problem bringing that pile of lumber in from outside. Just stick it under there," Ernesto instructs as he points to the space underneath the stove.

Ilian nods. His mind and heart whimper as he takes orders from another. But he must follow through. This is the only plan he has. And it cannot fail.

"Yes, sir," Ilian responds. He finishes his meal and stands with bowl in hand.

"Leave that there, Ilian. Cordaya can clean that right up," Nelida says. Ilian bows his head, offers his thanks to the gods above for his full stomach, and heads outside to collect the lumber.

Cordaya sits on the porch, staring at the forests and mountains in the distance.

"It's a beautiful view, isn't it?" Ilian asks in a soft tone, not wishing to scare her.

She nods as a response. Not one of many words.

"We don't have views like that in the city. Nothing but buildings and people, a lot of people. All the time. Not peaceful and quiet like here."

"Yeah, barbarian attacks are real peaceful," Cordaya states in a sarcastic tone. "I'm sure you don't get those in the city."

"No, no we don't." Ilian takes a moment of silence before continuing. "The brutes would never think to attack because of our military force. They would fall in seconds, as if asking for their own deaths."

"You speak as if they deserve to die."

"Don't they? They pillage and raze villages, kill innocents... The gods do not condone such acts-"

"Amazing you speak of the gods while you worship a man who sits on a throne supported by our backs and bare hands and ignores our existence."

"The gods chose Governor Caseto as their divine representative on this abysmal planet. He will bring peace and justice to the nations."

"Peace? There is an ongoing war in the countryside, and he chooses to ignore it."

"This is not his war. I understand as little as you do about why these barbarians are attacking villages and small towns."

"But you saw it. And you choose to deny it."

Ilian pauses to think about her words. The image of the sword with the alexandrite sliver enters his mind. The design of the weapons used in Niekalarah, a bordering nation not far from the villages being attacked. No more than a few mountains separate him and the nation now. Ilian shakes his head. He works close with the Governor. There may be conflict in trades but no talks of war between the nations. There must be another rational cause for the attacks.

"You insult my gods but look where your gods have left you. Why aren't they protecting you and your people?"

Cordaya turns her head to the ground and goes silent. She bites her lip in anger and frustration. Ilian takes a bundle of logs into the house and returns to find her in the same position. She had not left the argument, or she would have physically walked away. Or perhaps it's a stubborn, territorial wrath. Ilian stares at her.

"The gods sent me on a mission to find you. That is why Governor Caseto wishes to speak with you. The gods have instructed him to do so. We cannot deny their requests. Greater punishment may fall upon your people if we do not obey."

Cordaya's eyes meet his. The rich cocoa color of her irises blends into her pupils. She peers into the depths of his soul, unearthing the truth within him, attempting to bury her own truth.

"Have you ever talked to the gods?"

Ilian looks at her in confusion as if the question amuses him yet begs the question of her own beliefs.

"No." His simple, honest answer. "I have not heard their voices. But I have felt their presences. I know them to exist, and I will do as their word teaches. And I will do as His Grace, the Governor, commands. Do not doubt in my faith."

"I do not doubt your faith, only question its existence and place in our world."

Her last words linger in the air.

Our world.

Not hers. Not his. Not of any one person but of every.

Her tone bled with innocence, asking for a forgiveness if offensive.

Cordaya closes her eyes and absorbs the sounds and the scents through her pores. The soldier watches her in observation. Her wisdom and assurance stretch beyond the fabrics of their world, as if the universal truths bind together to form her being. Yet, he cannot prevent his pride from fuming. Ilian takes a deep breath, knowing he cannot anger with her if he wishes to succeed in his quest.

He picks the last of the lumber from the ground, ensuring to lift every last piece so he does not have to return. Stacking the branches and sticks in the space under the fire pit, Ilian works fast, the heat brushing his face adding to his irritation. He wipes the drops of sweat from his forehead and the speckles of bark and dirt from his hands.

Nelida sits at the table with two bowls in front of her. One contains unopened, dried bean shells and the other beans she removes from within, throwing the dried shells to the ground. Ilian takes his seat across from her and helps. On his first attempt, he slices his finger, the dried shell sharper than he thought. Nelida's eyes meet his, and she demonstrates how to do it. With both hands, she pushes with her thumbs where the shell comes together and then pulls apart. Ilian, wondering why he had not done it as so in the first place, picks up his next and follows her steps. The shell splits without much force, the beans within falling out. He scoops them up and puts them in the bowl, grabbing a handful of unopened shells and placing them in front of him. Nelida grins.

"Mrs. Morez," Ilian begins after he accustoms himself to the task, a conversation not a sufficient distraction to slow his hands. "I do not wish to get too political, but can you tell me when these attacks began? As far back as you can remember."

"The barbarian raids? We've had troubles with them for centuries now. But, recently, in the past six months, they've gotten worse."

"Worse? How so?"

"They've been happening more often, and in larger groups. Before it was the same few tribes making threats and asking for ransoms. In these past months, they ask for nothing in return. They just want to see destruction."

"But what do they gain from simply destroying?"

"I'm no politician," Nelida says with raised eyebrows at Ilian, as if knowing he will deny her opinions to protect his Governor. "But I feel these attacks are political. They're gaining something by wreaking havoc. It's their purpose. Their mission."

"And these towns and villages have absolutely no defenses, even with the threat of future attack?"

"With what money would we do that, may I ask? As of now our disciplinary force is made of volunteers, and only when they have time. Listen. Our people are descended from ancient tribes of warriors. We all have a bit of warrior in us. When they come, every man, woman, and child grab their weapons and defend what is ours. It's all we can do. Each other. That's all we've got."

Ilian releases a swift exhale, wishing to retort but unable to find suitable words. Another of the dried shells slices under his fingernail. He winces and shakes his hand with the sharp pain. Nelida ignores it, focusing on the work in front of her. The bowl fills with beans. Ilian thinks they arrive at the end when Nelida removes a handful more from the sack at her side.

"And Cordaya... She's not married?"

Nelida laughs. She shakes her head and glances at the soldier with suspicious eyes.

"No, no. Don't go thinking she's undesirable. She's had many an offer."

"I would never think that," Ilian answers with a straight face. Nelida raises an eyebrow. Ilian reddens in the face and clears his throat. "That she's undesirable, that is. I would never think that. But I wonder why she has not accepted any offers. Surely there are gentlemen in this village."

"She says we're the only family she'll ever need. Absolutely no interest in any of them. I doubt she even thinks about getting married and having children. Work. It's all she ever wants to do. Work. It's probably all she ever thinks about."

A new strategy enters Ilian's mind, though he wipes it away, knowing it will not work if Nelida speaks the truth. And yet he understands after his short talks with Cordaya that it is not so. Her mind wanders as a hummingbird through the landscape in search of sweet nectar. She dips a cup into the countless fountains of knowledge, through her work and expression of faith. It all comes together to nourish her. Cordaya exists beyond the humans of this world. Perhaps a divine being sent by the gods, similar but not equal to the Governor. Her rough beauty, calloused hands with a flawless copper face that glows as the gods shine the rays upon her. Hair like soft strands of obsidian, scraped from the volcano's wrath and transformed into fine threads. Ilian knows why they believe her to be a demigoddess. For there are no other natural explanations sufficient outside of the divine to categorize the warrior of the glass sword.

"As a child, Cordaya never believed me that school and worship were important. I had to bribe her with work. That's the only way she'd go. When her grades slipped, I told her she couldn't come with us to our plots of land unless she improved her scores." Nelida giggles. "And what do you know? Not a month later and she went from being the bottom of her class straight to the top. Teachers couldn't believe it."

Nelida takes the full bowl of beans to her food preparation table and brings an empty bowl, which hangs from nails on the wall, back to the table with her. She takes her seat and continues.

"Worship was different. After convincing her to attend her first service, she wanted to keep going back. Cordaya watched and listened in awe as the leader talked of the gods and spirits. She came home and constructed her own altar in dedication and thanks to them."

"And what exactly do you all believe?" Ilian asks, trying to mask his doubt with an open mind.

Nelida looks at him with a shocked expression, knowing the people of the capital to have a fervent affirmation of their religion with plenty of doubts cast upon others. She shares a grin of appreciation and takes a deep breath, for this may be her only chance to convert or at least instill the belief of a member of the higher class.

"As most belief systems, we believe many gods work together, each with their own purpose in making our world function. Sometimes they bless us. Other times they punish. They operate from the heavens, using spirits as their messengers and laborers. In Hoja Rosa, the god which affects us most is the God of the Forest. His wishes determine the yield of our harvest."

Nelida bites her lip, carefully deciding each word before it leaves her mouth. She peers into the soldier's eyes. Ilian notices the tears build up.

"They're angry with us, Ilian. The gods are angry."

"You think they're the ones sending the barbarians?" the soldier asks, confused. Nelida shakes her head, her bottom lip quivering and the tears forming waterfalls down her cheeks.

"The attackers are cutting down trees, burning fields. They take from the land without thanks. Our people, in their desperation, are beginning to do the same. The spirits of the forest are angry at us. Punishing us. Soon they will rise against us, Ilian. Cordaya does what she can to protect and preserve these lands. But she is only one. I'm afraid her efforts won't be enough."

Ilian reaches out and grabs Nelida's hand. The comforting sensation soothes the woman and she takes a deep breath.

"I will not let your people fall or allow your home to be taken from you. You have shown great hospitality, the gods notice this whether you worship them or not. I will not let Cordaya fall. I will protect her. I promise."

Nelida bows her head in thanks and they return to their work in silence.

Chapter Three

Ilian wakes up the next morning with a stiff neck and a collection of bites on his legs. He shivers as he thought he'd only need one blanket, for the concrete walls radiate immense heat after having absorbed the sun's rays all day. But the morning meets him with its cool, brisk air. He swings his legs over the edge of his mattress, which sits no more than a few inches from the floor. With a deep breath, he dresses himself before heading to wash.

Ilian wipes his face clean. The smell of black beans and fresh tortilla meets his nose. His hands grasp the concrete water tank. He stares into its depths, the light catching the dust particles floating on the surface. Scooping into its water with the designated bowl, Ilian cups a handful of the cold water and splashes his face. Drying his skin with a nearby towel, Ilian keeps his eyes closed, listening to his surroundings. The chickens call as the sun's light escapes from behind the mountains. Workers talk as they pass on their way to work. He hears the chatter of Nelida and Ernesto in the kitchen. Ilian takes a deep breath, knowing he's entered no dream.

Ilian makes his bed before heading to the kitchen. Passing through the dark corridor, he enters into the light and warmth of the concrete room. His senses awaken and his mouth waters as he sees the food Nelida prepares.

"Good morning, Ilian. Hope you slept well," Nelida greets as she places his plate on the table.

"Good morning, Mr. Morez. Mrs. Morez. And yes. Thank you for your generous hospitality."

"Just wait til we put you to work today," Ernesto chuckles, taking a drink from his cup of coffee.

"Ernesto, Ilian looks like a strong, young man. It's not gonna kill him," Nelida says, wagging her wooden spoon at her husband. Ilian smiles. "Do you have a change of clothes, or only that uniform?"

"I have others," Ilian answers, chewing his beans and tortilla before answering. "I wear this uniform as a symbol of pride and faith in the Governor."

"You're not gonna need much pride in the middle of the forest," Ernesto says with raised eyebrows. "I suggest you change. You'll sweat up an ocean in that thick uniform jacket. You want long sleeves, but a light fabric. Something you don't mind dirtying."

Ilian takes a deep breath, understanding they know more of this work than him. "Yes, sir."

He'll listen to their words of wisdom for today. But he understands they underestimate his strength. He spent years training as a soldier, his muscles built and formed to perform physical tasks. Ilian smirks as he thinks of the shock they'll wear when he demonstrates his abilities. They may compare him to Cordaya, who is known as the fastest worker in these parts.

They finish their coffee and prepare to leave. Ilian looks around.

"Where's Cordaya?" he asks, having not seen her all morning.

"She was working a different job early this morning. Said she'll meet us," Ernesto responds, securing his baskets and sacks with lasso to his person. Nelida carries a tweed tote and a metal pot of food. "You take the machetes," Ernesto instructs the soldier.

Ilian picks up the machetes, sheathed in a simple leather pocket with a thick string hanging from a loop. He hangs it over his shoulders and helps carry the other supplies in his personal satchel. He keeps his saber on his belt, Nelida and Ernesto glancing at the weapon from time to time, knowing its purpose is not intended for the work they will be performing.

They nod at one another when ready and walk uphill.

Many who live in the town center started the morning cleaning the mess left by the barbarians the day before. The dead have been placed on the tables within their homes, a leader of the church passing from house to house to bless the dead and gift them safe passage on their journeys to the heavens. Ilian bows his head and issues his own prayer, begging the gods to forgive their ignorance.

Once out of the town, they take a thin dirt path off road and up the mountainside. Ilian's feet slip as they climb, no solid ground to grip. The dry earth runs downhill as they trod upward. Ilian follows from behind and watches as Nelida and Ernesto ascend with ease, Nelida in no more than thin, worn-out sandals. The fresh air of the misty morning caresses his exposed cheeks. The flowering trees and weeds add purples and yellows to the landscape. Ilian smiles at its natural beauty.

After five minutes of hiking, Ilian breathes heavily, his sides hurting. Exhausted. The older couple climb, as they've done several times before, no troubles. Ilian shakes his head in shame. But a grin manages to find its way to his face. The irony, he thinks, that a young soldier cannot endure the scaling of a mountainside when those more than double his age could.

They arrive at a wide road at the top and follow it to another snaking, dirt road, leading down the other side of the mountain. The sun heats the air of day as it performs its own tiresome work, never failing to deliver full intensity in the valley.

"The gods have incredible endurance," Ilian whispers to himself. He refuses to stop despite his legs trembling and his lungs aching. The soldier trudges forward, awaiting the collapse when they arrive at long last.

They arrive at a clearing in the forest. A dirt circle with old ash in the center and logs placed around. Nelida and Ernesto place their possessions on the ground and take a seat on the logs. Ilian gives his thanks to the gods. He stares at the log nearest him, wondering if he'll be able to stand again afterwards.

"Take a rest, Ilian. We won't start for awhile," Nelida says, easing his thoughts. Ilian inhales deeply and collapses onto the log. Never had a hard wood surface felt so comfortable.

Ilian observes the forest, many coffee trees filled the plot, along with those of banana and mandarin. He absorbs the cool breeze in the shade through his pores, calming his heart and breathing. The longer he sits, his legs transform into gelatin. No training had prepared him for this. Soldiers traveled on roads, mounting their horses if they grew tired. Their stamina paled in comparison to the laborers of the mountains.

Ernesto stands and ties a basket about his waist. He tightens the lasso as well as he can and hangs a small sack from his shoulder. Grabbing a few larger sacks, Ernesto examines the land, strategizing the best plan for tackling the area.

"I'll start at the right and work to the left... No, no.... I'll start at the bottom and work up," Ernesto decides, rubbing his sweaty brow. Nelida nods with a smile.

"Just like always, Ern. No need to over think it."

"Yep. Well, let's get to it."

Ilian watches as Ernesto works his way down the mountainside and begins his day's labor. Ernesto picks the red coffee fruit from the trees, placing every one in his basket as he goes. When he happens upon a green, immature fruit, the man places it in the small sack to his side. As he gets into the motions of the work again, his hands do no more than slide along the branches, the fruits finding their way to the correct place. He works from the bottom of the plant to the top, making certain not to miss or drop even one fruit. Ilian analyzes the plants, noticing the scarce amount of fruit they bear. Nelida, who also watches, frowns.

"They don't give fruit like they used to," she says in a solemn tone. "Even the newer plants. Maybe it's a plague. Other workers have said the same thing. These trees used to fill with fruit. Not anymore. Ten days. Before it took the three of us ten days to harvest the fruits from the trees. Last year it took us seven. This year is even worse."

"And you believe the gods are responsible?"

"The forest spirits allow us to use their lands to grow our food and crops necessary to live. But, when we damage the land, dump our waste, cut down trees, burn entire mountainsides, they anger with us all."

"That is why we must continue to thank the spirits and give offerings to appease them," Cordaya says, setting her bag on the ground and sitting near Nelida. Ilian wonders when she arrived, having not heard her footsteps as she drew near. Nelida, accustomed to Cordaya's silent entrances, shares a smile and wraps an arm about the warrior.

"It doesn't seem to be helping," Ilian responds as he thinks about Nelida's words. Cordaya bites her lip and shakes her head. Nelida's smile drops.

"Things could be much worse, Ilian. That is why we thank them, no matter the complaints we could make. Things could be much worse," Nelida says, her eyes masking a sadness and foresight his own must lack.

Cordaya stretches her arms and stands, Nelida following her lead. They make their way to a small creek running through the land, nearby a large, wooden tub. Ilian rises, with difficulty and pain, and walks over to watch the process. Cordaya fills a bucket with water and dumps it into the tub, which is filled with slimy coffee beans they will be cleaning.

Nelida moves her hands in the water, removing the pulp from the beans. Tiny sticks and leaves rise to the top as Cordaya fills the tub. They remove the contaminants from their coffee, Nelida using her arm to stir the water about. Her fingers scrape the sides of the tub, every piece as important as the other. The slime covers her arms, taking care not to splash the water on her clothes. Cordaya places the bucket on the ground and helps Nelida with the cleaning process. Her hands move with lightning speed as she removes the twigs and leaves, along with the empty shells of the coffee fruit that fell in during the depulping process.

Ilian smiles as he watches, never having seen the process before. Everyone in the capital drinks coffee, but he is certain none know of the work behind it. Nelida grins, hoping Ilian to grow in his understanding of the work of the laborers of the nation. Cordaya pays him no attention, her work more important than worrying about what he may think.

"I think that's good," Nelida says, pulling her hands from the pulpy water. "We'll give it another go and then bag it."

Cordaya nods and reaches further into the tub. With one hand she unscrews a cap from the outside, the hand within blocking the hole to prevent the beans from flowing with the water. The dirty water splashes to the ground like a powerful tsunami. Cordaya bites her lip with the force, despite having done the work many times before. When the stream grows thin and the tub empties, Cordaya screws the cap to block the hole and grabs the bucket to start the process once more.

"I'll begin my work then, I suppose," Ilian states, nodding to the working women. He stretches his arms and removes his machete.

"Only those branches and sticks you find on the ground. We wouldn't wish to anger the forest spirits," Nelida instructs with a light tone.

"Right..." Ilian says, sliding the machete through its leather pocket. As he turns, he raises his eyebrows and releases an airy chuckle.

He walks through the Morez's plot of land, told the yucca spikes signified the border on all sides. He kicks about the dead leaves, scavenging for the sticks underneath. He jumps as the large insects and spiders run from his kicking feet, their disturbed homes crashing and crunching with his footsteps. He grabs the sticks from the ground, collecting them in his arm. His abdomen and back scream in pain as he bends over time and time again. His duties as soldier involved him standing guard, observation duties done in a cushioned chair at times. He starts to miss those days but realizes his mission is far from complete.

Ilian looks ahead and sees a circle of geraniums and petunias. The breeze brings the sweet scent to his nose, the smell of decomposing coffee shells near the cleaning tub finally leaving. A tall coffee tree stands in the middle of the ring, untouched by Ernesto as he makes his way uphill. Unlike the others, fruits fill the branches, the leaves shining like emeralds in the sun. Ilian steps near and touches one of the fruits.

"What are you doing?"

Ilian turns to see Cordaya behind, three beautiful, glowing mandarins in her hand. Ilian wipes the sweat from his forehead, thinking about a sweet juice made from the fruits to hydrate himself. Cordaya glares at him as she sets the mandarins at the base of the tree and offers a prayer. The soldier observes her, marveling at her faith despite their conditions.

"How often do you make these offerings?" Ilian asks as Cordaya stands and gazes at the tree.

"As often as I can," she responds, guilt lacing her voice as though the answer is insufficient. Ilian puts a hand on her shoulder.

"I'm certain the gods are grateful."

She brushes his hand away and shakes her head.

"I can ask for forgiveness of the sins of my family and myself, but my offerings will not cover for all of those of the village."

"But they are grateful for your attempts. Why would they gift you the glass sword otherwise?"

Cordaya closes her eyes and releases a vocalized exhale. Upon opening them, her eyes scan the blooming flowers, the reds, pinks, and purples a sign of hope in the landscape. The forest spirits had not abandoned them yet. She glances at the tree, full of fruit.

"The sword is not a gift," Cordaya says. She opens her mouth to speak but promptly closes it, unable to find the necessary words. She shakes her head. "Nelida invites you to join us for lunch should you be hungry."

Ilian's stomach growls at the sound of the word. The thought of food brings the scents of fried beans and tamalitos, no more than cooked balls of corn dough, fly to him in the air.

"What do you mean it's not a gift?" he asks, trying not to grow distracted by his hunger. "Your fighting abilities compare to none I know of in the guard. No blade reaches your skin, no cut nor scratch to be seen after any fights. A sword of glass is nothing other than legend. A gift from the gods."

"I don't wish to hear it. Especially from one who does not believe in my gods."

"No matter our beliefs, I cannot deny that you are gifted, Cordaya."

"Being able to kill and fight is not a gift. It is a curse that I must protect those the gods would otherwise punish. That violence is the only solution they have given me to solve our problems."

"But it doesn't have to be," Ilian interrupts with enthusiasm, the light in the tunnel reaching him. His chance arrived. "Violence does not have to be the only answer. Come with me. To the capital. We can talk with the Governor and find other solutions. You will find him to be wise and compassionate. He will listen. We will find a-"

"There is nothing your governor can do to help us. He ignited this flame. The gods anger with the rulers of these nations, destroying and killing in their pride and greed. Acting as gods of the world. You question their anger-"

"Then why don't they punish us? Why only your kind?"

"Because my kind do not have the money nor the means to prevent this. We have no voice-"

"You do. That is exactly what the Governor is offering. He wants to meet with you to give your people a voice."

"I represent no one. I am a servant to the gods, their spirits and to no one else."

"Why don't you give it a chance? Nothing bad can come from talking."

"And abandoning the villages I'm sworn to protect in this time of war is wise? Who will protect these villages if not I?"

"We will ask the Governor to send his armies. They can fight this battle better than an individual. Even if you are the warrior of the glass sword. It's too risky."

"I'm not afraid of my death, Ilian." The soldier pauses and steps back. It was the first he'd heard her say his name. Cordaya takes a deep breath and recollects herself. "Nations rise and fall. So it has been since the beginning of time. But something darker is at work here. Unless I figure out what, it won't just be me or you. Life as we know it will end. The gods do not wish for that. Neither do I."

She turns and walks to the clearing. Nelida kneels by the heated ash of the fire, warming the tamalitos wrapped in banana leaf. The woman smiles as they approach. Ernesto holds his bowl of beans, utilizing a flat wood chip as a spoon.

"Here's yours, Ilian," Nelida offers him a bowl full of beans. Cordaya fixes her own, grabbing a tamalito from the ashes, and takes a seat. Ilian accepts his bowl, bowing his head in thanks and sits before eating his lunch.

The soldier observes the small pile of sticks he collected thus far and shakes his head. He looks over and sees Ernesto has filled a sack with the mature coffee fruit. Though his eyes wander to find a distraction, Cordaya's words echo in his ears. Had the Governor known, by message of the gods, about the fate the warrior spoke of? The Governor knew the gravity of the situation, the reason why he chose his top guard. But no fear covered the face of His Grace, nor did his tone suggest urgency. The command issued was no different than ordinary, only a harsher tone would have come was his dinner served later than usual.

Ilian stares into the ashes. The glowing coals remind him of the lava flowing from a volcano. The mountain range not far from here includes a few active volcanoes, sleeping and in wait of their chamber's pressure to grow beyond control. Ilian wonders if the gods anger enough if they'll trigger an eruption. Or perhaps a massive earthquake, for small tremors were quite common in the area. The gods could perform any number of horrors if punishment was their aim.

The soldier finishes his lunch and returns to work. The others stare at him, as they absorb the shade and relax before throwing themselves into work again. Nelida and Ernesto share a smile, wondering if the soldier begins to understand their livelihoods. Cordaya takes off in the direction to continue cleaning the coffee beans. The old couple share confused expressions, wondering what may have been said between the two, wondering in the silence of their lunch. Ernesto shrugs and stretches before heading to where he left off.

Ilian grunts as he bends over to grab a piece of log, a large stack of sticks and branches in his arms. The sun descends after having reached its peak not long before. Sweat drips from the soldier, happy he listened to the couple's words of wisdom about clothing choice. If he had brought his uniform, he'd be working in no more than his underclothes by now. When his arms tire from the weight he carries, Ilian returns to the clearing to drop his findings into the pile.

Cordaya stands near the equipment, tying a lasso about herself to secure a basket. She glances at him when he drops the sticks and examines his work.

"Are you going to help?" Ilian asks, taking a seat to rest his aching body. Cordaya notices his pain.

"I'm going to cut some beans from the stalks," she replies, tying the final knot in the lasso. She starts to walk away when she turns to face the soldier. He looks up at her and their eyes meet. "I'll take you there. The home of the forest spirits."

"You know where they live?"

"It's a sacred place. Few know of it. Those who do understand the importance of preserving it. I happened to stumble upon it five years back. I want you to come with me."

Ilian squints, trying to see through a lie for his doubts in their gods fed his uncertainty. However, the longer he observes the warrior, he sees the truth glimmer like crystal in her eyes. His eyes move to the ground in deep thought. To most it would be an honor, but he feels like it may be a trap. Cordaya averts her eyes, knowing it would be risky to take him there. But she knows he must see it for himself.

"Cordaya. I believe in different gods than your people. I do not want my own to think I have betrayed them through conversion-"

"If you come, I will go with you to your capital. I will speak with your governor. You are right. As a single individual, I cannot do this alone. We must find the root of the problem. The cause for the gods' anger. Help me and I will meet with your leader."

Ilian's eyes widen. He knows what he must do.

Chapter Four

The roosters crow as a new day dawns. Ilian fights to open his eyes. His body cries in pain as he sits up. He flexes his arms, his muscles screaming underneath his skin. He grits his teeth. Running his hands along his shoulders, Ilian feels the indentation of the lasso from the day before. Carrying the weight of the lumber he collected during the day on his back at the end, as if he hadn't exhausted himself already. He prayed to the gods every second of their way home to give him strength.

The smell of fried onion and eggs finds its way to him. His stomach growls for nourishment to rebuild his torn muscles. Ilian wishes to sleep once more, finding comfort in the thin mattress after a hard day's work. He had never slept so well, passing so quickly into the dream realm. To think he'd face another day, the same work, the same torture.

Ilian readies himself and heads to the kitchen. Nelida sits alone at the table, sipping at a cup of coffee and nibbling at a piece of sweet bread. She shares a smile as Ilian enters in hunched form.

"How are you feeling?"

"I'm well," Ilian lies, not wanting to be seen as weak. As a soldier of the royal guard, this type of work was often joked about. If only he had known then what he knows now. "And yourself?" he questions, trying to prevent his voice from cracking as he takes steps toward the table.

"I'm doing just fine, dear," Nelida says. She stands and walks to the concrete stove, a covered pan sitting atop the metal containing his warm breakfast. Ilian's mouth waters at the sight. He never thought this class of food would look appealing to him. He hadn't eaten meat in days, craving a plate-sized, well-done steak in his weakness.

"And your husband?"

"He went to help with some cleanup of the town center before we head out today. There were nine deaths this last attack. Three of them children," Nelida says in a melancholic tone, shaking her head.

"I am sorry for the loss your village has faced due to these attacks."

"Not only ours, but many villages have faced far worse destruction than our own," Nelida's sensitive eyes brim with tears. "If it weren't for Cordaya, there may be no villages left in these mountain ranges."

"What of the governor's soldiers on the border?" Ilian asks.

In his thoughts the day before, he wondered why the soldiers based on the borders of Micacao did nothing to stop the trespassing of the barbarian troops. Perhaps they died in trying to stop the brutes. But that thought stood on the brink of impossibility seeing their more advanced weaponry and numbers. No message had even been sent to the capital about the attacks until the legend of the warrior with the glass sword spread. The barbarians must have found an entry point unguarded. It was the only plausible answer.

Nelida stares at Ilian in confusion, his perspective of the situation far different from their own. She thinks of her words with care, not wishing to insult the soldier.

"Many have said that the soldiers at the borders have begun accepting bribes."

Ilian shakes his head and laughs at the nonsense. The character of one of the Governor's army must have a strict moral code and loyalty to their nation. They are trained not only in body but in mind. They swear an oath and may the punishment of the gods be upon them should they break it. To suggest bribery is not only an offense to the soldiers but to the Governor and the gods as well.

"I apologize for the outburst, but I fear these rumors only work to further depreciate the value of our Governor and his godly work in this nation. Certainly, there are bad seeds that may begin to grow within our ranks, but the generals are certain to eradicate those weeds at first sight," Ilian says with utmost enthusiasm and trust in his comrades. Nelida offers a gentle grin and returns her attention to her drink. Ilian composes himself, taking a bite of the delicious fried egg. His stomach and taste buds savor every bite and yet his thoughts seek to ruin his meal.

The sound of Ernesto returning sends Nelida to her feet. She peeks her head out the door and mumbles indistinct words to her husband.

Ilian finishes his sweet bread and mentally prepares for the day ahead. They told him his day would be easier. His job: Picking coffee fruit from the trees. It didn't appear a difficult task, as one stood in the same spot while picking the fruit from the branches. Ilian breathes easy, knowing the journey to the plot would test his true strength and endurance as a soldier.

"Ready?" Ernesto asks as he enters the kitchen eating a banana.

"Yes, Mr. Morez."

"Then let's get to it."

They tie to their backs those things which they took the day before, but their load includes more baskets for all will be harvesting today. Ilian looks around and finds that Cordaya, once more, started the day before the rest of them. He wonders where she finds her energy.

When they arrive at the plot of land, Ilian takes a seat without hesitation. His legs burn, the raw muscles punishing him for giving them insufficient rest. But Ilian finds the hike decreased in distance. Perhaps this was due to the fact that he lacked anticipation in wondering when they would get the chance to rest. He knows what to expect, not that his legs scream any less.

"Let's get your basket fitted to you," Ernesto says, motioning for Ilian to come to him. Ilian looks to the ground in disappointment, having desired more time to rest. He walks to Ernesto Morez and stands with his arms outstretched. Ernesto observes him in amusement. "Give me a lasso with a pad attached, Nelida."

His wife does as he asks. Ernesto wraps the rope about Ilian's waist, the pad resting on his lower back. The pad is no more than folded up bits of an old sack, but he prefers it to the rope digging into him as the basket fills. Ernesto motions his finger and Nelida gives him a basket. Ernesto passes the rope through the loops on the sides of the basket and ties it off. He tightens the knot further and further, ensuring the basket will not fall during Ilian's work. The soldier grunts as the rounded edge of the basket digs into his stomach.

"Tight enough for you?" Ernesto asks, shaking the basket up and down, side to side, to see if the rope loosened with his force. Ilian grunts again. He holds up a thumb to show it is secure, not wishing his irritated tone to cause problems. "Good."

Ilian takes a seat and watches as Nelida and Ernesto tighten their baskets to themselves. They move with great speed, much quicker than it took to secure his own. Their many years of experience assist with their pace, even in their older age. Each nearing their sixties, and all Ilian can do is marvel at their condition and determination to work. Not that the couple have much choice. Cordaya is their only laborer outside of themselves, their profits from the harvest what they use to survive until the next year's harvest.

Nelida leads Ilian to the section where Ernesto left off the day before. They take a moment to look around and enjoy the breeze passing by, knowing in no time the sun will turn their cool day into an inferno. The birds and insects sing nearby, their songs for the spirits of the forest. Nelida grabs a branch and clears her throat, ready to begin the explanation.

"When you pick the coffee fruit from the tree, you want to use your thumbs in a snapping motion to remove it. One by one. We don't want the whole ball of fruit falling in the basket at the same time, it's harder to take the shells off that way. Jams the machine. If it does happen, just break apart the stems."

Nelida demonstrates with patience, letting Ilian try to see if he's got it. Ilian plucks at the fruits. He finds the more mature they are, the easier they fall from the system of stems. His large fingers, though strong in grasping a sword, lack nimbleness. The fruits fall to the ground rather than land in the basket. Nelida bends over to pick them up.

"It isn't a race. Take your time. As the day goes on, I'm sure you'll get faster. And the small sack hanging to your side is for the green fruits. There shouldn't be many, but when you come across them, pick 'em and stick 'em in the small sack. When your basket fills, we've got larger sacks you can dump it into."

Ilian shares a grateful smile, though again finds frustration that the task is harder than it looks. He glances at Mr. Morez, whose fingers barely brush along the fruit before they fall from the plant and straight into his basket. Nelida starts on a plant next to the one they've started, leaving Ilian to finish it. As he tries to pick the fruit, the force in his fingers break the shell and the beans within come flying out. He clenches his jaw in panic and quickly hides it amongst the others in his basket.

After a few minutes, Cordaya makes her way down the slope, basket tied and ready to go. Her eyes meet Ilian, who shares a smile she chooses not to reciprocate. Her hands dirtied from her earlier work, Cordaya finds a tree nearby and begins to pick the fruit from its branches. Ilian thought Ernesto made the job look easy. Cordaya's hands move like lightning along the branches. He barely notices the fruits fall into the basket as she goes, every once in a while moving her hand to the small sack at her side to deposit the green.

Ilian examines the plant in front of him, wondering the best way to complete the task. He squats down to the lower branches, trying to position the basket under the fruit he currently picks. The higher branches hit him in the face, the leaves caressing his neck and cheeks. He shakes his head, trying to get a clear visual on the fruits he picks near the trunk so he does not miss one.

Beginning to feel confident, he works his way down the branch, plucking the fruits from their tiny stems one by one. He stands and starts on the next branch, then the next. When he finishes one side, he rotates to the other, an accomplished grin spreading across his face. It does not last long, for he looks over and sees Cordaya has her basket more than a quarter filled. He looks down at his own, the fruits barely covering the wicker bottom. Ilian ignores it, or so he attempts to convince himself, and squats to start this side of the tree.

While picking the coffee from the plant, he notices fruit he left behind on the other side. He growls in irritation. Nelida glances at the soldier and a proud, motherly smile spreads across her face. She slows her pace, not wishing to get far from Ilian if he happens upon a question. Another fruit falls to the ground, Ilian biting his lip to hold back a curse. A silent giggle issues from Nelida as she turns her head to hide it.

At long last, Ilian picks the final red fruit from the limbs of the coffee plants and moves to the next. He looks down at his basket, satisfaction filling him in seeing the coffee fruits piling up.

The sun creeps higher into the sky, the days growing hotter as summer approaches. Ilian wipes the sweat from his forehead and hunches over to reach for the fruit in the lower branches. As his basket fills, the back pain returns. His legs grow tired, but he concentrates on his work. He looks down at his basket. Almost full.

With a deep breath he pushes forward. When he finds his rhythm, an interruption breaks his focus.

"Ilian, time to break for lunch. Go ahead and empty your basket and head on up," Nelida says as she slips off her own empty basket and goes to warm the food. Ilian turns and sees that Ernesto and Cordaya continue, probably waiting for the food to warm before heading up.

The soldier tops off his basket with the last of the fruits on the plant he works from and walks to the sack, dumping the mature into one and the green into another. He fights with the knot in the lasso, grunting as the wicker edge of the basket digs into his stomach, raw from the weight pushed against it for the past few hours. As Ilian heads to the clearing, he glances at Cordaya, who is well on her way to filling her basket for the third time. He grins and shakes his head.

He walks to the creek they used to wash the beans with the day before, to clean the dirt and sticky pulp from his fingers. He splashes his face with the cool water, taking a deep breath as it absorbs into his pores. The soldier licks his lips, salty and rough. His stomach calls to him, the scent of the warming food always finding its way to him in his moments of hunger.

Ilian takes his seat on a log and spreads out his legs, hoping they rest before heading back to work. He arches backward, cracking his stressed back and limbs. Nelida offers him a cup of water, which he readily accepts.

"So, this is what you all do every year?" Ilian asks, his eyes scanning the forest, attempting to calculate how much they've finished and what remains. Nelida nods as she stirs the beans. Ilian leans forward, resting his elbows on his knees. A gentle breeze finds him, and unfortunately carries the smoke from the fire pit to his face. He coughs.

"What do you think?" Nelida asks, her eyes meeting his. With every day's work, her skin darkens and the wrinkles around her eyes grow more prominent. He smiles.

"About what do you refer?"

"The work. The land. Nature. What do you think about it all?"

"It's definitely different than the work I am accustomed to. I thought my body would perform well in this work, but it seems I have all the wrong muscles trained in terms of strength."

"It is different, yes. And everything in this world takes time to get used to."

"In terms of nature, I've always enjoyed being amongst the trees and the serenity of a quiet, starry night."

"But you never picture the countryside with poverty and trash in those visions of tranquility, or yes?"

Ilian looks to the ground. Guilt fills his eyes. In truth, whenever the images of the countryside enter his mind, he ignores the negative bits. As if they don't exist, he sweeps himself away with his dreams of beautiful flowers filling a forested landscape, silence and isolation. A vast difference to the crowded city. Ilian lets out a large exhale and dons a sympathetic grin. Nelida understands.

"Sometimes always finding the good in things is a problem, too, you know. How can we fix the bad if we continue to ignore it?" Nelida says, scooping beans on to a plate for the soldier. He accepts it and picks up his tamalito heating on the ashes.

Ilian averts his eyes from the woman, believing she could read his mind. However, she doesn't refer to him explicitly, more so discussing the topic as if it were a widespread pandemic.

Ilian hates how he can never go a meal without so many thoughts flooding his head. Like a tsunami, they smash and crash his very ideals. All he's ever known. In his meditation and prayers, the soldier asks for strength and patience. Open-mindedness. The trials he face challenge him, tempting and swaying his cause from that which he swore upon. He is a royal soldier. A high-ranking member of the guard. Ilian refuses to allow these obstacles become roadblocks. He knows his path, thanks be to the gods and His Grace. He will perform his duties at all costs. No matter the opposition.

The crunching of the dead leaves occurs behind as Ernesto and Cordaya join them for lunch. They pour water from a jug to wash their hands, the dirt and pulp running to the ground. Ernesto accepts his bowl and Cordaya hers. She holds the plate firm in her hands and closes her eyes as she mumbles her prayer of thanks. Nelida, as always, serves herself last.

"How are your fingers holding up?" Ernesto asks before slurping at his beans. Ilian looks up from his bowl and nods his head.

"They're fine-"

"You've got soft skin still. Just wait until it toughens up a bit."

Ilian bites his tongue at the comment. The term "soft hands" in the city referring to the young ladies. He understands the sentiment and takes minimal offense. Cordaya glances between the two, examining Ilian's hands for a second before turning her eyes back to her meal.

"I think he's got potential, Ernesto. He's already faster than those laborers from Cooducahm."

"Yeah, but they're lazy workers who want high pay for sitting around. No wonder their economy is worse off than ours."

"Ernesto," Nelida says with a shocked expression. She gives her husband the expression that tempts him to pass his limits to see what punishment he lands. Rather, the wise husband closes his mouth and moves from the thought. Nelida continues. "What I meant was that Ilian is a fast worker. He'll find his rhythm in no time."

Ilian grins at her compliment, knowing the woman can say nothing unkind or without gentleness in her tone. Her character and personality differs from his mother, whose callous and harsh words brought tears to his eyes almost every day of his childhood. However, thanks to his parents he grew stronger. He would have never been made a member of the royal guard without their support.

"I'll get the hang of it," Ilian says, coughing to clear his throat after for his insecurity in speaking casually.

He was never one to stray from an educated vocabulary, his own comrades often joking with him about it. However, Ernesto and Nelida turn to one another with confused expressions which transform into smiles. Ernesto lets out a laugh, choking on a bean, once stuck in his tooth now in his throat.

Ilian displays a nervous grin and continues. "I wish you all to not think ill of the royal soldiers. We are strong. Trained for near impossible tasks. This is no more than exercising the finger's strength."

Ernesto rolls his eyes, the smile dropping. Cordaya places her tamalito into her bowl of beans and scowls at the soldier.

"You have no idea or respect for what we do," she says, wrath lacing her tone as she tries to contain the bittered flames. Ernesto holds up his hand and she stops, her breathing heavy as her heart races. Ilian gazes at her in confusion, having meant no harm with his comment.

"We'll see about that, soldier. Two days ain't nothing compared to a lifetime. You haven't even had to carry that full sack up the hill to the road yet. Then we'll see how handy your training is," Ernesto says with a tip of his head.

Ilian glances at Nelida, who wears a sympathetic grin. He cannot determine whether her husband's statement is a threat or truth, but he figures come the end of the day his sore muscles will find out.

When they return to work, Ilian feels refreshed and ready to go. His fingers move faster than before, the fruits falling in their place. A grin spreads on Ilian's face as he thinks he may understand the best way to go about this type of work. His heart calms as his pride swells, watching his basket fill at a much faster speed than earlier. As he moves from one plant to the next, he glances at the tree designated as a shrine to the gods.

Fruit fills its branches, large, crimson, and round, ready to fall with the slightest of touch. Ilian knows his basket would fill from that one tree alone, the collection of coffee fruits forming balls all the way up the branches. Truly a plant blessed by the gods for the gods. The temptation grows as Ilian eyes the plant. He shakes his head and continues his work, filling a basket and then beginning on the next.

At the end of the day, the four laborers tie off the sacks, creating four fulls and leaving them with one partial of mature and one full of green. Ernesto tightens the string about the top of his sack and Cordaya hers. Nelida takes their baskets and heads to the clearing to pack up their belongings. Ilian watches as they throw their lassos about the sacks, laying it near the bottom. They take a seat on the ground in front of their sacks, positioning the piece of fabric against their foreheads. Ilian looks at the lasso in his hand and then back at the two.

With a push, Cordaya forces herself upward. The lasso tightens, the weight of the sack falling upon it and preventing it from falling. Sweat drips from her face, as the full sack of coffee hangs off her back, her head supporting the weight. Her hands raise to grab the lasso at the sides of her head, and she begins her trek. One heavy step at a time, Cordaya builds up momentum. She helps lift Ernesto from the ground, every year standing with the weight growing harder. Ilian watches as they make their way uphill to the clearing.

Ilian attempts to repeat what he saw them doing. He throws his lasso about the sack. He tries to move the sack to a better position, only then realizing how much it weighs. Putting the fabric against his head, Ilian leans forward in an attempt to throw himself up. The sack doesn't move. His neck cracks. The soldier takes a deep breath and tries again. In standing straight up, the lasso works its way about the sack and flies off. Ilian falls forward.

Brushing the dead leaves, twigs, and dirt from his hands, Ilian throws the lasso about the sack for another attempt. He takes a deep breath, frustration growing within him. Ilian sits near the sack and presses his hands against the fabric on his forehead. He pushes forward with his feet, falling forward to his knees. But a smile bursts when he realizes the sack sits upon his back, lifted from the ground. He tries to push upward with his feet, but his knees lock underneath him. With a profound inhale and a bit of a battle cry, he tries again. The sacks falls backward as his knees push up and he lands in the position he started in.

Cordaya returns, breathing heavy with her hands on her hips. She analyzes the soldier and shakes her head.

"You're going to hurt yourself doing it like that."

"How?"

"With your knees so far together. You need to spread them out a bit to sustain the weight when you eventually rise. If you can, that is."

Ilian shakes his head, but after a second thought listens to her advice. He spreads his feet on the forest floor more than before and pushes off. Though they tremble with the weight underneath him, his knees do not lock nor prevent his movement. He tries to take a step forward, almost falling backward with the weight. He feels the stress on his neck, but he pushes his head forward, staring at the ground rather than look ahead.

Cordaya places her back against the full sack of green fruit and lifts from the ground, leaving the partial for Ernesto to take. Ilian repeats her movements in moving her hands to her head, pulling against the lasso digging into the side of her head. She passes Ilian, her legs shaking as she climbs the incline. Ilian watches in awe until she makes her way from his vision. He begins his journey forward, wondering if he remembers the path to the clearing.

Ernesto passes Ilian as he makes it to the halfway point, or at least what he believes to be.

"Bet you never did this as a soldier," the man said with an exhausted laugh.

"No," was the only word Ilian could summon, his entire strength focused on getting the sack uphill. They were lucky they didn't need to take it to the road today. Ilian couldn't imagine lasting all the way uphill.

After many respites and prayers, Ilian makes it to the clearing, dropping the sack backwards and falling atop it as soon as he can. Cordaya stands not far, sweat dripping from her head and soaking her shirt. Carrying the sacks was by far the hardest part of the job.

"Heavy, aren't they? I never could manage a full," Nelida says offering Ilian a drink of water. He takes a sip, any more than that and he fears nausea may strike. He takes a deep, shaky breath.

"I'll have to recommend something like this for soldier training. Definitely strengthens the muscles, after completely destroying them first that is," the soldier responds, a breathy laugh to follow.

After a few minutes, Ernesto arrives with the last sack. Ilian stares at the old man, wondering by which strength he is able to do so. Ilian believes himself to be in his prime, the greatest shape he will be in his life. Yet this work challenges those beliefs, and those thoughts he had about the people in the countryside. His legs cry, knowing if they do the same work the next day, his muscles may never regrow.

"Well, are we ready to head home, or do we need another moment?" Nelida asks, sliding the plates, cups, and eating utensils into her thatch tote. Cordaya glances at Ernesto who stands with a nod. Ilian leans his head back in despair. He stands with aching legs, dripping sweat in the ferocious sun. Cordaya and Ernesto carry the baskets and lassos, Nelida no more than her tote and a pot with little bean left within. Ilian slides the two machetes over his shoulder, his only cargo, and they head uphill.

Cordaya leads the way, baskets balanced atop her head with one hand supporting them as she goes. They pass other laborers heading to their villages and houses in the opposite direction from which they head. Ilian stares forward as he feels their gazes fall upon him, surprised to see the soldier working in the countryside.

"Back to it tomorrow, I suppose," Ilian whispers more so to himself than to another. However, Nelida, walking at his side, overhears and turns her head to him.

"No work tomorrow. We never work on days of worship," Nelida responds.

Ilian's eyes grow wide. He had yet to see the worship of the people from the mountains. Curiosity fills him as he wonders what songs and prayers they perform, wondering if any similarities occur between the two.

"And you are going to join us, correct?" Cordaya shouts back to the soldier from over her shoulder.

He looks up with jaw agape, not certain of the answer he should give. He wishes not to anger the gods by going to the worship of other deities. The mission given to him by the Governor crosses his mind.

"Yes. Of course."

Chapter Five

As expected, Ilian fails to sit up with ease and free of pain the next morning. His back and legs cry as if he had undergone torture the night before. The soldier takes a deep breath and exhales with a swift blow as he stands from the mattress. A wince accompanies every step to the wash tank. The cold water shocks his muscles and senses awake, despite his desire to return under the covers. Per routine, as his senses leave their sleep behind, the smells from the kitchen find their way to him. The thought of no work on this day gives him hope and motivation to eat breakfast without fear of what the day holds.

But a different anxiety grips the soldier. A fear rooted in his soul and spirit as he worries about angering the gods with their plans for the day. They invited him to worship and, as a gentleman does, he accepted the invitation. To say his intentions were true and honest may be deceitful, for Ilian understands the strategy he employs. If he can build a bond of trust with Cordaya, she will take him to the home of the forest spirits. And after that, she will go with him to the capital to meet with the Governor. The pieces fall into place in his head. His task appears simple and straightforward, however, the time it will take to check off the items on the list is uncertain.

Ilian limps into the kitchen and takes a seat at the table. Cordaya cooks their meal, Nelida and Ernesto sipping at their coffee as they talk with one another.

"Good morning, Ilian. How are you feeling today?" Nelida asks, her motherly concern always refreshing for the soldier.

"Good morning. I'm... well," Ilian begins with a chuckle, that which his lungs pierce his ribs in more pain. "I'm sore and my entire body aches, but I am certain your worship will lift my spirits and make me forget all about that."

The variety of expressions jolts Ilian's nerves. Nelida offers a grin, Ernesto a raised eyebrow, and Cordaya a stern glare. He looks to the table, repeating the words in his head to determine what term may be the cause of the mixed reactions.

"Well," Nelida says, cutting the tension in the air with a knife. "I hope it opens your mind and cleanses your spirit as it has done for all of us."

Cordaya places a bowl of warm, mashed camote in front of Ilian. He stares at the food for a moment, unsure if he wishes to simply pass breakfast. The light lilac colored vegetable appears and smells of sweet potato. A sweet, sugary scent, that which met his nose through the corridor, finds him once again. Cordaya stands in wait. Ilian wonders if she wishes to see his reaction, until he realizes his manners.

"Thank you," the soldier says. Cordaya walks back to the metal slab and serves bowls for her guardians as well. They dig into their meal, their eyes lighting up in the rich flavor of the mashed vegetable. Ilian takes a bite. As he chews, the savory yet sweet flavors ignite his taste buds. Cordaya takes a seat and glances at all, perhaps self-conscious of her cooking. Nelida offers a smile and a wink to the warrior. Ilian thinks he sees a slight grin on her face before it disappears in the stonework once more.

"Cordaya woke up early to harvest these. Fresh from the earth, thanks be to the forest spirits," Nelida comments, this last line almost a chant-like prayer.

Ernesto finishes his food and leaves to ready himself for worship. When Nelida clears her plate, she stands from her chair and looks to Ilian.

"For worship, put on some nice clothes, not that uniform though. We'll be leaving in thirty minutes. Oh, and wear shoes you can comfortably walk in."

After finishing his meal, Ilian sits at the table and thinks of what to expect. He had heard crazy stories of the religions of the mountains. Stories of strange dances, rituals, and sacrifices. He hopes it won't appear rude to stand in the back and be no more than an observer. Analyzing Nelida's attire, Ilian supposes it may not be as eccentric as he heard. Granted most stories he's heard of the mountain dwelling people stray far from the actual truth.

Once he deems his appearance suitable for the worship of gods, he kneels at the side of his mattress and prays to his own.

"Beloved gods who have granted me health and wisdom, food and drink at my table, and a place to lay my head. Watch over me as I venture into the unknown. Protect me from the devils and temptations that may linger there. Forgive me if this is to be seen as betrayal. You have demanded the Governor to ask this task of me. In accepting this invitation, I grow ever closer. Shield me and may I not be swayed. Or brainwashed. My thanks and the honor of the Governor, His Grace and the honor of the celestial bodies."

Ilian stands and takes a deep breath. Cordaya walks through in a long, emerald skirt and a cream, cotton blouse. Ilian smiles. The warrior rolls her eyes and deposits the dirty dishes on the platform near the wash tank to be cleaned later. Upon her return, she stops and stares at the soldier.

"Are you ready?" she asks, her eyes masking all emotion as Ilian tries to read her.

"Yes," he responds, his nerves creeping up on him. To think he's stood in the presence of His Grace several times without the anxiety he experiences now. Ilian barely believes himself the same man he was when he left the capital. Perhaps he isn't.

The journey to the worship grounds leads them from their small village and through another. Ilian believes they grow close, as the occurrence of houses increases. However, they take a path off the main road, an upward climb. The soldier exhales in disbelief, having believed this to be his day of rest.

After fifty minutes of walking, they arrive at the peak. Ilian looks down to see a structure built of concrete. Tarps tied together at their sides stretch from corner to corner. A crowd of people gather at the site. The playing of children occurs behind him as more people, following the same path, arrive at the worship site. Ilian sees the main road snake up the mountain on the other side. If they wouldn't have taken this shortcut, their elapsed travel time may have been double.

A chorus of singing rings out. The forest fills with the sound of drums and lute, or what Ilian believes to be a lute. When he arrives, he sees this is not the case.

"Oh no, we must be late," Nelida says in panic.

"As if we ever make it for the opening hymn," Cordaya responds.

"Cordaya, Nelida, calm down. We'll be fine. People always show up after the start," Ernesto says, finding a tree to lean against and pick the dirt from under his fingernails. In no hurry, to his wife's despair.

Nelida marches down the hill at a faster speed, Cordaya following behind in worry the older woman may trip. Ilian shakes his head in disbelief. The thought of arriving late to worship boggles him. And to think it's as so for them and many others every week.

They arrive at the flat clearing where the worship site has been constructed. Several benches made of wood fill the pavilion. At the front of their sanctuary stand several tall vases and urns containing flowers from the gardens of some of the worshipers. Tables to the sides hold bowls overflowing with fruits and vegetables. All offerings for their gods and the spirits.

Cordaya walks up to the altar of flowers and fruits. Kneeling before it, she throws her body to the ground in praise. Upon rising, she wipes the tears away and dips her hand into the cloth satchel hanging at her side. From it she withdraws a mango and places it in one of the bowls. She returns down the aisle, singing along to the hymn, and takes a seat on the third bench from the front.

Nelida touches Ilian's arm, her eyes asking if he will be alright. He turns to see Ernesto at his side and gives a nod. She smiles and makes her way down the aisle to sit at Cordaya's side.

Ilian realizes the women and children sit on one side while the men sit on the other, the latter's section paling in comparison to the women. Many of the men remain standing at the back, Ernesto included. Ilian stands at Ernesto's side and observes every sight and sound the worship offers.

What he earlier assumed to be a strange lute turns out to a be guitar with twelve strings. The fingers of the one who plays the instrument move with ease, their eyes staring at the congregation rather than their instrument. A woman, a necklace made of avocado pits around her neck, stands nearby the band and leads the songs. No books, no papers, all from memory. And the others in the pavilion sing along.

When the songs end, the congregation kneel and switch directly into prayer. Their voices fill the forest, each with their own thanks and praise, their own wishes and devotions. The collections of prayers offer a haunting sound to Ilian's ears as they mix with one another, some sobbing and crying, others yelling at the top of their lungs, their voices attempting to pierce the barriers of the heavens.

In the churches and other worship sites in the city, prayers are often done as a collective verse followed by silent prayer. Their priests and leaders say the omnipotent gods hear all. He attended the services of many different religious sects in his days in the city. None compared to this.

Their worship leader brings all the voices together in a common close to their prayer, "Praise be to the skies and seas, the forests and the earth beneath. Praise to the worthy spirits and their work. Praise to the almighty Gods. Thank you. You may take your seats," he directs to the congregation.

Ilian notices three people, two women and a man taking their seat behind the worship leader. From their position in the pavilion, he guesses they must be significant or have some form of power within the church.

"Who are those with their seats beyond?" Ilian questions Ernesto, who uses a post to support himself as his drowsiness fights to take him. Walking such distance takes a toll on the man at his age. The scalding sun rises, making the fight all the more difficult.

"Those are the leaders of the different seasons under the different Gods. The current leader connects us to the God of the Forest in the season of harvest. That first woman there connects us to the God of the Seas, the next woman to the God of the Skies. And that man there connects us to the God of the Earth."

"The season determines who will lead your worship?"

"Yeah. And also if some natural disaster or plague occurs. They hold specialized services outside of normal worship for those."

Ilian processes what Ernesto tells him, piecing together their religion a little at a time. His attention shifts to Cordaya, who stares with immense interest at the leader, absorbing every word he offers.

"So," the leader continues, his sermon only just begun. "In this time of harvest, it is important to give thanks to the God of the Forest. Respect and grant offerings to the spirits of the forest. Preserve those lands which are ours. And those which are not. Harvest only from those trees which you have been granted permission. Cut down none. Trust they will provide sufficient lumber in the branches upon the forest floor. And with faith, it will be given. With faith, we will not go hungry. We will not go thirsty. The Gods will care for us if we do so for them. We must nourish our souls. Giving our own spirits as laborers for the Gods."

The sermon continues along the same themes of having faith and trusting in the gods. Ilian listens, intently at first, but with time his attention slowly fades away. The thoughts clouding his mind succeed in distracting him. He wonders how he must help Cordaya in order to get her to the capital as soon as possible. They claim the recent attacks and the acts of desperation from the townspeople anger the forest spirits. But how can he convince them to act otherwise? How could he prevent the attacks? The more Ilian tries to find the answer, the further he finds himself from his mission.

Before he realizes how much time has passed, the congregation drops to their knees and offers their prayers once more. Ilian closes his eyes and folds his hands, offering his prayer to his own gods. The other voices distract him at first, but he slowly drowns them out with the power of his thoughts.

"By the grace of the gods, grant me strength. Grant me mercy in the form of His Grace's forgiveness for this obstacle which I face. That these trials may test me but not defeat me. Grant me strength."

He opens his eyes and many of the congregation stands once more. Cordaya is one of few who remains kneeling. Ilian grows confused by the warrior's vulnerability. Inside the pavilion, Cordaya appears a different person entirely. Ilian does not wish to misinterpret her faith for weakness, but he wonders why the warrior crumbles in tears with her devotion to the gods.

The woman who sang before returns to the front, along with those members who play the instruments. They begin their song and the others join in. Some raise their hands into the air. Others sway from side to side.

God of Harvest grant to me
That which we have earned
May we grow and eat with thee
When it is our turn
Spirits of the Forest be

Our help for our crops still
May they grow and bare for me
That which is your will
God of Harvest grant to me
That which we have earned
May we grow and eat with thee
When it is our turn

Their songs continue, one song flowing into the next. Ilian listens to the craft of words, amazed at the members who sing verse to verse without text or sheets of music in front of them.

Rivers flowing down the hill
We look around
At all the gods have given us
Gifted and have granted us
Blessed and their honor just
From the skies and to the ground
Sun and rain, wind and fog
We hear their call
We praise the gods for giving us
Gifting and for granting us
Their blessing and their honor just
For one and all
Up on the mountaintop
Our lives fulfilled
We trust the gods will give to us
Will gift and they will grant to us
They will bless us with their honor just
Peace to the world

The congregation offers a short prayer at the song's end and promptly takes their seat. The woman Ernesto claims to be their connection to the God of the Skies rises. Tears stream down her face, one hand covering her heart the other raised into the air. She shakes her head and meets the eyes of the congregation in her sadness. They mumble their prayers, asking for forgiveness, knowing this leader to only bring bad news from the gods.

"My fellow worshipers. My family. My friends. My brothers and sisters, all who are present and believe in the true presence of our Gods. We have been met with bad news since our last meeting. A few of our members left this world. Climbing the treacherous path that leads to the skies. To the heavens. We must keep them in our prayers that they may make it. That they may rest at last. Away from the violence. Away from the destruction."

Ilian knows she speaks of those lost in the barbarian attacks. He looks to the ground, not able to stop the compassion swelling in his own heart for those who lost a dear friend or family member in the raids. The face of the shopkeeper enters his mind, the before and after searing into his brain. As a soldier, he'd seen a few comrades fall. But they knew it was the risk of the job. These innocents were doing no more than living their lives and working to earn a wage. Truly a loss to all when innocents get caught up in the violence.

The soldier looks to Cordaya. She trembles and stares at the bench in front of her. Biting her lip, guilt overwhelms her with the loss of lives she believes she could have prevented. Had she been faster, stronger, had she'd known, perhaps those innocents would still be alive. As he told her, no one person can do it alone. And though she accepts this statement, the guilt fills her nonetheless.

"Our battle is not over. Nor will it ever be upon this planet. There are forces working against the Gods at all times. We must remain vigilant and faithful. We must not sway to temptation and that which leads to sin. We must understand that our work in this world is not done."

Some of the members in the congregation shout out, "Praise to the Gods." Nelida raises her hand to the heavens, soaking in her divine task in this world. Cordaya closes her eyes and mumbles her prayer. A strange sensation courses through Ilian with the breeze that enters and leaves the pavilion. As if a thousand eyes fall upon them, a pressure and weight without natural origins. The soldier looks around, wondering if any of the others feel the same. He realizes the only other one to react is Cordaya, with knees slightly bent and eyes gazing to the skies, as if looking past the tarp roofing the pavilion.

Ilian shakes his head in disbelief, clenching his fist in anger of his own doubts.

"I cannot abandon my Gods. I will not abandon my Gods," he repeats over and over, hoping it will erase any other thoughts from his mind.

"We will not falter from our faith," the woman screams in enthusiasm. The congregation cheers. "We will not stray from our paths. Our trust is in them. Our love abides by their rules. We will not falter. We will not falter!"

As her volume increases, so does that of the worshipers. They raise both their hands in the air in praise.

"And when our day comes that we begin that upward climb to the skies, we will thank the Gods for the time we had. We will thank the Gods for the love we experienced. We will thank them for everything. The good and the bad. Because life is made up of both. We live and we learn. But no matter what obstacles we face, we will continue that upward climb. Because our faith and our trust in the Gods will give us strength to do so."

The sound of sobs and prayers fill the sanctuary. Ilian examines the solemn faces of the congregation, almost in disbelief of their level of faith and spirituality in exhibiting such emotions. His eyes meet with that of the woman preaching. She shares a gentle smile with fiery eyes. His heart beats faster as he begins to question all his life choices. Should he walk that path, he wonders how far he'll make it. He believed him strong in terms of physical and mental strength before he arrived. But his perspective has all but been flipped on its head. With the trials to come, Ilian faces uncertainty in the results. And if Cordaya speaks the truth, failure could mean disaster of unimaginable proportions. Not just for the nation of Micacao, but every nation on the planet.

Whether by the doing of his gods or hers, Ilian does not doubt in his connection to this mission. Fate, whether by the Governor's knowing or some other divine being, placed him here, sent him to find Cordaya. Fate ties them together and may pull them apart if it so chooses. One may die. Or both. Ilian accepts whichever end he meets. But he refuses to deny the existence of his gods simply because those of Cordaya and her community may undeniably present themselves to exist.

When the leader representing the God of the Skies steps back, the man leading previously takes her place.

"We will now begin our offering of coins. Though we grant fruit, vegetable, flowers, and other such gifts to the Gods, let us not forget of those material needs of the assembly and pavilion."

Two men who stand in the back step forward to the front, grabbing collection dishes, no more than wicker bowls, in their hands. They start on opposite sides, going from row to row to collect the offering of coins. Ilian searches his own person, knowing this to be a tradition across religions. He finds a silver piece and sighs, not having any of lesser value. He accepts this and places the piece in the dish as it passes. Ernesto looks at him with raised eyebrows, as if impressed the soldier would agree to give so much.

As the dish carriers walk to the front of the pavilion, the leader leads the worshipers in their closing song. Ilian peeks about the tarp to see the sun's position in the sky. About four hours have passed since the start of the service, his legs growing weary at standing without movement for so long. In the city, most services last no more than two hours, two and a half at longest. The city people have other chores and work to attend to before their work week begins, making time for church an added difficulty and one some choose to ignore all together. Their dedication to their gods and abundant faith leaves Ilian in awe, ashamed of his own worship.

The song ends and the leaders share the announcements of further events in the weeks, along with a remembrance service for those who passed in the attacks. The congregation stands and makes their way to the back of the pavilion where they socialize with one another before heading home.

Cordaya joins Ernesto at his side while Nelida talks with family. A young man, who appears to have money judging from his clothes, approaches and offers his hand to Ernesto first, then Ilian, then to Cordaya, placing a kiss upon hers. She recoils and glares in disgust. Ilian peers at the man who continues to smile and playfully gaze at the warrior.

"Crazy the attack this past week, right?" the man says to Ernesto, who nods in agreement.

"Our little town's got no hope when faced with those barbarians."

"And the governor ignores it. As if he's got better things to do than protecting his own citizens." The man glares at Ilian who matches it. An anger rises within him, but he refuses to have an outburst, especially in the pavilion on a worship site.

"I heard you tried to fight them," the man directs at the soldier, his menacing tone laced with maliciousness.

"It's more than you tried to do," Cordaya speaks up, wearing a straight face. Ilian looks to her in shock. Her defensive comment of him not one he'd ever expect.

"That's sweet." The man says in reply to Cordaya's statement. "And I'm sure the dog is a good laborer, too. How much are you paying him?"

"He can fill a basket faster than you could ever hope to," Cordaya says again, her frustration of this man's refusal to leave them alone growing.

"Right. Well, good day to you, Mr. Morez. Cordaya." He gazes at Ilian with a raised eyebrow and says nothing more.

"Don't mind him," Ernesto says once the man is out of earshot. "His family owns a lot of land and they've got a lot of workers. They think they're better than us for the money they've got. Don't be bothered. Then again, I'd say you got more." He tells Ilian with a wink. Ilian gulps and forces a grin. To think he feels guilty for having money, as if wishing to experience life the way they felt it. But he knew it would never be possible. Despite how Nelida tries, Ilian may never truly understand them.

Nelida joins them and they discuss their departure. Ilian glances around at the faces that remain. His eyes find the leaders, who gaze upon him with interest, grins worn on their faces. Ilian averts his eyes, turning his head back toward Ernesto and Nelida. A pressure drops upon Ilian's shoulder. He rotates and sees Cordaya standing near.

"I'll take you there. To the home of the spirits of the forest. I'll take you there tomorrow if you'd like."

Ilian's eyes widen. He shakes his head in disbelief, unable to imagine how he'd gained her trust so quickly. His head turns to the leaders who continue to gaze in his direction. His jaw drops, a realization hits him. Before he can ask questions, Ernesto announces it's time to begin their walk.

Cordaya bows her head and leads the way. They take their spots in the line following the snaky paths through the mountains. Ilian smiles as his legs no longer feel sore, though perhaps the thought comes too quickly as they'd only just begun. Ilian thinks about the next day's adventures. He thinks about how close he may be to completing his mission.

His eyes scan the forest, knowing its beauty will relax him in such times. His thoughts slow and a glowing form passes through the trees. Ilian jumps and turns to see what it may be. He loses the image, the light fading into the sun's rays slipping through the forest canopy. Perhaps that was all he saw. A trick of light. Or a mirage of his manifesting thoughts. He shakes his head and continues the climb uphill.

Cordaya glances back. When she turns to face the front once more, her eyes grow serious, forming no more than slits. She scans the forest and sees nothing. A hand moves to her side, ready to withdraw the sword if she must.

Chapter Six

I lian rises from bed the next morning, feeling refreshed and rejuvenated. Strength and energy course through him. He firmly places his feet on the ground and heads to the wash tank, clean face and teeth making him feel all the better. In walking to the kitchen, he notices the silence to fill the house. Cordaya sits in a chair, eyes closed and face rested, as if in a state of meditation.

"Good morning," she says, causing Ilian to jump and wonder how she knew he stood there.

"Good morning," he repeats, scratching at his forehead and looking around. "Where are Mr. and Mrs. Morez?"

"They headed off to work. I told them we had other work for today."

Ilian clenches his jaw and gulps at the thought of physical labor. His body feels rested for the first time since he arrived in Hoja Rosa. To think he'd torture himself yet again with such tasks so soon, even though he knew it inevitable, worries him. To think Cordaya mentions their plans for the day as work, whether to mislead the Morezes or says so in truth. His nerves grow as he thinks what visiting the forest spirits may entail.

"We've got a long journey ahead of us," Cordaya starts, as suspected by Ilian. "I've prepared rice and beans to take along with us. There are avocados on the path to their home. The spirits grant permission for us to pick what we may need to nourish ourselves."

Ilian's eyes stop wandering the kitchen in his thoughts and meet hers. He questions whether he heard correctly. The spirits granted their permission. As in she asked and received an answer. He wishes to shake his head in disbelief, release a chuckle at the joke. Yet, he prevents himself from doing so, at the cost of losing the invitation. Rather he stems his doubts into a question.

"You speak with them? The forest spirits?"

"And you don't speak with your gods?" Cordaya questions, dodging the one posed by Ilian. He opens his mouth to respond but understands it to be rhetorical.

"And how long will it take until we arrive?"

"That depends how fast you walk."

"I was thinking we could ride," Ilian says with a smile, nodding to the outside, where his horse stood tied to a post, watching those who passed by.

"I didn't ask permission to bring your horse-"

"We can tie her to a tree when we draw near. She'll refuse to go with anyone who's not me," Ilian reassures her. Cordaya takes a deep breath, indecision on her face. The soldier walks to the warrior, invites her to place her hand in his, and leads her outside.

"This is Pinto," he introduces, rubbing the horse's snout. Her tail swishes from side to side in happiness to see her partner. "Come on," Ilian says, telling Cordaya to place her hand on the horse's head. Cordaya moves forward with hesitation, interaction with animals never having been something she was accustomed to. Her hands reach and fall upon the head of the horse. She runs her fingers through her mane, her jaw falling in her awe of the beautiful creature.

"And you take her into battle?" Cordaya asks, looking into the eyes of Pinto.

"She's more so a messenger horse than a member of the cavalry. I don't often fight battles on the ground. My top priority is the Governor's protection."

"She's beautiful," Cordaya says with a glitter in her eyes. Ilian double checks to see if a smile breaks through the stone mask she consistently wears. But nothing more than her eyes reveal happiness.

"Thank you," Ilian replies, disappointed he cannot break her shell. "So. Can we bring her along? You said yourself, it's a long journey."

Cordaya stares at the horse and thinks for a moment. She runs her hands down its neck and to its saddle, dropping her fingers away. With a nod, she accepts, and Ilian clenches his fists in victory.

"We need to tie her up outside of their territory. Even if she peers within, I'm sure they won't mind." Cordaya refers to the spirits of the forest. With every mention, they transform from mountain myth to rare creatures in Ilian's mind. He thinks through the paintings and art of the spirits depicted by the ancient tribes of the land. Small, green men with large ears in some paintings while others show tall, wispy figures with several eyes and vines for hair. The religion of these ancient tribes greatly influences those in the mountain, perhaps where the rumors of sacrifices and blood offerings began despite these modern times.

Nonetheless, Ilian wonders if their journey will come up with any results. Cordaya wishes to find the cause to the angering of her gods. Ilian fails to understand how going to the tree will help them find these answers. It would only make sense if she had direct communication with the forest spirits. This idea sends his thoughts spiraling. He looks to Cordaya, who continues to gently stroke the mare. The air about her is in its own mystical, her abilities remain a mystery to him. No passion presents itself but that side of her that wishes to work and worship. No more, no less. The warrior of the glass sword, humble in nature, strong in body and mind from years of labor and practicing her faith, possesses qualities not many humans achieve until later in life. As if wisdom above all else was her gift from the gods.

"Are you ready?" Ilian asks Cordaya, eager to find out what awaits them. The warrior nods and returns to the kitchen to grab their pots of food. Ilian unties the lasso from Pinto's neck, looping it to take with them on their journey. He runs to grab his saber. As he exits, Cordaya stares at him in shock.

"What are you doing?"

"What if we are attacked on the road? The barbarians could be anywhere."

"Do you trust in the gods?"

"Yes, but-"

"Then you don't need that."

Ilian thinks about her words and ultimately agrees. As a soldier, he learned that it was better to be prepared than not, a saber at his side a comfort to him at all times. He felt prepared. Cordaya speaks from a place of faith, and though he wishes to show utmost trust in the gods, he knows there are demons at work in this world. He respects her wishes, primarily because he knows of her fighting skills and the ability to call the glass sword when in need. For this reason, and this reason alone, he accepts her request.

He closes the door as he exits for the final time. They stand at the horse's side, and he offers her a hand. She stares at it for a moment then returns her gaze to the horse.

"Can you mount her?" Ilian asks, not knowing if her stubborn, independent nature forces her to refuse his help.

Cordaya places her hand on the saddle, no more than a rectangular piece of leather sewn into a colorful, thick cloth, a leather strap belting it underneath the horse's belly. She pulls at the piece to see how it slides with a slight pull.

"Stand here," Ilian suggests backing away from his position at the horse's shoulder. Cordaya walks to his previous position. "Now, wrap your hands by the neck, pull up, and swing your leg over."

Cordaya nods and follows his steps, accomplishing the task of mounting on the first attempt. Ilian shakes his head in disbelief, remembering the number of falls he had his first time. No doubt the God of the Forest looks down and smiles upon her.

Ilian motions for the warrior to edge to the back of the saddle, trying not to kick her as he swings his leg over. He never rode with another behind. Nerves settle in. He takes the lasso looped around the horse's neck in his hands.

"If you need to hold on, I can attach a second lasso or simply grab around my waist," Ilian says, trying not to embarrass or frustrate her. According to Nelida, Cordaya takes no romantic action with humor. The warrior wears a straight face and nods.

She does not bother with what he says but rather observes the world from her new perspective. Her hands rest on the horse's side, feeling its heartbeat and breath. Cordaya closes her eyes and absorbs it all in with a profound inhale. Ilian smiles, her connection to nature innate. Ilian bets not even the stray wolves growl as she walks by. If anything, they part their pack so she may pass.

Ilian clicks his tongue and brushes his hand along the neck of Pinto. He leans over and whispers in her ear. "Ride like the wind poses no competition."

A soft whinny issues from the horse and she begins her trot through the town. Once outside of its limit, not much traffic of concern, Ilian taps his heel to the horse's side, and she picks up speed. Cordaya jerks back with the sudden shift of speed, her hands clenching tight to the saddle. Her heart races with the fear that struck her and continues to race as the horse darts down the road. The trees speed by on either side of her. She grows dizzy as she scans the forest for signs of the spirits, knowing her eyes will never be able to focus in on time. Outside of the loud gallop of the horse, dust flying up behind them, no other sound but the calls of songbirds and insects can be heard.

They reach another town and Ilian slows the horse, not wishing for an accident. A man with a scarf covering his white hair wanders the streets selling coconuts and cacao. Ilian figures the poor man must be from Niekalarah, as Micacao does not have the tropical lands for such crops.

"Do you want something?" Ilian asks the warrior, as his eyes scan the wares and crops of the vendors in the street.

"No."

Trotting with care through the crowded marketplace, Ilian watches the path in front, not wishing to bump into anyone. This task proves near impossible in the narrow streets of the town. The townspeople scurry about, with no concern of the horse, pushing and shoving one another to get to their next location. Glares meet Ilian, as his identification as a soldier, or simply as one from the capital, fails to go unnoticed in the mountains. Stares and whispers find Cordaya, her legend far spread. The hope she brings as the warrior of the glass sword placing her among the praises of the gods. Cordaya ignores it, staring ever forward in steadfast focus of their destination.

A little girl, no more than four years of age, approaches the horse's side and tugs at Ilian's pant leg. He halts the horse and greets the child with a smile. She holds up a mango, offering it to the soldier. His jaw drops in shock and confusion, his eyes scanning for any sign of her parents.

"It's for the glass sword fighter," the girl mumbles. Ilian rotates to face Cordaya, who sits with her eyes closed.

"Where are your-"

"She help my town from the bad people. And my papas always say to give offerings in thanks. I want to be just like her."

Ilian accepts the mango with a gracious smile and places it in a sack tied to the saddle.

"Thank you."

"Hey, you!"

A shopkeeper, burly and fuming, approaches and grabs the little girl by the wrist. She lets out a wince of pain as he raises her into the air, her feet dangling with no way to run.

"You steal from my shop, you pay the price, you street rat!"

Some of the passerby eavesdrop on the conversation but continue on their way with nothing to say. Ilian notices a blade dangle from the merchant's belt. His eyes widen when he catches the glimmer of a sliver of alexandrite, similar to the swords used by the barbarians and of Niekalaran design. He wonders why there are so many of these weapons in this region.

The soldier reaches for his own blade. Its absence reminds him that at Cordaya's request, he did not bring it. Ilian mutters but Cordaya says nothing. She does not even open her eyes to glance at the scene. In his panic, Ilian readjusts his posture as one of intimidation and looks down upon the riled merchant.

"Unhand her," he demands, his voice deep in doing his best imitation of the Governor. "She is no more than a child."

"A child who steals from my shop!" the merchant yells, tone laced with spite. His flushed face sweats with the rising heat. He uses his scarf and free hand to wipe away the drop running down his cheek, the little girl struggling all the while. With a growl issued to her, the girl stops squirming and the scared tears flow. "And this rat will get some punishment as the rest of 'em. Parents sendin' them here to grab what they can get their grubby, little hands on. Well, this rat's not gettin' away!"

"Here," Cordaya holds her closed hand to the man who places his open palm beneath it. She drops in three bronze pieces, equal that of six times what the girl gifted. "I sent her to see what they cost. She must have misunderstood. Forgive me."

The merchant glances between Cordaya and the little girl. He releases his grip, the girl sprinting from his side and clutching at the tights revealed from under Cordaya's skirt. He grunts and mumbles before walking away.

"Go now. You are safe," Cordaya whispers to the girl. The child nods and runs off. Ilian marvels at how quickly the warrior deescalated the situation, yet his satisfaction of the final result remains minimal.

"Why did you pay him so much? And why didn't you send that girl back to her parents? Did you see the sword at his side?" Ilian asks, question after question leaving his mouth as his thoughts swirl. His fingers continue to search the empty space at his waist, wishing to fall upon the grip of his saber. The situation should not have ended in the favor of the merchant as it did. Those who act through impulse and ignorance should not be rewarded. In his frustration, Ilian tightens his grip on the lasso and starts the horse into a slow trot once more.

They exit the busy street in silence, entering a part of town outside of the market.

"Why did you do that?" Ilian asks, his back remaining to the warrior as he watches ahead. He thinks of how hard she works for every bronze piece, the countless hours she spends for such low wages. For standing guard of the Governor within his court, no more than in preparation should an attack occur, Ilian earns three silver pieces every other week. One silver values that of five hundred of the small bronze Cordaya handed over. He sees their poverty and wonders why they don't find other work. Move to a larger city. Demand more for their crop. The solutions become endless in Ilian's mind. Yet, those of the mountains always choose to blame the Governor for their hardships.

"Why did-" Ilian's irritation cut off by Cordaya's words.

"Ilian," she starts, waiting to ensure he stops before continuing. "We don't need problems and you have no idea how out of proportion these foreign merchants make things to earn a bit of profit. They come here and cause a bit of trouble when the residents buy elsewhere. But they are the ones who caused the prices to plummet in the first place. Before them, a person could make enough to feed their family for the day by selling at the market. Now it's not that easy.

"As for that girl's parents. There's no saying they were even nearby. Truth is, they probably did send her to work or steal something so they could eat tonight. She should've run but decided to gift their meal to us instead."

Cordaya shakes her head in guilt as she thinks about it. Ilian's expression grows solemn at her words, not realizing the grim truth. To think, at four years of age, the little girl was expected to find a meal for her family and look for a way to earn a wage. She could be kidnapped, harassed, violated, yet the parents worried more about their meal than her safety. Ignorance was bliss. Ilian knows with certainty the Governor must not know about this, or he would have done something.

"Violence is not the answer, Ilian. Only the evil of this world fights to be the offensive, the first to attack. We, as servants of the gods, must only fight to protect. And only when lives are in danger. There are other ways to combat evil. Ways which do not displease the gods. We must be careful, Ilian. Even from here, they watch us."

Ilian takes a deep breath and says nothing. His eyes scan the forest in his paranoia, the slightest shift in the shadows causing him to tighten his grasp. The sounds of the townspeople fade into the distance as the insects and birds become a prominent sound once more. Rising into the mountains, a chilled breeze sweeps by, brushing against the steep cliff and returning to them. Upon looking over the edge on the other side, Ilian sees the thick, white clouds below, covering the town in the valley they left no more than an hour ago. His eyes grow tired as the wind pushes against them, but the soldier does not slow the horse's speed. They ride with haste, growing ever closer to their destination.

"To the left," Cordaya shouts from behind. Ilian barely catches her words when he arrives at the fork in the road. The left path slopes downward, that to the right continues around the mountains. Ilian steers to the left, Pinto racing downhill.

The sound of wagon wheels and the clicking of hooves hits his ears and Ilian pulls back on the lasso, Pinto's front heels leaving the ground. Cordaya lunges forward and grabs hold of Ilian's coat. The other horses appear from around the bend and stop upon seeing their obstructed path. Ilian pivots Pinto to the side and lowers himself from the horse. The maize-filled wagon pulled by the oncoming horses extends for the entirety of the narrow path. Ilian shakes his head in disbelief.

"Who believes they are so special as to command both sides of the path?" Ilian pleads in anger, not wishing for any other interruptions in their journey. Cordaya recognizes the horses and opens her mouth to answer when the owner's voice grates their ears.

"That would be me," the man responds. Ilian knows him to be the man which confronted him at the worship site. A smirk meets Ilian's face, for no qualms exist in this area. Yet he cannot forget Cordaya's words from earlier. The soldier calms his breathing and loosens the fingers forming fists. "And I'm the only one with horses in these parts. Well," he takes a pause and glances at Pinto with a disgusted face. "Was. And the name is Julio Montane Hernan. You'd do best to remember it, dog of the capital."

"Hernan? In relation to the president of Niekalarah, I suppose," Ilian says, his shock transforming to disgust. Examining Julio and his foreign laborers and equipment, Ilian understands his fortune does not derive from his work in Micacao, the connection all the more believable.

"What an inane and accurate assumption to make, soldier," Julio says with a mischievous grin. He turns to Cordaya and gives a friendly wave, flashing a smile which goes unreturned. "He's a distant cousin on my mother's side."

"You're of Niekalaran blood?"

"Yes. I traveled here ten years back to buy and tend these fertile lands. The crops I grow and reap are all exported and sold at low prices to the Niekalaran people, the government paying out wages."

"So that's why the prices plunged in past years," Cordaya inserts, sliding down the horse's back and marching forward, her anger evident in every footstep.

"Governor Ralfonso wanted to raise the prices on exports, going as far as taxing them, to line his own pockets rather than help the people of yours and all other of the mountain village. So President Isara, looking out for his people, took manners into his own hands. Those once impoverished no longer worry about where their meal may come, prices so low they can afford it on their feeble income. And every election ends the same. A reelection of Isara. People fear the rising prices and crumbling economy if he were to be voted out. And let's face it. I wouldn't be out here doing this dirty, sweaty labor for other blood. Well, unless it paid double."

"You're not only stealing from the villagers. You're stealing from all of Micacao and our Governor," Ilian states in his wrath. Cordaya joins at his side in anger. Not one of her village suspects Julio's selfish acts, having thought his fruitful lands bring him good fortune when selling to the government's distribution company. The question of his blood had never been brought up. Her shaky breath reveals the frustration pumping through her heart.

Julio snickers at the anger, tangible and filling the air. His laborers take their rest in the shade, not caring one way or another how the argument goes.

"Little by little, Niekalarah grows independent of Micacao's aid and influence. Not to mention our weapons are of great demand on a global scale at the moment."

"And the tensions continue to rise and people are dying because of the barbarians armed and sent by your president." Ilian steps toward Julio with clenched fists. Cordaya grabs his arm to stop him. Her glare penetrates the traitor with more ferocity than his own, yet she still refuses to resort to violence unless it's purely defensive. Ilian finds a different filter for his rage. "You truly are a greedy, apathetic bastard. Aren't you?"

"And you aren't a stinking government dog? Waiting to take Cordaya from her village only to protect the governor-"

"That's not true-"

"Letting all her people die while she stands and protects the one who's done nothing but make her life difficult. Stealing from her table and family-"

"Stop-"

"Not just her, but robbing from all of his citizens-"

"Stop spitting lies!"

"You call me apathetic. But what does that make you? I've helped to eliminate the poverty in my country. You perpetuate it-"

"You dirty-"

"Stop!" Cordaya shouts. Her tone deep and forceful, shaking the trees and mountains in its tremble, clapping like thunder. As if a command from the gods.

Julio licks his lips, shakes his head, and turns his head down in defeat. Ilian believes it to be a temporary surrender.

"Back up your horse to the fork and wait til we pass. We'll move fast."

Ilian takes a deep breath, staring at Julio as if his words hit a stone wall. He does not wish to abandon the fight so quickly and, given the final result, so much remains unsaid. The soldier questions

Niekalarah's plans, knowing much more happens behind the scenes than Julio reveals.

He hears Cordaya's footsteps behind him, her sandals leaving their imprint in the dusty path. She mounts the horse with no energy spent and leads it up the path. Ilian gazes at Julio, who averts his eyes from the two, focusing only on the dirt path and his horses. Ilian turns and follows Cordaya to the fork, mumbling to himself as the thoughts swirl, but saying no more.

After all pass, the maize-filled wagon on course for Niekalarah, Ilian and Cordaya continue on their journey. Pinto runs the fastest she can downhill without stumbling. Ilian focuses on their path, but the distractions creep up with every bend and curve. When the pressure grows too great to bear, he opens his mouth to yell back to Cordaya. But she taps his shoulder, interrupting his thoughts.

"We stop here."

Like a whisper it meets his ears. The impossibility of hearing the quiet voice at such high speeds causes him to question if it had been in his own mind. He wonders if he imagined it, but he slows the horse nonetheless. When Pinto comes to a full stop, Cordaya slides down.

"We tie her up here," Cordaya instructs, pointing out a specific tree.

Ilian dismounts and grabs the lasso to lead Pinto to the tree. She neighs and whinnies, trying to resist his pull. Shock covers Ilian's face, as he never saw her spooked by anything before. He tries to contain her, her resistance surpassing his physical strength. Cordaya approaches and rests her hand on the horse's snout. Pinto calms. Cordaya ties the lasso to the tree, the horse standing as still as a statue. The warrior senses his questioning thoughts.

"It's the spirits of the forest. She senses them. This way," Cordaya says as they continue their walk forward. They arrive at a narrow dirt path, large hydrangea bushes on either side of the entrance. One bush contains flowers bluer than the sky on a rainy day. The other in stark contrast, a pink so bright it cannot but spark joy to the one who views it.

Strange, tingling sensations course through the soldier as they walk the path through the untouched forest. Pines and trees tall and full, wildflowers finding their way along the ground to find the rays of sunlight breaking through the canopy. Ilian tries to determine if it's a change in the air, the humidity, or perhaps the temperature, or the mixed scents of the plants around them. No matter the rational thought, nothing fits the description Ilian's mind puts to it.

Mystical.

Chapter Seven

Ilian knows not by what divine forces the forest is ruled, but the lack of insects biting and vines pricking gives him the faith to believe something outside of mortal powers exists here. The farther they travel from the road, the greater paranoia Ilian experiences. As if something or someone watches from behind the trees. He suspects the spirits of the forest to be the cause. Ilian questions if they will ever reveal themselves, especially to him, the outsider.

The canopy grows thick above, the sun fighting to break through. Yet darkness struggles to win the battle on the forest floor. Insects illuminate the path in front of them, leading the way. The wildflowers, glowing every color known to man, fill the clear pasture between the trunks of trees. The emerald and sapphire grass and clover grows no higher than their ankles and glitters in the lights given by such sources. The gentle hum of a steady stream flows through the lands, cascading from the mountains climbing toward the heavens. Its clean, clear waters tempting to the soldier after their long journey. But these lands don't belong to him. This is the land of the forest spirits.

They continue their walk, Ilian wondering how they'll know when they've arrived. Every sight to his right and to his left appear magnificent in comparison to the forests he knows.

Smaller trees, whether younger or meant to maintain such a size, sprout from the land. Fruits hang from their branches, ripe and ready to eat. Mangoes and mandarins, pacaya and peaches, guyavas and apples. All growing under the same forest despite the differing conditions in which they thrive. Rows of bushes form the main path they follow, splitting into many dirt walkways to lead down the rows. Strawberries and blackberries, tomatoes and beans, endless rows spreading in both directions. An unlimited supply of crops, always ripe, never rotting.

The quetzals and hummingbirds fly closely overhead, their colors shining like gems in the air. To his left, a toucan sits on a low branch in one of the fruit trees and makes its call. Its long beak and golden and green plumes no less than beautiful.

Ilian's jaw opens in awe at the amazing nature around him. He absorbs the sights and sounds, the scents and sensations into every pore of his skin. One who would not marvel at such a sight surely does not contain the soul of man, Ilian believes.

Cordaya's face softens in the presence of such wonder. Her cocoa eyes scan the life surrounding them, the tranquility and peace far from the trash filled streets and dirty smelling water of the town center, Ilian also comparing the difference to the capital. The warrior treads with care along the path, not wishing to interrupt the traffic of the small creatures at work, doing the bidding of the spirits.

Shadows shift in the trees. Ilian moves his head from side to side, attempting to catch a glimpse of the movement's origins in his peripheral vision. Lights whiz past, never seen head on. The doubt of whether the images exist in reality or no more than fantasy float about Ilian's mind. Cordaya notices them as well, but her exploration of the sights stands in contrast to Ilian's own. She trusts in her senses, that they will not betray her. She trusts in the forest that nothing will harm her. And she trusts in the spirits, that they will reveal themselves when they see fit. The gods accept her trust, and her faith, placing her upon a pedestal in their eyes. For no other was worthy of their will.

Ilian's eyes widen more than he believes possible. His heart skips a beat, and he holds his breath, not wishing to ruin the movement.

Cordaya stops, Ilian running into the back of her. She says nothing, ignoring the act despite Ilian's whispered apology. Cordaya holds up her hand to silence him. She mumbles, her words indistinct. Ilian does not ask questions, figuring the words were not for his ears.

A gargantuan, ancient tree trunk extends upward toward the heavens, branches full of glittering leaves and shimmering white flowers, zebrina creating a halo at its base. Its shining grey bark drips with sap of liquid silver and gold. No shrubs nor trees grow along the path surrounding the tree. In front of it sits a stone font filled with crystal water. The sensation of eyes watching them grow stronger.

Cordaya motions for Ilian not to move. With deep, profound breaths she steps near the font. From the satchel at her side, Cordaya withdraws the mango given to them by the little girl at the market. She kneels on the ground, holding the fruit above her head to display her offering. Ilian watches, wondering why she waits.

A hum rings out through the forest, causing Ilian to jump in his surprise. Cordaya does not move a muscle, breathing carefully to avoid doing so. After the hum fades, the warrior stands and washes the mango in the font. With gentle fingers she rotates the fruit, the pad of her fingers rubbing any dirt or particles from its flesh. As these contaminants drop into the water, they dissolve and cease to exist. Ilian peeks to see the water as clear as it began. Cordaya inspects the mango, ensuring it is of quality to offer to the spirits of the forest. With a nod and deep breath, Cordaya treads around the font and places the fruit at the base of the tree. Ilian wonders how she learned of this ritual, wondering if she knew they would receive that which they would offer to the spirits when they arrived.

The fruit touches the earth at the tree's feet and sparks fly from the spot where it meets. Cordaya does not drop the fruit, her fingers firm in its flesh until it lies steady on the ground.

Ilian hears shifting behind him, light footsteps drawing near. He gulps and reaches for his invisible sword, fear overcoming him.

Cordaya stands and turns to face him. But her eyes do not connect with his. They look beyond him.

Ilian rotates his body in slow motion. Fighting the urge to jump back or run away, Ilian widens his stance. Countless small creatures, with olive-colored translucent skin, arms that extend to their feet the thickness of a twig, and bodies smooth and without a flaw, form their army about the tree, watching them. Their eye sockets exist for no more than to emit a faint glowing light, no noses, mouths, or ears visible. Ilian examines the creatures with shaky breath, afraid any movements may trigger them into an attack.

"Why do you come, my children?" the deep voice, like an echo reaching them, calls from behind. A large, charcoal black mountain lion licks at the mango at the base of the tree. Cordaya, upon seeing the beast, takes a few steps back. She and Ilian wear matching expressions. Such an animal draws out both terror and awe of its beauty and form, their shock not unexpected. The lion raises its head and sits, staring at the two. Although he cannot hear their footsteps, Ilian knows the forest spirits draw closer, tightening their circle.

"Why are you here?" the voice asks once more. The lion's mouth does not move but to lick its lips, yet, they intuitively understand it to be the origin. Ilian glances at Cordaya, knowing she should be the one to answer for her great faith.

"We've come to help. We ask what service you need of us, as we have been brought together by the fates for this purpose," Cordaya says. Ilian's body trembles, experiencing nerves even as she speaks. Cordaya maintains a calm composure, though Ilian knows she suppresses her own fears for sake of respect and trust in her gods. Ilian lacks the faith to remain so trustworthy, his instincts telling him to run and never look back.

"My child, while you possess the faith of a divine warrior, the human at your side lacks the will."

Ilian's eyes widen, knowing this beast to sense his fear or read his thoughts. He wonders if they've happened upon a god. The bright lime eyes of the lion pierce his soul, freezing him and his nerves. A chill rises up his spine as the pit falls into his stomach. An obstacle grows on the path where Ilian believed he would not falter. His once unshakable faith tested by the lion sitting at the base of the mystical tree. His heart and mind wish to defend himself, but the soldier succumbs to his mortality. He cannot question nor deny the claim of this ancient being.

"But..." Cordaya mumbles, her hope shattered with his simple answer. She fails to find the words to object, realizing as Ilian that she does not possess the authority to press the lion's wisdom. Her eyes sparkle with the tears that threaten to break through the stone walls she constructed.

A rich violet bubble, filled with dark smoke, grows from the tree behind. When it becomes too large, the bubble pops and releases a noxious gas from its core. It leaves a faint, rotted ring on the bark of the tree. As Ilian observes this occurrence, his eyes adjust and notice the other rings on the tree. Hundreds of them stain the bark, the older ones faded but leaving their mark. The true damage lies within, he thinks. The bark hides what plagues the tree within, the fibers rotting from the inside out.

The lion jumps back and hisses at the popping bubble. The gas dissipates and the lion turns to the two, fierce eyes scanning them to read their reactions. Ilian appears confused while Cordaya allows the tears to flow in disbelief and empathy. The beast sits and licks at its paw.

"As you both see, our tree is dying."

Ilian gasps, not believing such a mystical tree of being mortal. Cordaya wipes away her tears, as if the understanding hit her moments before the voice revealed the truth. Ilian knows not what this means for the forest, nor for the people who utilize it for crops.

But he understands the death of this tree would mean the deaths of many more, perhaps reaching as far as the capital.

"Our tree, named Arbagodaia by the ancients, provides these and all lands with the necessary nutrition to thrive. Its roots extend across the world, giving new life to barren lands and assisting those lands not in great need. Through flood, earthquake, hurricane, and volcanic eruptions, Arbagodaia ensures no lands will go without life. No matter the damage, our tree will heal."

"What plagues the tree? How do we stop it?" Cordaya asks, her voice strong and filled with resolve. Ilian admires her courage. No fear, nor wrath, nor sadness prevents her from doing what is right.

"Recklessness and revenge run rampant in these lands. While many do as they can to strengthen the tree, many more commit acts of evil, acts which the gods have warned against. The gods anger for lack of faith. Lack of morality. The God of the Forest is no exception. While the skies fill with rage, the ground below us ever moving, waters forming waves of insurmountable height, the trees rot from the inside with the plague she creates."

"If you are not a god, who are you?"

"I am no more than a leader of the spirits of the forest, a messenger from the God of the Forest. The gods threaten to wage war upon this world should the sin and evil continue to grow."

"But we cannot stop that! We are two people and no more than that. We do not have the power-"

"You do not have the power to stop the sin. But you, divine child chosen as a warrior by the God of the Earth, possess the ability to prove to the gods the consequences of their anger. This world holds much beauty. The gods, in observing the hate, fail to see this."

"How can I convince them when you cannot?" Cordaya asks, tears forming as the grim fate of the world grows inevitable. Ilian follows the conversation with as much dread as the warrior. While the responsibility placed on Cordaya appears unbearable, her words of their connected fate presses down upon his shoulders. The weight of the world shared between the two of them makes an impossible task. His legs tremble with the invisible weight, his heart racing and his breaths shallow.

Another toxic bubble pops from the tree. With each vision of the plague which strikes the ancient Arbagodaia, Ilian shakes his head in disbelief. He believed the threat to exist within the mountains, but the real threat extends any artificial borders and manmade construct. The existence of the world and life as they know it will crash to the will of the gods.

Ilian clenches his fist, his anger at the gods rising. His wrath at their lack of compassion for those beings which they've created surmounts his fear of his faith. He realizes he cannot fear them if he is to face them. His Grace must have known. Sending him on this mission, knowing that fate ties the soldier and warrior together.

"What do they gain from such destruction? Do they have no pity?" Ilian says in a low tone, his anger lacing his voice.

The lion watches him with squinting, glowing eyes. It steps closer to Ilian, the soldier refusing to step back. He holds his own, if an attack be his punishment for speaking out against the gods, it would be nothing less than he deserves for his disrespect. But the lion stops in front of him and sits down, inspecting the soldier, smelling his scent, or as Ilian believes, his emotions.

"You have much to learn, child. The gods create and destroy. Past, present, and future, this has not nor will ever change. They experiment as they can until they've created the perfect creations."

"Humans are not perfect. All life in this world contains flaws. There is no way to convince them otherwise," Ilian says, desperation leaking through his voice as he pleads for the answer.

"You believe the gods lack compassion. Yet their creation lacks more. What the gods lack they make up for in patience. If not, this world would have been remade centuries ago. Mortals do not comprehend the substance of what makes up a spirit and soul."

"If you speak of poverty and war, I cannot disagree. I feel more at fault than ever for such violations of humanity. But His Grace does what he can-"

"You dare compare a mortal to a god!" The lion roars and takes a defensive stance. Long, curved claws eject from his paws, no doubt with one swipe the lion could kill a man.

Ilian pauses and gulps. He knows not how to answer, his nerves eating away the brave front he built up. His own beliefs and faith place his governor no more than a steppingstones distance from the gods' authority. He may not be a god, but the Governor is far from mere mortal. At the least, those in the capital share this belief with the soldier. As if that was the only affirmation he needed, one from within an echo chamber. Ilian's doubts grow, his guilt doing so parallel to the other.

"Wise spirit," Cordaya begins before the lion cuts off her speech.

"You may call me Mizochtal."

"Mizochtal," Cordaya repeats and takes a deep breath, the name of the forest spirit lingering like the sweet juice of a fruit upon her lips. Her spirit sings and her heart soars to have the honor to learn the ancient being's name. "Though you cannot give us the answer, fate will deliver it. But how long do we have?"

Ilian stands to attention, wishing for the time to prepare, time to warn his people. The mountain lion expresses solemn eyes and walks to the base of the tree before lying down. Cordaya looks to the ground, understanding the answer.

"Not long," she whispers with trembling heart. Their minds fill with the endless possibilities, the limitless tasks which will be set.

"No," the lion says, sympathy in his voice. "There is no time. For it has already begun. The plague races for the heart of the tree. Subtle earthquakes will grow until all volcanoes awaken. The clouds continue to fill the sky, darker and darker they become. The waters sway with unease and indecision in their patterns. You have no time. For it has already begun. It is now up to fate and your faith."

"So what do we do?" Ilian interjects.

"Go about your lives until you find the answer. When we do not search for it, when we do not wait for it, fate arrives. When you least expect it," the lion answers.

Cordaya and Ilian turn to one another, wondering how they are to go about their lives as if nothing happened. As if fear of the unknown did not threaten to constrict them to place. The magic and tranquility of this enchanted land give them the strength to listen to the lion's wise words of warning. But outside of this place, where they are left to their own devices without the protection of this untainted land, they wonder by what power they will move forward.

Cordaya falls to her knees and mumbles her prayer. The lion watches, pleased with her reaction, satisfaction evident in his eyes as he absorbs her faith, as if it rejuvenates him. Ilian gazes at the warrior's form. He feels a slight pressure from behind and turns to see a couple of forest spirits peering at him in their curiosity. As if they had never seen a human so close. Ilian bows his head to the creatures who look to one another. Their blank expressions give nothing away, however the lights in their eyes illuminate brighter, as if struck by joy and hope. Ilian understands not only does the fate of the planet matter to the humans, animals, and plants, but to the spirits as well. This is their home, as much as it is his own, for they've cared for the land much longer than civilization. If anything, the rise of civilization created more problems for the spirits.

Ilian rotates to face the lion and takes a knee. He puts his fist to his heart and bows his head.

"I am a servant of the gods and of no mortal man. As the gods wish so I comply. My faith is my sword. My resolve is my hope. What

I lack I shall make up for. My mistakes past will be buried and I will start anew," Ilian says, as if taking an oath in front of a royal court.

The lion tilts his head and examines the soldier.

"May the words cease to flow from your mind and come from your heart. Words unmatched are empty caskets by the wayside. They lack life and soul. When the tests and trials arrive, your reaction is what will prove your faith. Your action what will prove your resolve. Until then, think wisely upon your stance and where fate may place you upon the end. For fate is one possibility of many in cause of an effect. Do not allow your confidence to distract nor detract from the situation. The same for your fears. You will learn, my child. You will learn."

"Yes. I promise."

The lion smiles, revealing its white fangs. Ilian bites his lip, a promise to the forest spirit a heavy weight to carry upon his shoulders. Ilian takes a deep breath and whispers his prayer to the gods, wondering if it is even his gods he addresses.

Cordaya rises and peers into the eyes of the lion.

"When the battle ends, what becomes of the glass sword?" Cordaya asks.

The lion gazes at the empty hoop dangling at the side of her leather sash. The warrior stands tall. The woman, in her long skirt and sandals, long, wavy, black hair, and defined muscles in her arms and hands, demonstrates the image of a divine warrior. Her humility and compassion shine in her eyes. No pride nor honor stem from killing another with her crystal weapon. She accepts the responsibility through grace, through her faith. Not abusive nor arrogant as the wielder. Not from royalty but from poverty. Not from palace but concrete hut.

"Fair warrior of the glass sword. The gods would never revoke this token through an act of thanks. But as one of spite."

They look to the mountain lion in confusion. Ilian believed through the gods' wrath they felt a noble warrior upon the planet necessary. Through their disappointment and disapproval they gifted the sword to one capable of judiciously eliminating the problems. The sinners. Cordaya closes her eyes. Guilt fills her as she imagines the result if the gods' rage disarms her of her village's last defense. She peers at the soldier, wondering of his thoughts. He stares at the earth, determining his place in the battle to come. If Cordaya loses the sword, does he assist in the protection of innocents? Or consider the mission complete, as the warrior of the glass sword would no longer be, and return home? If Cordaya loses the sword, the gods will have decided the fate of the world. Who can change or challenge the minds of the gods? The thought of the world ending without a farewell to his family causes him to pause and consider his options. Cordaya notes his hesitation of questioning the lion despite his confusion, uncharacteristic of the soldier.

"I will do what good I can with it while I can," Cordaya answers with head bowed down. Her clenched fists release, the sensation of the smooth crystal pressed against the palm of her hand lingers in her thoughts. Never experiencing the sword's strength and mystery leaves her fingers itching to find its grip. When left defenseless, she will need Ilian's help more than ever. She knows she can't fight this battle alone.

"You will always be the swordswoman of legend. Both of your names will go down in history as the saviors of our world. If that is the fate you so desire."

"Honor, fame, nor prestige hold us to our fate as strongly as our faith and morals. We will do what's right. Not in the name of temptation of greed, but for our hearts and souls."

Mizochtal, messenger from the God of the Forest to her spirits, rises from the earth and bows to the two. Ilian and Cordaya watch with wide eyes alike. Ilian turns his head to see the spirits of the forest repeat the action. They lower themselves in respect of the warrior. And Ilian as well. Their actions to decide the fate of the world. Cordaya's jaw drops in awe, knowing she is not worthy.

"In these trying times, we must have faith, children. We must remember why we are here."

Every statement from the lion transports Ilian further into his mind, driving his doubt and insecurity. With every comment, the purpose of his mission illuminates, but not that of Julio's deceit. The Governor waits for his return. The Governor wishes to know of the growing conflict. He wishes to help. If Cordaya's sword disappears, the Governor will provide what resources they need to continue the battle. As a chosen one of the divine, the Governor must have known all along.

Ilian raises his face to glare at the lion. The acclaimed forest spirit insults the Governor despite His Grace's superior knowledge of the situation. The lion leaves them to solve the problems, no assistance nor clues as to how. But the Governor contains the intelligence and ability to talk with the gods. He will help Ilian and Cordaya more than the spirits. Ilian's faith wavers.

"Cordaya. It's time to go."

"But-"

"It already told us it doesn't have the answers," Ilian states defiantly. His harsh tone causes Cordaya to lean back, shock worn upon her face.

"Ilian, there are so many questions left unanswered," Cordaya begs the soldier, with emotion he had never heard lace her tone.

"And death won't care one way or another. We need to return and find help. It's all we can do."

Cordaya peers at him, convinced they have much to learn from wise Mizochtal. The marvel and awe of the enchanted forest lose their effect on the soldier. Tense, with no sense of tranquility. She knows without a doubt the mountain lion senses his shaky faith. Cordaya glances at Mizochtal in apology and nods to Ilian.

The soldier releases a shallow breath, bows his head to the lion, and returns down the path. The spirits of the forest part to allow the passage of the two, eyes dimming in loss of hope. Mizochtal watches after them.

The lion squints in observation of the soldier, solemn surrender shown in its expression. No miracle convinces one nailed to their faith. Conversion only works on the two extremes of the spectrum of intelligence, those in the middle too stubborn to move no matter what presents itself to the being. Those without said intelligence fall prey too easily. But those with the capacity to think through, admit to their mistakes when greater evidence reveals itself, may always convert when the time comes. The soldier falls in the middle. Properly brainwashed and stubborn. Mizochtal understands it stands no chance in changing the soldier's mind. Only the gods can do so, and only if they choose.

When gone from its vision, the lion disappears behind the trunk of the ancient tree. No more than an indent in the dirt where the offering lie.

Ilian and Cordaya exit the forest in silence. When they arrive at Pinto's side, Ilian looks to the clouding sky. The villagers may be pleased their prayer for rain has been answered in the dry heat of summer. But fear will flood them when the waters fail to cease. Another sign of the beginning of the end.

Chapter Eight

Nightmares and apparitions overcome the soldier as he tries to sleep that night. Upon opening his eyes, the shadow beings dart to the corners, where their forms grow indistinguishable from those natural shadows of the house. Beads of sweat form on his brow, forcing him to kick the blankets away despite the threat of mosquitoes. In the shadows, Ilian cannot help but imagine the dark outline of the lion watching him. No spirit of the gods. One of the demons from below.

Ilian tries to wipe what may be blasphemous thoughts from his head. The claim of being a messenger of a god lies in direct contradiction to all the Governor has taught him. His Grace speaks to the divine, clear answers given to him when he does so. Yet a messenger claims it cannot provide a message from the gods. The hypocrisy.

Ilian gently bangs the back of his head against his pillow. It follows the rhythm of his heartbeat, thumping against his chest. His questions push him to the limits of his own faith. And the fate of the world dangles from that string. His fear is that he may cut it too short, never able to recover.

Noises and shuffles occur in the kitchen. Ilian, deciding sleep lies far from reach, rises to investigate the sounds.

Nelida tiptoes about, sweeping the kitchen and moving about the chairs to reach under the table. Ilian jumps in and helps, grabbing a chair in each arm and moving them from her path. Nelida smiles. When she passes, Ilian takes a seat and stares at the old, patchwork tablecloth. Nelida sweeps up the dirt and dust and jogs to the kitchen to heat the kettle of coffee. Once the fire sparks, she takes a seat at the table.

"What are you doing up so soon? With that long day, you should be resting."

Ilian grins, thinking that the ability to sleep would be ideal. His drowsy eyes fight him as he looks up to the woman.

"Too much on my mind right now," Ilian answers. He rests his elbows on the table and shakes his head, as if thinking the thoughts may detach themselves.

Nelida stands, leaving the room before quickly entering once more, supplies in her hand. She lays several colors of thin paper on the table along with a pair of scissors.

"I suppose you wouldn't mind helping me while I cook breakfast then, would you?"

Ilian shakes his head with a smile.

"Good."

She grabs a sheet of the thin paper and begins to fold it, again and again and again. She grabs the scissors and cuts slits into the folded paper.

"Just like this," Nelida says while staring at the piece in concentration.

Ilian watches, reminded of the crafts they would do in primary school. He wonders what they're for, but his unknowing does not prevent him from joining in. He grabs a turquoise sheet and begins to fold it in the same way Nelida demonstrated. Ilian looks over to see Nelida has several strands of the thin, scarlet paper on the table in front of her. He cuts his paper into strands and grabs the next color.

Nelida stands and prepares breakfast while Ilian continues to cut the paper. The distraction of the stress-free task helps Ilian clear his mind of the tormenting thoughts. Though the cutting of paper would not lead to the answers he searches, the task was therapeutic nonetheless.

An hour later, as the sun cracks the mountains to allow some of its rays to enter the land, Cordaya enters. The circles around her eyes demonstrate her similar inability to sleep.

"Where were you, sweetie?" Nelida asks in concern. She stirs the scrambled eggs in the pan, not wanting the edges to burn. "Didn't hear you come in last night."

"I had work to do," Cordaya answers without looking up. She grabs a bucket of corn flour dough and begins to make tortillas alongside Mrs. Morez.

"All night? Did you manage to get some rest?"

"I'm not tired, really."

Nelida gazes at the warrior with sympathy, knowing how she's willing to sacrifice anything and everything for more work. Nelida wishes to tell her that they'll get by without that extra bronze coin, but she knows Cordaya enjoys it. Cordaya saves up every coin until she can purchase more land, giving her even more work.

"You're going to the cemetery today?" Cordaya asks, picking up some of the thin strands of paper and examining them. Nelida nods. Ilian looks up and returns his focus to the shreds wondering how these papers could mean they're going to the cemetery.

"Yes. Today would have been my sister's seventieth birthday. Would you like to join us, Ilian?"

The soldier nods and returns to cutting. Knowing the papers will be used to honor the dead, Ilian now cuts with great precision, his heart racing as he attempts to make the lines straight as can be, following the folded crease as if his own life depended on it.

After a quick breakfast, the three head to the cemetery to pay their respects. They take the road further down the mountain, one Ilian had not yet traveled. From above he remembers seeing a smaller town stem from the path. They stray from the paved path and follow a thin dirt road uphill. Every time he climbs the inclines, Ilian believes they get easier. However, when he looks ahead, and they appear to scale straight upward, he loses hope once more. He never realized how grateful he was to the level paths of the capital.

On the top of the hill, overlooking the entire countryside, they arrive at the cemetery. Ilian pauses in awe at the gates. He had never seen such a lovely, joyful sight, especially when concerning death. The concrete caskets sit on the earth, flowering bushes and trees growing near the base of each one. Ilian frowns as he notices smaller caskets, no more than the bones of children within them. Dates and verses from their worship literature etched into the stone. Paper decoration hangs from the stones and posts pushed into the ground. The rainbow of colors offering brightness in the dark hour of those who have died.

Nelida leads the way to her sister's site. When they arrive, she kneels at its side, Cordaya waiting patiently behind her to do the same once she's finished. Nelida rises and places the bag on the flat concrete top of the casket. Cordaya arrives with a broken branch with its leaves still attached and sweeps the dirt and debris from the top.

Ilian watches, wishing to help but unaccustomed to the culture. Rather he stands back and learns from their customs, not a problem for Nelida who wishes for his mind to open.

Nelida removes string from the bag. Cordaya picks it up and ties one end to a tall stick acting as a post. Ilian notices there is one on each corner of the casket, Cordaya tying the strings from one to the next, forming a rectangle around the area. Nelida grabs a few strands of paper from the bag and walks to the hanging strings. She ties the strands about them, leaving space in between every one. Cordaya helps. Ilian watches as the colors brighten the area. Nelida notices Ilian's urges to assist.

"Here, you try. I'm sure my sister would have loved to meet you," Nelida says with her gentle, warming smile.

Ilian returns it and accepts the strands of paper in his hand. He analyzes how Cordaya ties the strands, wondering if there is a special way to do so. When he becomes comfortable with the method in his head, he begins to tie the pieces to the string.

When the strands run out and the string is filled, the three step back and look with joy at the sight.

"A birthday celebration indeed," Nelida says with a tear streaming from her eye. Ilian places a hand on her shoulder. She grabs it in her own and squeezes. Ilian glances at the clouds in the distance, hoping the rain allows the monument to stand for the day before wiping the memories away.

"Do you all believe in heaven?" Ilian asks, his eyes unmoving from the clouds.

Nelida looks to him with a gentle expression.

"Why yes, we do. We believe when a person dies, they begin their journey to the skies. They'll take what they've learned in life and happen upon many different obstacles on the way there. With prayer, they may gain more strength or surpass tasks. It is not a punishment by the gods, rather a test to prove a person's faith. Those without faith will wander centuries before reaching heaven. They say some still haven't made it."

"And does a person's religion matter to you all. If I die, though I do not believe in your gods, will they still permit me to attempt the journey or simply force me to wander forever?"

Cordaya turns to Ilian with a sour expression. She wishes not to believe his words, thinking that after seeing such sights his doubts would have vanished. Yet, the stubborn soldier stuck in his ways chooses to deny their faith. She shakes her head and looks to the skies, her eyes begging the gods to give her guidance.

"Ilian. We believe all have their chance at redemption in the afterlife. It does not matter whether one worshiped the correct gods. It does not require a person to have worshiped any gods in their time on this planet. But faith and compassion do come in handy. The tasks will not seem as grand as mountains to those with faith."

"And how do you know how much faith is needed to surpass those obstacles?"

"We don't," Nelida answers honestly. "And that is the mystery of faith. Sometimes we question if those with the most faith are tested with harder obstacles just to prove so. But that is often a reflection of life itself and not the journey we take after death."

"Right..." Ilian mumbles, reaching his hand up to stroke the dangling paper strand in front of him.

Cordaya gets to work on pulling the weeds around the casket, Ilian and Nelida watching in silence. When she finishes, Nelida grabs the bag, and they make their trip back to the house.

Upon arrival, they grab a quick bite and head out to the harvest, taking Pinto along with them. They go to a different plot of land, one that is not too far. It contains fewer coffee plants than the other, many banana trees climbing the side of the mountain along with lemon and mandarin bushes.

Ilian, machete in hand, cuts at the stalk the bushel of bananas hang from. He forms a pile of them on the ground, taking them near the road where Pinto waits when he finishes. He returns to help Cordaya with her task.

She stands at the base of the mandarin bush with a long stick in hand. Cordaya pokes at the fruit, hoping it to fall so she may reach it. Ilian grabs a stick and mimics her strategy with a different bush not far from her. The orange fruit bounces to the ground as he hits it, sometimes rolling down the hill, forcing him to give chase. Ilian laughs at himself, but Cordaya wears a straight expression, no joke in the work for her. Ilian sighs, wondering if all her positive emotions were drained in exchange for the sword. An argument she would likely debate.

"You know, the cemeteries where I'm from are quite different. We place flowers at the base of a decorative concrete stone. The dead buried under the ground in marble caskets."

"They must be super happy to be so fortunate as to have such wealth in their deaths. You know, even though they can no longer spend it or use it. Because they're dead."

"Well, except those without the money for such luxuries, normally substituting a wooden crate. It's not like it matters, as you say." Ilian scratches his head in irritation, feeling as if nothing he says will spark a smile from the warrior.

"Except it does matter. Your class will throw away their money to the dead while the living starve. Where is the compassion in that thought process?"

"It's a tradition. I don't know why or how it started-"

"But your class continue to propagate it as a show of money and nothing else. Trying to impress others when oneself mourns for loss is a strange level of greed I will never understand. And don't ask me to. And your governor is no better. Generations throwing gold about as if it means nothing to them yet ignore what they can do to help those without. They always ignore. Act as if we don't exist. But when they need crop to feed their people, or laborers to tend their land or excavate their mines, they come calling for our aid. And pay us next to nothing in return."

"Why do you stay if it's so miserable here? Why don't you go somewhere else rather than complaining about it?"

"Where would I go? You tell me, soldier. Your capital? With high rent and low paying wages to anyone outside of the blood line? With what money would I travel there? Should I just walk? How will I eat? Scavenge the land every night and day just to survive? Just because you were lucky enough to be born into a family with money and connections, do not assume all have that privilege."

"I worked hard to get to where I am. I trained night and day, yes, to have the strength to rise to the top of the Governor's guard. To have the honor to work with His Grace is a privilege. But it was not luck."

"Luck is getting a good education, well fed, and not being distracted by your own growling stomach. Having the time to train night and day rather than working to put food on the table. Being able to sleep at night because you don't have to worry about the insects and other animals that may bother you as you lie on the forest floor, not enough energy or light to find your way home. Luck is knowing your parents can help you through all, rather than having to help them through all."

"I didn't choose this life."

"Well neither did I."

"But you've had some luck. Finding the Morezes."

"I will never say I am not fortunate. I am grateful with all the gods have graced me with. The Morezes have helped me through much. They've provided shelter and food as long as I can remember."

"And you were lucky to receive the glass sword."

Cordaya freezes. She turns to Ilian with furrowed brow. Throwing her stick to the ground, she approaches him with anger in every step. Ilian gulps and crosses his stick in front of him, trying to create a barrier between the two of them. Cordaya clenches her fists, staring at the ground while biting her lip. Her chest rises and falls as her heavy breaths inflate and deflate her lungs.

"Listen," Ilian begins attempting to deescalate the conversation. His calm voice fills with guilt as he knows his own insecurities lead him to offend others, even those who do not deserve it. He stares at Cordaya, despite never appearing happy, she is only capable of good. Ilian understands this. Yet, a contorted envy stands between them. "I know you do not consider the sword a gift. But there are many who would've loved being in your place. With that strength and power... one could do so much."

"And yet they shouldn't. That is why it is my responsibility and of no one else. Understand?" Cordaya looks up with tears pushed to the brink of her eyes. "It is not a gift. It was not by luck. It was of desperation, and I was the only one there to receive the call. It was fate. No more. No less. The gods decided long before I was brought into this world that this would be my responsibility. Have you learned nothing of how fate works in the past few days? It was not by your training that you are here. It is because this is the fate the gods chose for you. Stop ignoring the signs. You know we don't have long-"

"Until what? Until the world ends? If the gods wish for it, why should I be against it? If the gods wish for it, I should be at my home, praying with my family that they will grant us mercy and allow us into our heaven. If the gods wish for it, you think two humans will stand in their way?" Ilian releases a breathy chuckle and shakes his head. "I bet you believed every word that lion said."

Cordaya stares at him, her facial expression as if she no longer recognizes the soldier. She mirrors his reaction to his own statement, disbelief spelled across her face.

"And you didn't?" she asks in shock, hoping her doubts to be misguided, her hearing flawed.

All which occurred the day before appears no more than an imagined tale, a fantasy, in Ilian's eyes. She wonders the fate of the world if not even the one destined to help follows through in their plan.

"How can you stand face to face with the mystical being and not believe even a word? Many believe without ever seeing at all. That is the beauty of faith. And yet you see and continue to deny."

"For that reason, I deny. Why would they reveal themselves to us but to misguide us? Not all mystical forces of the world work for good."

"And you believe the spirits of the forest are one of these contrary forces? Which sins do they possess to demonstrate such an idea in your mind?"

"Pride."

"And like your governor doesn't have that and much more?"

"His Grace is better informed of the happenings and future of the world than that being. That is why he sent me to find you."

"And you honestly believe I'll go with you knowing what I know now? I could lose the sword."

"The Governor has plenty of weapons to spare."

"Oh. So stockpiling weapons is now a divine act?"

"He's prepared. A message from the gods delivered to him describing the events to come. The Governor must protect his people."

"And I must protect mine."

"How do you expect to do so alone?"

"My faith will lead me."

"And what if your gods aren't real?"

Cordaya pauses. She bites her lip and shakes her head, wondering how his doubts perpetuate to such an extreme. All she wishes to say, to scream, at the soldier swirl in her head, the uncontrolled tornado sucking all her energy from her. The thoughts, and her own doubt in the past, about her faith circulate through her veins, getting the power they need from her heart.

"When I fight... when I kill those evil soldiers, warmongers, barbarians, whatever you wish to call them, I don't think about whether the gods exist. I don't question where their death will take them. I don't pause to think about the lives they've lived up until that point. I grip my glass sword and I swing it to protect those innocents who cannot protect themselves. It's not about my salvation. It's not about their sins. The people I protect could very well be greater sinners than those I kill. I've thought about that one. When I sit alone in my bed, I consider that I may be the evil. That those sent to the villages are the good of their own stories. That they believe it their purpose from the gods to kill those sinners and wrongdoers of the villages. I consider all of this. And yet, the next time it happens, without hesitation, I take up my sword and I strike them down."

"You protect them because they are not fighters. Because they don't have weapons to protect themselves."

"They are warriors by blood. They very well could protect themselves. But... there's something else in the air. A strange thickness that clouds the mind. As if they've forgotten. Their aggression cut out and replaced with a desire to protect their possessions and what little fortune they have."

Ilian thinks back to when he first arrived at the village. The townspeople ran as if in fear, yet not even that stopped them from stealing some of his belongings. Ilian looks up, searching for another mandarin to prod from the bush.

"I'm not sure what will become of the mountain villages," Cordaya says with defeat in her tone. "I'm not even sure we're meant to make it out alive. But what I do know is that more than a few thousand lives hang in the balance. Millions. Millions will feel the effect. Strange how guilty I feel knowing I can't save them all. It eats away at me every time I think about it."

"In training, we soldiers learn that sacrifice is a part of the job. Death will never be too far from our line of duty. We must accept and come to terms with it before we take up our post. It feels... dehumanizing, almost, to cut out this part of me. I wonder if the gods can forgive me."

"I wonder the same," Cordaya answers, lifting her hands to see the phantom blood covering her palms and fingertips. She bends down to grab her stick and walks back to her tree. They continue their work in silence for some time before Ilian speaks up.

"You can't blame yourself. Not for what you can't control. You shouldn't blame yourself even for things you can. You can give it your all and still come up short."

"I was chosen by the gods for a reason. And though you may doubt, I never will again," Cordaya says, poking at a mandarin, nudging it to her pile once it hits the earth. Her expression reads amusement, her eyes, and not mouth, doing the smiling. She shakes her head. "Sometimes I believe I had more faith before attaining the glass sword. Perhaps it's all going to my head. Hearing my name as if in a legend. Little girls coming up to me saying they wish to be like me one day. I couldn't imagine the guilt I would feel if those dreams came true. That's why I force myself to work and work and work. So I don't forget where I came from. So I don't forget that I'm still there. A glass sword doesn't change anything."

"That's where you're wrong," Ilian contests. She glances at him. "You've done so much good with that gift. And don't correct me again. It is a gift. You don't have to be here. Doing this physical labor. Straining yourself night and day just like everyone else. You're capable of so much more."

"Ilian-"

"Meet with the Governor. Listen to what he has to say. I'd bet that if you do him that favor, you nor the Morezes would ever have to worry about that next meal ever again. Nelida and Ernesto are growing old. They can't do this work for much longer."

Cordaya's eyes turn to the ground and her grip tightens on the stick. His statement catches her off guard, using her weakness to attack her heart. She wonders the sacrifices she'll need to make. Many new paths form in front of her, tempting her to journey down them, to see what awaits. As her eyes absorb the nature around her, the trees and flowers, her ears listening to the singing of the birds and insects, and every other sense tuned in to her environment. Cordaya pokes at another mandarin, this one not falling from her jabs.

"And after this is all over. The battle won. You're going to return to your normal life, right? Forget all about us. It won't matter because you believe it ceases to affect you. Your governor will continue pretending as if we are not his citizens. Therefore, not his problem."

"Cordaya, don't make such rash assumptions," Ilian says, his voice as if begging her to listen. He thinks about how coming to the mountains transformed and reshaped his thoughts, his beliefs. Before it was pure imagination. He heard the rumors, the stories, all about those who live in the rural regions. Though many stereotypes have been broken, many have also been strengthened. Those back in the capital speak of the mountain people's strength, but to be put up to the challenge grows an appreciation before unknown. They hear of the poverty, but to see its face and ugly effects burns a scar into the heart.

"It's not rash, Ilian. It's the truth. You want to believe you've changed, but in the end, it's no more than a memory. In a few years, we'll be no more than a story you think you remember hearing. Not shortly after it will be a dream you once had. They'll call you brave, courageous, a soldier for the people. The governor will raise your pay and create a new, higher rank of official just for you. And we'll be here, struggling to win the war he started yet refuses to fight." With her last sentence, Cordaya's volume raises as if crying into the air, wishing for the gods to hear, wishing they would do something. Her eyes, full of rage and despair, pierce him like a dagger to the heart.

"The Governor fights his battles. He's strategic. He does so to cause the minimal amount of casualties among his men. He-"

"You didn't even know about these attacks until you came here! Since they've began, not one soldier from your capital has arrived to save the day. But the tax collectors don't miss a day, do they? Neither do the trucks they send from the cities to buy our goods with the low prices the Governor dictates. But this is war! People here die from starvation and illness. We're accustomed to such deaths by now. But battles on our land, destroying that which we fight to preserve, we will not tolerate such reckless violence. And we shouldn't have to."

"That is why we must talk to the Governor. Help him plan so the troops arrive sooner than later."

"No one is coming to save us, Ilian."

"You don't know that."

"Yeah, I-"

"Cordaya!" Nelida's scream carries downhill to the two. Their eyes widen. They drop their sticks and dart up the mountain, panic coursing through them as their hearts race with the infinite possibilities filling their minds. Not one of their thoughts possesses a favorable outcome.

When they arrive at the dirt road, out of breath, they join the Morezes at their side. Nelida and Ernesto stare off into the distance, distraught expressions carving fear and despair into their faces. Smoke rises in the direction of a small village not far east. A barbarian attack. Cordaya's fingers reach for the loop of her sash. The glass sword, transparent but gaining definition, forms from nothing more than the air around it. The moment she feels its sensation caress her fingertip, Cordaya sprints at full speed for the village.

"Stay here but move from the road. If the enemy heads this way, you won't want them to see you," Ilian instructs. Nelida and Ernesto nod. The soldier whistles and runs after Cordaya.

The patting of hooves throwing up dust sounds behind Ilian. A grin forms and his eyes illuminate with determination. Pinto arrives at his side. He mounts the horse and doesn't hesitate before taking off.

Before long he catches up to Cordaya, her pace never slowing. Her skirt billows in the wind she creates and dirt fills her sandals. He decreases the speed of the horse once he arrives at her side.

"Jump on. We'll make it much faster on horseback."

Cordaya nods. Without stopping, she grips the saddle and throws her leg over the horse. Their anger and tension from earlier vanish as worry overtakes them. At lightning speeds, granted by the gods, they make haste for the village.

Chapter Nine

Pure devastation meets them upon their arrival. The rising smoke could not have prepared them for the sights they were about to witness.

Children hide in the shadows and bushes, gazing with tear-filled eyes at their parents and family lying in the street, blood pouring out. Sporadic, scared chirps issue from the chicks running about, their sound quenching the haunting silence. Smoke escapes from the doors and windows of the concrete houses and structures, all that lies beyond the scorched walls turned to ash. Cordaya and Ilian intently listen, scanning the streets and alleys in search of the enemy.

Cordaya jumps down from Pinto and examines the wound of one lying on the street. She drops her head to the young woman's chest. Cordaya's expression reveals the absence of sound to reach her ears. The warrior stands and looks around. Vultures circle above. Stray wolves wander the streets for a fresh meal.

"Let's split up. These barbarians couldn't have gotten far. At least I hope," Cordaya says, running her sweaty hand through her hair as she looks around. She shakes her head and sprints down the street, turning to the right at the first corner.

Ilian, approving of the plan, takes the left turn. The hoof steps of the horse echo in the emptiness of the landscape. His eyes scan the houses to his sides, nothing remains. He wonders if most of the people ran away, not noticing an abundance of bodies in the street. However, the number far surpasses the number of dead he would have wished for.

"The attack must have happened hours ago. There is no sign of anyone left. Only some children. The lucky ones, I'm guessing," Ilian mumbles to himself. Blood trails, as if bodies dragged away, create a path down the streets. Ilian tries to decipher which direction they were taken, the painted lines sporadic and without reason. Perhaps survivors attempting to get away. Perhaps torturous play by the brutes.

Ilian turns down the next street. He slides from Pinto's back and pulls the lead behind him as he examines the remains of the city. The wooden structures built on top smolder as the flames cease to find fuel to satisfy their hunger. Homes, workplaces, no longer present in the town. The humble establishments all the citizens of the small village could afford. In death, they would no longer need to.

Ilian hears the whimpers of a child further up the road. He directs Pinto to the location, wondering if any of the brutes continue to torment, even after such destruction. As he grows closer, his eyes scan for his or her location, unable to distinguish where they come from.

He pauses as the noise occurs to a place to the right of him. Ilian sprints and kicks in the scorched, metal door of the residence, its hinges weak from the flames. Smoke hits the soldier in the face, the heat brushing his cheeks, burning his skin. When the dark air filters through the entrance, drifting heavenward, Ilian's vision clears. He looks around the room, searching for the origin of the noise. A whimper leaves like an exhale, growing softer every time. Ilian turns to see a shelf, fallen over from its burnt supports. He bends down and lifts it, revealing a young boy underneath,

Ilian throws the shelf, which crumbles with the gravity of being lifted. The soldier then grabs the boy under the arms and pulls him from the pile of ashes and debris. The boy clings to Ilian, trembling and fighting to breathe. Ilian bats at the smoke in front of him, his eyes watering and lungs filling with the foul air. The soldier races for the door, stumbling over the debris in the walkway, trying his best to maintain balance with the boy in his arms.

When they arrive at the outside world, a breeze of fresh air greets them. He sets the boy on the ground and takes deep breaths, peering up and down the street to get eyes on an attacker. Not one shows. The soldier scratches his head, wondering where the enemy could be.

"Are you alright?" he asks the boy, whose face glows red in the sun with ash in his hair and on his clothes. He nods in response, his lip trembling as the tears form and the suppressed screams fight to be held back. Ilian looks upon the boy with sympathy but understands he cannot spend his time protecting the child.

Ilian holds out his hand, inviting the boy to stand. The boy's legs, weakened and bruised by the shelf to lay atop them, cannot find the strength to do so. Ilian picks him up and moves him behind a bush, whose leaves and blooms wither in the heat but whose resilience inspires Ilian to move forward.

"Stay behind here and say nothing. Not until you have the strength to run. When that happens, go to the nearest village and seek help. Do not approach any strangers on your path. If anything, hide from those on the road until you arrive at the next town. Trust no one. Do I make myself clear?" Ilian asks, knowing he provides a long list of instructions for the young boy to follow. The soldier can do no more than have faith that the boy will arrive unharmed. The young boy nods and cowers behind the bush.

Ilian stands and looks around, paranoia settling in further and further the longer he goes without seeing anyone. He closes his eyes and listens to his surroundings. Nothing meets him. He shakes his head and whistles for Pinto to follow as he continues his search of the town.

The next street over, Ilian finds a corpse on the ground. He creeps toward it, wondering if it could be a trap placed by the enemy to lure in others. When no sounds or movements reach him, he bends down to inspect the middle-aged man. A machete lays on the ground at his side, not going down without a fight. A warrior by blood.

Ilian places his trembling fingers on the man's neck. No pulse, as expected. Ilian shakes his head, knowing there to not be much else he can do.

Curiosity finds the soldier the longer his eyes examine the dead man. Unlike the other woman, his blood does not spill into the street from his wound. Rather his shirt absorbs what blood leaves him. And not from the slice nor stab of a sword. But from a hole, no larger than the pit of a peach. Ilian's eyes grow wide, the type of weapon to be used unlike any he had ever seen. Ilian's paranoia forces him to glance about his surroundings, the enemy more terrifying than he could imagine.

"What technology is this?" Ilian questions.

He walks down the road, wondering if Cordaya found anything similar. Thoughts spin in his head, doubts form about his defenses, no more than the machete at his side. His best chance for survival is to avoid the enemy altogether. Or a surprise attack. He continues to question if the enemy remains within the town or moving on to their next victim.

A rancid smell joins with the breeze. Ilian covers his nose, the repulsive scent stirring his stomach. Ilian turns his head to the concrete building next to him, mostly unaffected by the flames ravaging the rest of the village. He scales to the second floor, looking over the balcony in an attempt to see the cause.

In the distance, large smokestacks billow into the air. Ilian gasps as the black smog fills the green hills of their village. Hoja Rosa burns in another attack. Two attacks in one day. Ilian curses at the merciless barbarians, their stratagem cruel and unyielding. Threatening to destroy every village until none remain, their endless attempts to begin a war anger the soldier. Knowing that the Governor refuses to answer these attempts creates a bitter taste in his mouth. Countless deaths of the citizens of Micacao. No government, not even their own, believing them significant to save.

Ilian climbs down the rails. His feet hit the earth sending a flurry of dust upward. He waves it away, not knowing what to do. He knows if Cordaya realizes the attack on Hoja Rosa, her priorities lie in her home village. But if she doesn't know... he must tell her. He has not seen sight of the enemy within this city. They must have moved on.

The soldier runs down the street, turning down roadways not yet traveled in search of Cordaya. He doesn't wish to scream her name, not knowing if he is able between shallow inhales of the air and smoke to enter his lungs. The flurry in his mind and racing heart force his legs to keep moving, the feeling of tiring overcome by a numb sensation. Pinto follows behind, galloping to keep up with the soldier. Ilian's breath grows shallow as his panic deepens and his search brings no results.

A loud bang occurs not far from him.

Ilian freezes. He attempts to decipher the sound but fails to do so. Like an explosion from a cannon and with the force of a firework sent into the air, the sharp bang crackles at his eardrums yet leaves no residual marks. No residue or smoke filters into the air. No crashing of houses and crumbling mountainsides resound to the effects of the cause. A sound with no consequence?

Ilian unsheathes his machete and tightens his grip. The wound of the man from earlier flashes in his mind, a hole singed through him of unknown origin. And Cordaya, her location unknown to him, sends a haunting thought. The soldier swallows his fear and runs toward the danger.

The putrid fumes grow stronger as he approaches where he believes the sound boomed. Before he rounds a corner wall to the town center, he observes the charcoal black smoke to rise, wood never producing a colored haze so toxic and horrifying. Fire crackles as it eats at materials Ilian has never heard it feed upon, ongoing and fresh, consuming more material by the minute. The soldier, with a calming breath and reminder of the necessity of bravery, peeks his head about the concrete wall. His jaw drops.

In the town's center, a pile of corpses mounds into the air. Brute and citizens alike burn, their bodies dowsed with some form of oil to spark the flames. The burning clothes, hair, and flesh sends foul fumes into the pure air. Black clouds form from the smoke, travelling to the next towns as a warning.

A stash of swords with a sliver of alexandrite lay not far from the pile.

"Who did this?" Ilian whispers, begging the gods for an answer and their assistance. Those who came to the aid of the village did not do so as friends, but as another set of enemies. More barbarians? Or worse? Ilian hears voices from behind the pile. He fights to get a look but finds the task difficult if he wishes not to be caught.

"This one was hiding behind a bush. Thought he could get away," the voice says, lacking all emotion.

"Throw him in with the rest of them. We never know who could be a spy for the enemy," a different voice responds.

The shadows move closer to the pile, throwing another smaller shadow into it. The dead corpses shift with the added weight. Ilian bites his lip, debating what should be done. He gazes behind him hoping to see Cordaya. He wonders if she watches from afar as well, planning her attack.

The boots of the ones hidden by the pile click against the ground as they approach where Ilian hides, forms gaining distinct features as they pass through the countless veils of smog. Ilian lowers himself further to the ground, using a water barrel as cover. He peeks through the crack where the barrel does not quite touch the concrete wall and catches the glimpse of two soldiers, in their uniform jackets and with their caps on their head, uniforms familiar to his memory. He squints at the weapons. Sabers hang at their sides, Micacaoan military grade weapons of an alloy only slightly better than those of the interior forces, but the one soldier grips a strange combination of wood and metal in his hand. Unable to contain his vehement disgust, Ilian stands.

"General Victorino?" Ilian questions, scowl forming despite the fear racing through his heart.

The two soldiers jump in shock of the voice and turn to face him, weapons at the ready. Ilian throws up his hands and observes their expressions. Blood stains their pants, sweat lining their brow, yet no fear can be seen coursing through them, not even adrenaline. They read calm and collected, burning bodies as if it were no more than an outdoor feast for the family.

"Grace's Guard Ilian? Is that you?" Victorino asks, clearing his throat as he steps through the final veils of smoke to separate them. A golden snake badge shines on his chest, revealing him to be the Appointed General of the Perimeter, the other man no more than an unranked soldier.

"Yes, it's me. What are you doing here?" Ilian questions, his eyes moving from the General to the pile of corpses behind. Shock and denial enter him as he wonders whose orders they follow. General Victorino's role entails border security, ensuring no military powers nor threats cross those lines. Not only has he failed to comply with those orders, but Ilian finds him committing dishonorable acts upon their own. Possible treason?

The General glances to his underling, turning back to Ilian with a smirk. The other soldier flashes his weapon at Ilian, who gazes at the unknown with wide eyes.

"The Governor has given us our orders. New orders."

His malicious smile sends a flurry of butterflies into flight in Ilian's stomach. A throbbing pound, like a pulse in his head, reverberates the muscles in his skull. The hot blood flows through those veins, expanding them and putting pressure against his forehead. Ilian hears a distant prayer, as if his voice detached from himself, his soul begging the gods before it is too late. But Ilian refuses to show weakness, especially to one ranked below him.

"New orders?" he questions, not sure where to begin nor if he even wants to hear the answer. "And who protects the borders while your troops execute these new orders? Who's preventing more of these brutes from entering?"

Ilian, not wishing to disrespect nor comment on the failures of General Victorino chooses to ignore them altogether. But the shine in the General's eyes... the twist at the corner of his mouth... the way his fingers grip the saber. All key signs that nothing happened unintentionally. The General did not view the attacks as a failure on his part nor cared of the outcomes.

"His Grace has no concern of these pesky battles in the mountains. They don't affect us in the slightest. If anything, these begging rats prove more of a problem," the General snickers, the soldier at his side following suit. Ilian stares at the two in disbelief. He wonders where they hide their honor and by what laws they feel secure in their doings.

"Rats? Innocent citizens of Micacao are dying because you refuse to do your job!"

"Don't act as if they contribute anything to society. Since the trade wars have begun, their product no longer brings profits to the government. If anything, it costs the government more continuing to buy from their own rather than from foreign exports. Niekalarah offers their crops at a much fairer rate."

"And what of the nation's independence? Are we going to continue feeding into the pockets of Hernan while he sends armed men to kill the mountain laborers and steal their land for his own?"

"These are lands of Micacao. His Grace has sold nothing."

"Yet Hernan sends laborers to transport crops from these fertile lands to his country so he can continue to lower their worth and profit from this nation without paying out a cent. And you let them pass the borders as if you see nothing."

The General straightens his posture and squints at Ilian. His face spells his surprise.

"How do you-"

"Do they bribe you? Does the Governor know?"

The soldier at the General's side raises the unknown weapon. Ilian takes a deep breath and puffs out his chest. The General looks to the ground but uses his hand to lower the weapon. A malevolent chuckle, starting low then growing into a bellow, rings through the empty city. Any still alive and in hiding would have heard it and been paralyzed. Ilian freezes any and all movement, preventing the slightest twitch of a finger.

"My Lord's Guard..."

"And these barbaric threats, with their Niekalaran weapons. How is this not an act of war? Why has the Governor not sent troops to respond to these attacks?"

"Lord Guard Ilian. Your heart is good and your mind, its thoughts. Governor Caseto sent a messenger at dawn, giving us new orders. To find the warrior of the glass sword."

Ilian's eyes widen. His desire to scan the surroundings in search of her collides with his instinct to avoid doing so. If they remain in the city, if they remain talking to him, it means they have not yet found her. The thought strikes.

"The barbarians... you let them-"

"Are you beginning to understand now, Ilian? What's a better way to call the warrior from hiding than through an attack."

"And you let the others move onto the next village."

His eyes look to the smokestacks in the distance, the black smog covering Hoja Rosa. His heart beats with the desire to escape.

"Yes, some of our soldiers followed not far behind. You see, we made a deal with them. They can do as they please, as they're ordered, if we can claim the warrior. We'll search village after village until we find him. Surprisingly these brutes know their way well. He can't hide for long. We'll find him."

Ilian refuses to correct their mistake. If they believe they search for a man, they'll be even more shocked when they see her and her capabilities. Perhaps so much so they will fall to her sword. Anger grows within him to think of the origin of the cruel plan.

"The Governor, His Grace, could not have agreed that this is the best way."

"He gives us the orders. We execute them as we see fit."

"This is against everything we learned. Every code of honor, every religious law, it's-"

"The gods will forgive us through the pardon from the Governor."

Ilian shakes his head, disgust worn on his face.

"There is no forgiveness for such heinous acts."

"And that is not for you to decide, Guard." The General's smirk and piercing eyes shake Ilian to his core. His refusal to permit such evils, knowing the gods look down upon him, send his hand to his saber. The two step back, taking defensive stances. Ilian takes a deep breath and releases his grip.

"And what of my mission?" Ilian mumbles, fighting for the words to escape.

"I suggest you return to the capital. You're no longer needed here."

Ilian nods and turns away. His hand meets the neck of Pinto, her hair in his fingers, like soft wire, provides a comfort and nostalgia he longs to return to. He remembers arriving to the mountains, not more than a week back. The hospitality he met, the kind acts of grace he received. All from those with less. Those who understood his wealth, his position. Yet they never failed to make him feel welcome. He couldn't say the same for all. Some villagers didn't like the idea of a soldier of the government within their once peaceful village, now targets for the barbarians. Ilian wonders how the world arrived to this, understanding why the gods anger.

His head jerks up as he hears a clicking sound behind him. Ilian turns to see the soldier aiming the strange weapon at him, its unknown power and capabilities sending a number of fears through him. A pit falls into his stomach.

"What are you doing?"

"The Governor doesn't need to know about any of this. In fact, if we told him we found out you'd died, well... that would solve a lot of problems. Wouldn't it?" The General speaks with a venomous tone. Bloodlust laces his voice, glazing his eyes.

Ilian pats the shoulder of Pinto, warning her to run. She trots away, Ilian following after. A loud bang rings out behind him. Not a second later, a concrete post not far ahead of him emits a puff of dust as debris. The metal pellet cuts through the strong pillar, leaving its mark by scraping off the corner. Ilian turns to see they prepare another shot. He grabs for Pinto's saddle, throwing himself over as he saw Cordaya do earlier.

They dart from the burning village, to be abandoned, the gods taking back their land. The images of the piled corpses, his fellow comrades, those strange weapons spiral in his head. He thinks of Cordaya, praying she is safe, unharmed.

He stops on a road with view of the villages beneath. He sees the village he escaped. Hoja Rosa, not far, blazes with great flames. All which survived the first attack now crumbles to the ground. He thinks of the Morezes. All they have is that which they earned through blood, sweat, tears, and years of merciless wages for their crop. Gone. Erased by the fire, ashes taken with the wind to a place they'll never be able to reforge them. Ilian thinks of the others in the village, hoping most, if not all, succeeded in their escape. And Cordaya...

Ilian cannot stop thinking about her. He imagines the possibility presented by Mizochtal, the messenger spirit of the forest. If her sword disappears, she will be unable to defend herself. Ilian shakes his head. He knows even if her sword vanishes, she will search for a weapon, anything nearby, to protect those in the village. She won't stop, not if the sword disappears, not if she takes her last breath. The warrior will fight until no longer capable. The gods chose her, not only for her faith, but for her strength. Her resolve. Her selflessness. Ilian wishes he can grow to be the warrior she is.

The thoughts swarm him. He wonders what he is to do next. Ilian rubs Pinto's neck, trying to calm both of their racing hearts. The only solution forming in his mind is to return to the capital. He must tell the Governor.

Ilian finds difficulty swallowing. The whispers of the forest, though perhaps the voices within his own mind, fill his ears with words of caution. The statement of the lion rings out in his mind. Could His Grace truly be no more than human? Could the talk of the divine, being the one chosen for royalty, could it all be a lie?

Ilian watches the smoke rise. A bright sun glare shines in the distance, disappearing as soon as it came, forcing Ilian to wonder if his imagination tricks him. He nudges Pinto's side, and the horse continues down the path, in the direction of the capital.

The sun beats down on him, sweat dripping from his forehead, back, and chest. As they climb the mountain, Ilian allows a stop at a creek passing the road for himself and Pinto. Ilian strays from the path, noticing a blackberry bush not far. He winces as the thorns stick into his hands and sleeves. He uses his free hand to detach those piercing his skin, some preferring his hand to their place of the branch. He brings the wild fruit to his mouth and enjoys their bitter taste and sour juice, his stomach only caring for the nourishment.

Ilian walks back to Pinto, thinking of their situation in despair. He would've thought he'd want to reunite with his family after all that transpired. Yet his wishes and desires include sitting at the dinner table with the Morezes, learning of the village and listening to their gossip. The amount of information the two managed to learn in short conversations with the other townspeople amuses the soldier. He chuckles, the memories flowing freely. But the feeling grows distant. Blown away like ashes.

Mounting Pinto, Ilian trots to a nearby village to buy some supplies with what little he brought with him. He exits the shop and takes a seat on a concrete block outside.

Children run past, playing and laughing, a little one trailing behind with a stream of tears, wanting to join the fun. Quickly with the sight of a dried mango pit, a smile springs forth and the small child rejoices in her treasure. The adults form groups in the streets, talking about the soldiers who recently passed through. They glance at Ilian, knowing him to be one of them. He notices their lack of fear, the smoke rising from those destroyed villages hidden by a mountain. The only sign comes from the fogging air, a dense cloud of smoke covering the landscape.

Ilian eats a mango sprinkled with chile powder, debating his next move. Does he warn the village? Or should he head straight to the capital for help? Ilian refuses to believe General Victorino's troops act in accordance with the Governor, who very well knows their acts to be against the code of conduct of a soldier. Were the forces of evil corrupting their minds? Hitting where it would affect the nations most, attacking the government? Ilian shakes his head, trying to clear his thoughts despite the burning smell forcing his attention back to the innocents' unnecessary deaths. Ilian clenches his fists, tears forming. He made an oath, several years ago. An oath that doesn't disappear with age, rather further engraves itself into the heart and soul. A promise to the gods, whether it be his or theirs. It no longer mattered.

Ilian throws the mango pit to the ground and stands from the block. The huddled adults stare wide-eyed in his direction, murmuring about what the soldier may do next. Guilt fills him. The thought of causing fear to the very people the soldiers promise to protect. Ilian avoids eye contact with them as he walks past, Pinto following close behind.

When Ilian arrives at the road's intersection, he turns his head from left to right. Right will take him back to the other side of the mountain. Left leads to the capital. The images of Cordaya, distressed yet fighting until her last breath, no glass sword in sight, blur his mind and vision. To imagine the Morezes arriving, only to be killed by the strange weapon Victorino's men carry. Ilian shakes his head, almost as if hearing their screams echo in his ears.

A rustling in the bushes on the other side of the dirt road catches his attention. Ilian squints, trying to examine the creature to hide in its branches. He moves closer. Breaking of twigs occurs to his right. Ilian's head darts to find the origin. A small figure, similar to the form of a tree with foliage, runs away. Ilian blinks, wondering if the vision came from no more than his need to sleep. A delusion. Or could it be... Ilian glances about him before mounting Pinto and heading toward the capital. Paranoia fills him as he believes they may be watching. They await his next move. Ilian gulps, anticipating it himself.

Chapter Ten

After the sun descends and ascends twice, the world seemingly rotating faster and the journey home longer than before, Ilian rounds the mountain bend to see the familiar plains spread out below, rows of corn and wheat, fenced fields with cows and sheep. A smile forms as exhaustion fails to consume him entirely. The soldier follows the curving path down the mountain, counting the horse's steps until they reach the capital.

With every minute the clouds change to a darker shade of grey. If they happen to reach black, Ilian wonders if that signifies the end. The spirits of the air act quickly, demonstrating their god's anger.

The ground rumbles underneath them. Ilian slides from Pinto and looks behind, hoping the tremor will not cause a landslide. The earthquake passes, not enough to shake the trees to the ground but enough to shake him. Only deep in the mountains had he known earthquakes to occur at such magnitude. Most tremors near the capital barely manage to cause destruction, let alone turn heads. Every time they occur, they grow stronger. The spirits of the earth must be causing movement below. Ilian looks to the sea, wondering what the spirits of the water could be up to.

Ilian leads Pinto down the road. He stretches his muscles with his strides, sitting on horseback for so long straining his back and cramping his legs. With every step, time passes. The divine clock ticks, their distance decreasing but their speed doing the same. Each tick aligns with his heart's beat, his march in rhythm. Ilian struggles to swallow, his dry throat from the heat and his own fears another discomfort. Ilian wonders when it will get easier.

He thinks about Mizochtal's hint. To appease the gods, he and Cordaya must convince them to stop the spread of evil. He and Cordaya must convince the gods that the human race, the entire world, is worth saving. Yet Ilian finds himself in the countryside not far from Diodios, the capital of Micacao. Cordaya's location unknown. The chance she escaped from the barbarians and soldiers both don't lean in their favor. Ilian offers a silent prayer and looks to the sky. He believes he sees a ray of light break through the layers of clouds, but after blinking it disappears. Cordaya proves time and time again her strength and faith. Ilian hopes it was enough this time.

A tall tower, every brick growing distinct from the other as he nears, stands as a monument to the defensive prowess of the capital. A watchtower, as looming as it is hopeful. As it stands, calm and quiet, it delivers a silent assurance of their divine protection. A single light or horn blare could change all in a matter of seconds and chaos would be unleashed. A smile reaches Ilian's face to think about his fellow soldiers, performing their duties even in the darkest of times due to their loyalty to His Grace, the Governor. But that smile does not stay as realization hits and Ilian pauses. In times of trouble, a beacon at the tower's side illuminates with flames to signal danger. Yet the branches and dry brush remain untouched. Not the start of embers, nor even a sign of early smoke makes itself visible to Ilian from the distance. Confusion fills him.

The images of war and destruction further in the mountains fill his mind. General Victorino and his men, weapons in hand, killing barbarians and civilians in their search for Cordaya. The glimpse of an ancient, mystical tree, plagued and rotting from the inside out. The threat of all life ending with it. The menacing storm to approach yet the unbearable, dry heat held below. Earthquakes shake with greater and greater force. Volcanoes build with the pressure to burst as the lava boils within. The rising tides, growing waves, the warnings of a tsunami sent to wipe out civilization from existence. Natural disasters to clear the land and any proof it may hold of life. All destroyed, left to decay by the temperaments of the gods.

Ilian kicks a rock on the road in front of him. It hops into the ditch with long grass and wildflowers, vanishing from sight. He lets out a groan of defeat, a plea. The Governor must realize. He must notice the signs. Out of fear of widespread panic, the Governor refuses to tell the people. The beacons remain unlit for no other reason. To disturb the peace would mean robbing what happiness the citizens of Micacao have before the end strikes. Ilian tries to convince himself of the false narrative. His heart swells, as does his anger with His Grace.

"Have I lost faith?" Ilian mumbles, clenching his fists and feeling the rough, calloused skin of his palms cracking.

The houses on the outskirts of the capital take form beyond the watchtowers. Ilian imagines his family, delighted yet deceived. Their son is not who he used to be.

As Ilian arrives at the watchtower, a soldier steps out from within.

"Hold up just a minute, sir," the watchman calls out.

Ilian stops, his eyes gazing upon the great palace, built upon the small hill in the center of the capital. It stands in great majesty as if a monument to the gods, built by ancient kings in their times and standing the test of harsh winds and weather. The only damage lies in a northeast pillar, chipped by an obsidian tipped arrow from a war long ago. Victory sides with the hands of the divine. Obsidian shatters, as did the warriors and civilizations long passed to use such weapons, and the palace and its citizens remain. Ilian wonders if the capital's history proves enough to stand up to the task they now face.

The watchman approaches Ilian, one hand finds the saber at his side in the chance he may need to protect himself. His face lights up, an odd confusion in his eyes as he recognizes the soldier in front of him.

"Private Guard Ilian? Is that you?" the watchman asks.

Ilian knows him to be Olivio, having sat with him during a feast of thanks held by the Governor for every branch of the military and protections units. His parents were good friends of his own, their coming together sprouting from devotion for the gods and the interest in spirited social commentary with the finest wines one could procure in these parts. And they meet once more. Ilian thinks it must be luck, knowing he will not be poked and prodded before entering the capital.

"Yes, it is I," Ilian responds, shame covering his face as he recalls his dirty form, boots covered in mud and specks of blood and ash on his coat. To think a Private Guard would have dirtied themselves for the ungrateful civilians. This either proves their good heart or their stupidity, most from the capital considering it the latter. "I need to deliver a message to the capital. It's urgent."

"I'm afraid to inform you that the Governor is away. He should be back within the day. He left days past for counsel with the nation of Vangur concerning the tactics and underhanded strategies of Niekalarah."

"But..." Ilian mumbles, shock covering his face. "What is there to discuss? War has already begun."

"Do not be a fearmonger, Private Guard. Otherwise, I cannot let you pass into the city with such propaganda."

"But war has broken out in the mountainous regions. Barbaric tribes armed by Niekalarah are attacking our citizens. I saw it myself. Their weapons contain the sliver of alexandrite popularized by the Niekalaran army. The Governor has sent troops to respond and-"

"Ilian, you cannot go spreading rumors about the capital that the Governor himself has not approved. You know that."

"That is why I must speak with him."

"You mean His Grace," Olivio says with such lack of respect Ilian leans back. Before he left, all considered Ilian to be the Governor's right hand. He proved the most loyal, faithful, and respected guard of the palace. What had changed?

"Yes, that is what I meant to say."

Ilian blinks a few times to discover if he in fact remains in reality or has fallen into a different realm. Were the gods punishing him? His urgency to arrive was met with misfortune, one that serves to punish all should time run out. He misstepped. At the fork in the road, was it possible Ilian made the wrong choice? If fate planned for this, perhaps he still had the chance. But with Cordaya's location unknown, fate appeared too twisted and contorted for Ilian to decipher. He must follow his heart. He must trust in the gods.

"Listen, Olivio," Ilian starts with quiet tone. "I've seen a lot these past few days and I may not ever return to the man I was before His Grace sent me on my mission. But I do know that my faith has multiplied in the greatest of ways and I've experienced a revelation within myself. Allow me passage to speak with my family. Allow me passage to seek counsel with the Governor upon his return. I have not been removed from my post, or have I?"

Olivio scans the soldier's form up and down, knowing his only choice. He releases a loud exhale and walks over to Pinto to poke at the saddlebags, taking a peek at the items inside. Olivio studies Ilian again.

"All appears well. You may pass."

Olivio stands back. With a sigh of relief, Ilian takes up Pinto's lead and marches forward.

"Ilian," Olivio calls to him, solemn and quiet his tone. "Please, I say this as a friend. Be careful with the words you choose to speak. I would hate to see tragedy fall upon you and your family."

The soldier nods with serious face and moves forward.

The chatter of the city, the traffic of the merchants and shopkeepers, native and foreign, fill the streets of the capital. The aromas of fresh fruits and vegetables, herbs and flowers, meet him in that grim hour. The sweet smells reminding him of a funeral march. But this does not prevent his stomach from growling for roasted cow tongue and spiced ribs. The days of baked beans and rice may well be behind the soldier. The thought perhaps contradictory of his own hypocritical desires.

Familiar faces spring up, shock and welcome fill expressions and collide with him all in swift hugs and handshakes by the women and men alike. A couple of cousins tug on his dirty clothes, wondering of his travels.

"None of the women down there wanted to take care of a soldier?" One jabs, brushing some bits of ash from Ilian's shoulder.

"No, they only take care of the handsome ones," another laughs, pinching at Ilian's cheeks.

"But the question is, did you take care of them?" the first jokes with a loud bellow and making an obscene gesture, calling the attention and scowls of others in the busy streets. "I hear they're a strong bunch. Maybe a bit hard-headed. Probably like it rough. What d'you say, Ilian? Am I right?"

Ilian swats away their hands and gestures, knowing despite being his elders they continue to lack in maturity, a reason they never made it to the royal guard. And despite being of his blood, Ilian wishes he did not have to associate with them in public, especially at the expense of his own pride and integrity. Many from this town often said those who act out as so surely have blood that runs from the mountains, an insult to the intelligence and strength of those Ilian now considers family. An insult laced in ignorance, for Ilian now knows the truth.

"Enough, you two. I don't have time to waste."

"Gotta get back to your women?"

The laughs explode once more. They hold their abdomens, tears of amusement forming in their eyes. Ilian clenches his fists as anger rises within him. The clouds draw near, the quakes more powerful, to think of what else may be lurking sends a chill down Ilian's spine. No others in the town worry, nor do they appear as if they even know. And Ilian finds his irritating bloodline standing in his way of fate. One of his cousins nears and Ilian grabs his shirt collar, pulling him close. The other prepares to defend but Ilian withdraws his saber and points it at his cousin's throat. His cousin stops, eyes wide, not knowing the origin of Ilian's rage, as they always used to joke as so.

"I. Do. Not. Have. Time. For. This," Ilian says, wrath lacing his voice.

He drops his cousin's collar, no more laughs to be had. His cousins scan the soldier, wondering what demon may possess him. No doubt blaming the witches of the mountains they claim exist in the countryside, Ilian thinks. He shakes his head and bites his lip, looking around for an escape.

Finding no other excuse, Ilian says, "I must go."

He marches away. Puzzled expressions follow him but not even the pressure from their looks causes him to look back.

Ilian marches down the streets, squeezing and releasing the leather lead of Pinto. His neighbors wave and smile, Ilian attempting to return their welcoming gestures but unable as his nerves build within him. With every step, his thoughts form and dissolve.

To think of an explanation, any explanation, any word of warning, words of the end... Ilian takes shallow breaths knowing any second it could be upon them. He wonders if it better to warn and cause panic or to ignore and allow the joys of a city without fear. If he cannot control it, nor anyone for that matter, why would he wish to place himself in such a vulnerable position in the first place? The Governor would be displeased.

Tears form in his eyes as he turns to the turquoise metal door and window shutters. Plants in their pots hang from the crossbars of the windows, geraniums, anthurium, and syngonium. Ilian notices the few spice plants, oregano and cilantro, in a wooden crate not far from the door, trimmed back since he left for the mountains. The concrete walls, peach colored paint weathered from heavy rain, stand with minimal cracks for the quakes experienced in its lifetime. The carving of a sun sits at waist level near the door, a sign that Ilian arrives. The light to escape his dark. Home.

Ilian ties Pinto to a wooden post and taps his knuckles against the metal door, praying someone to answer with haste. A young woman, nursing a baby with mounds of thick, black hair upon his head, comes to the door. Her face changes from shock to happiness. Ilian's face a mirror to her reaction. She opens the door, and he wraps his arms about her in an embrace and she kisses his cheek. He never thought a few days without his family would bring him such jubilation upon his return.

Ilian's sister moves behind the open door to allow Ilian to pass. The soldier looks about his home, furnished with large, ornately designed rugs, tables, dressers, and shelves made of pine, and a religious painting, gifted to them by the Governor, hangs opposite the entrance. All illuminated brilliantly with the newest model of lightbulbs hanging from ornate fixtures on the walls. The stark contrast to the Morez's house, faded and flickering light, no furniture other than beds to be found outside of the kitchen. The thoughts of his home grow clouded by the thoughts of his travels. Guilt makes the fog toxic. With a subtle head shake, Ilian offers a prayer of thanks for his good fortune in life.

His sister, Alidora, watches him with wide smile, amazed by his incredible faith. She grabs the shoulder of her older brother.

"Long travels?"

"Yes."

"I can tell. You look like you need to bathe."

"Thank you and your concern for my smell," Ilian says with a tinge of sarcasm. He wipes at his brow with his hand, feeling the grains of dust and dirt lodged into his sweaty, greasy skin. Alidora giggles.

"How was it? The mountains?"

"The views were beautiful. Up until..." Ilian's thoughts trail off. He recalls the smoke rising high into the sky, entering a city that reeked of death and destruction. If despair had a smell, it would be a mix of that combination. Alidora senses a profound sadness within her brother, she takes a deep breath.

"And the people? I've heard they worship, well, differently than us."

"They do. I attended one of their services. It was incredible."

His sister scrunches her nose in confusion, as if taken aback by his reply. She expected a description of horrifying, fearful, blasphemous. The term incredible parts a cloud in her mind, shedding light onto her preconceived notion.

"Incredible? How so?"

"They sing from memory. More than twenty songs and they know all the words without looking at paper sheets. To arrive at the church, or worship site, they walk several kilometers from their homes. No matter the ages, the members find their way. And the paths aren't pretty and paved like we have here. Despite their poverty, they give offerings, bountiful. Their faith is so great they look down at ours from the mountain top. They trust in their gods with their entire livelihoods. There is truly no other word. Incredible."

"Hmmm," Alidora sounds as she takes it all in.

A shuffling noise occurs outside and Ilian peeks through the window to see his mother arrives. She carries several cloth bags, each filled with vegetables, fruits, and fresh meat. He opens the door to assist her, a large smile springing forth to her face. He rushes the produce to the kitchen, setting it atop the smoothed, concrete counter tops. The moment he spins his mother embraces him.

"Ay, mijo," she says, looking up to her son who stands taller than her. "Oh, how I prayed and prayed you'd be safe and come home soon. And by the grace of the gods..." His mother bites her lips and spreads her arms, palm up, in prayer. "My prayers. My son." The tears form for both of them.

Alidora pulls her sleeve up over her shoulder and stands with her sleeping baby in the entrance. Her eyes move from her mother to her brother, a watery glaze covering the cocoa irises, as the aches of tired muscles wish for her lids to shut and rest with her child. She licks her bottom lip and continues swaying, a hand slightly covering an ear of the baby as their mother mutters and mumbles thanks and prayer to the gods.

Ilian glances at his sister, his smile dropping at her worried gazes. As his mother squeezes at his arms, he forces a grin as their eyes meet, not wishing to disrespect the one to provide him life in the first place.

"Are you hungry? I bet you're starving. Dora, send your husband to pick up a chicken. Whole and sliced. Make sure it's fresh. Don't want yesterday's kill. Only one from this morning. Or tell them to make a fresh kill. Plucked, sliced. Never mind. I'll get it. Dora, cut the vegetables will you. No, it's fine. Let me..."

His mother's voice trails off, characteristic of his and his sister both, and she paces about the kitchen. She lowers a pot from the wall, observes it for a moment, and returns it to the same position. In a flustered state, his mother grabs her purse and rushes out the door. Ilian opens his mouth to interrupt her tangent, but, as if like a lightning strike, she disappears down the street.

Ilian's and Alidora's eyes meet, and they both release a breathy chuckle.

Alidora gazes at the soldier. Ilian averts his eyes and takes a seat at the dining table. He touches the soft, cotton cloth and observes the beautiful cartuchos in a vase at the center. His mother replaces the flowers every other day. She always loved the look and smell of them. This memory causes Ilian to chuckle.

His eyes scan the kitchen, tiled backsplash behind the gas stove and above the counter. Their sink had a faucet with water piped directly to it, simply turning the knob would let the water run. No concrete tanks or barrels with water. No open flames and escaping smoke. No hanging food from the rafters while it dries or matures. No sacks on the floors of corn, potatoes, or coffee beans ready to be sold. No Nelida or Ernesto. No Cordaya.

Ilian stares at his hands on the table, his fingers pressing against each other his only ability while his thoughts distract him. Alidora, who had snuck away to put the baby in the crib, returns to the kitchen and sits across from her brother. She stares at him with wide eyes while he avoids connecting with that gaze at all costs. His eyes focus on his fidgeting fingers.

"Ilian," she starts, trying to get him to look at her. He refuses. Alidora sighs. "What happened? What did you see out there?"

Ilian squeezes his eyes shut, seeing the images display themselves as his mind reveals the answers. He wants to tell his sister, to tell someone he can trust. Thoughts of excommunication from the church and the faithful government of Micacao prevent his voice from escaping. A sibling bond he never thought he'd question fills with doubt, paranoia escalates.

"Ilian," Alidora starts with a gentle, calming tone. "Your mission. What did it concern?"

The soldier turns to her, wide eyes spelling his shock. All within the capital know missions given directly from the Governor to his Private Guard involve confidential matters. Not to be spoken about. All know not to ask about mission of the like, no matter how hard their curiosity bites. As if an unwritten law, not set by rules but understood by all. His sister asks from a place of deep concern for her brother, Ilian knows this. Yet, if he were the type, he could take her to prison. The sentence would be life. If his dedication to the Governor and his gods guided his actions, he would not question to do so. Though Ilian may have been of the mind and spirit to do so before, he wasn't now. A creeping desire and increasing despair tempt Ilian to break his oath. At this point, he wonders if the soldier's code of honor exists no more than in the fabric of his mind, due to his own past hubris given his position.

"I promise you can trust me," Alidora says, her eyes begging not the soldier, but her brother.

His wide eyes slim and Ilian leans back in his chair, his hands moving to his lap. His fingers rub his dirty uniform pants, every particle a reminder.

"Dora... It's much worse than everything we've been taught. All we've been told. Hearing the stories affects perception. But living the life impacts a person. Down to the soul, I feel it. Every fiber, every opinion I held. It's all changed. I've changed."

"I noticed. You're not the same Ilian you were before."

"You wouldn't believe their strength. Their faith. It's unbelievable."

"Their strength maybe. I've heard stories of them carrying baskets of fruits on their head."

"That's not even-"

"But their faith? Be honest with yourself. Is it really impressive worshiping false gods?"

A loud clap of thunder rings out. Ilian looks out the window to see the sky burst with light as dark clouds make work at covering the sun. Alidora shakes her head.

"Almost every night for the past week we've experienced storms. They seem to come from nowhere. You should have heard it at the biannual worship service dedicated to our divine government. It was as if the gods applauded and exalted alongside us in the sanctuary."

A chill courses through Ilian as he considers his sister's words. He gazes at the swirling, dark clouds, hoping they'll bring no more than rain upon the capital. He trembles as his faith wobbles from equilibrium. His beliefs evolve of their own accord. His mind breaks through the cave he finds himself in, opening him up to a whole new world on the other side. His heart screams, demanding him to speak.

"We've been lied to," Ilian says, his statement enough to spark fear within him. The blasphemy. The lack of faith. A betrayal. If his gods were not angry before, they were furious now. Ilian fears their wrath. But the disasters falling upon the planet push him past his limits. The need for action overtakes his fear.

"What do you mean?"

"War has broken out in the south. Men, women, children, all innocent, killed by barbarians armed by Niekalarah. But not only here. All around the world. War, destruction, hatred. The gods are angry. And someone has to stop this, or we will all pay a steep price."

Another voluminous clap, with its long, vicious growl fills the land. The walls tremble with its strength. Ilian's ears ring from the sound. Rain pounds the street as if a barrage from the heavens. Spirits send their god's message.

Though surprised by the thunder, Alidora never peers from Ilian. A slight head wobble proves to Ilian that his sister wishes to believe she's misunderstood. But in her eyes, he sees his reflection that which she observes now. Unkempt hair, dirtied uniform with dingey badge, and calloused hands from days of hard labor. He grits his teeth understanding the superficial to be an understatement of the actual transformation to have taken place. An entire cornerstone has been removed and replaced. His world threatened to crash down around him, it may still. Ilian meets her troubled gaze with a serious expression. If not even she could accept his change, he wonders how the Governor will react.

"This could be the end of our world as we know it. These storms, the earthquakes. They are not the last to come. Things far worse. Plagues not sent by demons but by the gods and their wrath. Only we can convince them otherwise."

"This is ridiculous. Do you hear yourself? You will bring shame upon this family spouting such... such..."

"Blasphemy?"

"Yes," Alidora whispers, barely audible over the boisterous rain.

"But it's not. Everything we know, Dora. Everything. Destroyed. It's hard to imagine until you see it with your own eyes. It's hard to believe even after... you see it... with your own eyes."

The tree of life plagued and poisoned. Spirits of the forest and Mizochtal with their plea. Cordaya, the legendary warrior of the glass sword, more faithful and selfless than he. The burning buildings. The corpses piled into lifeless hills. Screams. Cries. The bang of that weapon killing another. The words of Mizochtal about the lies of the Governor, words that never stop echoing in Ilian's head.

"There's a woman. In the mountain village to the south where my mission brought me. She possesses amazing abilities, but nothing she hasn't earned through hard work and unwavering faith. It is true, she believes in different gods than us. But I owe her more than every gold piece I possess."

"She's the reason you've changed. She's the reason you've lost your mind."

"This is serious."

"Yes, it is. You are a Private Guard of the Governor, His Grace. You hold a near divine position in this city. A position that requires selflessness, courage, and faith. When your trust in the gods wavers, the entire kingdom will feel it. The Governor, His Grace, will know the words you've spoken. You must repent."

The thunder roars like a beast awakened from its slumber.

"Listen to the storm," Alidora continues in panic, tears forming. "The gods are angry. They will punish us all for your impunity. Why have you brought these demons from the mountains to our lands? We must pray. We must-"

"But it's the Governor who's-"

A violent knock at the door interrupts them. Alidora dashes and their mother enters, soaking wet from head to toe but with her ingredients to prepare Ilian's supper. Alidora stands in the entryway to the kitchen, her eyes unmoving from Ilian.

"That storm came out of nowhere, didn't it?" Their mother asks with a giggle, wiping her face with a cloth pulled from the wicker basket on the counter. She lowers a soup pot, ready to begin the chicken broth. As she turns to her children, her eyes squint to observe the tension between them.

No longer able to hold back her tears, Alidora sprints to her room. Ilian turns his head to the table, his finger picking starting to draw blood. His mother walks over to him and puts her hands on his shoulders.

"Anything you need to tell me?"

"No."

"Not even a little?"

"Not now."

"Do we need to pray?"

"Maybe later."

"But don't you need to get back to the palace after you eat? After all, the Governor's arrived."

"What?" Ilian perks his head up and looks to the window, hoping to see it for himself.

"The Governor's arrived. He'll probably be expecting you."

Ilian chooses not to correct his mother. Rather his anxiety climbs as the pit drops into his stomach. He no longer feels the pain of digging his nails into his fingers. His thoughts scream at him. The storm howls as if screaming itself. Urgency to speak with the governor overwhelms him, alongside his nerves.

His mother leaves his side to cook with haste, knowing her child must be hungry. But he no longer possesses the desire to eat. Nor to drink. Nor to shower. Nor to breathe. Ilian refuses to tell her this, hoping to buy himself time. But with every raindrop that hits, he hears the ticking clock. With every flash of lightning, he sees the glint of the glass sword. Every roar of thunder, the lion messenger sending another warning.

If in fact the Governor has arrived, Ilian knows what he must do. And, by the grace of the gods, he will find his voice to do so.

Chapter Eleven

Ilian panics as a slim ray of sunshine hits his face. He springs out of bed, wondering how he fell into such a slumber with his nerves. The promise he made to himself set the terms he'd close his eyes for no more than a few seconds, but like a shadow falling over him the weight forced his eyes closed. In a sprint, he throws on his uniform jacket and pants, finding his way to the bathroom to take care of his hygienic needs, all which had fallen behind on his journey. With a fine comb, the soldier slicks his black hair back. He observes his reflection, hoping he could not see himself trembling from the outside. With a deep breath, he heads for the kitchen.

The smell of the food does not greet him as it once had. No beans nor eggs lay out on the table when he arrives. No coffee in a mug, the rising steam a warm welcome after waking to the cold morning air. But the necessity for such warmth and comfort disappears as the luxury of his home proves sufficient, no apparent discomfort, drafts, or hunger to meet him. The bug bites scab over, and his muscles relax in knowing they will not be exerted in the day to come.

Ilian sits at the dining table and runs his fingers along the flower design on the tablecloth. Lilies... The soldier grins.

"Do you want breakfast before heading to the palace?"

Ilian turns to see Alidora standing in the doorway, her child tied in a burgundy scarf onto her back. Her crusted, swollen eyes force a guilt on the soldier. He averts his eyes, wishing to forget the sight, but realizing many images would never be cleansed from his mind.

"Don't worry about me. I'll be fine."

"What do you plan on saying to the Governor?"

"I plan on telling him the truth."

Alidora bites her lip and wraps her arms about herself. Correcting or advising her brother may be improper, given his position in their society in comparison to her own. She bows her head as the tears flow once more.

"I'm terrified for you. I do not wish the gods to punish you so."

"If I do not act, the gods will punish us all."

"Those with faith will be saved. Trust in the Governor. The answers will come to you."

"If I wait for an epiphany of sorts, many will already have suffered. I trust in the Governor, as much if not more than you. I will express my concerns. His Grace, in his intelligence and divinity will lead us in this. He's the only hope I can think of."

"You're convinced this will be the end?"

Ilian opens his mouth to respond, but his voice fails to find him. He licks his lips and, with a deep breath, he nods. Alidora wipes the tears away and rushes to embrace her brother. In his seated position, Ilian moves his hands to stroke his sister's arms around his neck. As she loosens her grip, Ilian stands and looks her in the eyes. His resolve and her faith evident as they glimpse into the other's soul. Ilian, with loss of appetite, walks out the front door. Alidora peers as he unties Pinto from the post, an expression of confusion spells across her face as the shape of his eyes transformed into those of a predator. Thirst and determination fill them, yet the glimmer reflected was not his own. Alidora steps away from the door and folds her hands to pray for the safety of her brother.

The burden of disappointment and hopelessness weighing down on him, Ilian pats the snout of his horse and rests his head on hers.

"May the gods look after us," he whispers. He swings himself onto her back and they race down the cobblestone road. The faces to gaze upon him as he passes express no solemnity nor dread. Not a frown finds a face on this tranquil morning in the capital. Joyous shouts and laughter fill the air as the children skip and walk to school. Seniors stand outside of the shops talking their early morning gossip, peering at the young as their minds cloud with images of their youth. Ilian wishes to feel as carefree as the townspeople, but he cannot shake the thoughts fogging his reality.

Creating nightmares by day and night. No matter where he goes, he senses the gods' gazes upon him. Paranoia and tension converge before him. Despite the heresy of witchcraft, Ilian wishes a clairvoyant to allude to his fate. The future appears grim as far as he can see. He only wonders which omens and instincts to listen to and take to heart.

A chill courses through the soldier as he rides into the shadow of the goliath wall constructed of auburn concrete brick. The outer wall of the palace rises into the sky, hiding the living quarters within. The guards standing watch from the tower above recognize Ilian's uniform. They spin the wheel to roll the log wall upon itself, opening an entrance to the soldier. Ilian tips his head to those above and continues forward. Pinto slows to a trot as they approach the gate and maintains a steady speed upon entering the courtyard.

Stone statues of gods, the ancients, and kings erected and scattered throughout stand tall with meticulous detail in the yard. Some show wear of rain and weathering. Others appear newer, their smooth faces and intricately designed clothing and headdress a symbol of the great honor and pride held by those who paid for such works. All follow a similar style, no matter the age or the sculptor. The Governor shows great appreciation for the culture of the kings of old. Some remain standing from such ancient times, others carved by the order of the Governor so as to continue their legacy. Claiming a legacy of his own.

The lifeless, stone eyes stare at Ilian as he passes. Paranoia grows as the faces contort to show pain and despair, as if prophesying their demise. The shrill of the wind creeping over the wall and passing through the maze of statues sounds as a scream traveling from afar. Ilian turns to find the origin when the steps of others come from the entrance to the palace. A sigh of relief issues from Ilian as he recognizes the guards in front of him. He slides from Pinto's back and makes for the doorway.

"Private Guard Ilian," Enamias, a castle guard calls out. They share a salute. "Welcome back."

"Thank you, Enamias," Ilian bows his head in respect. He turns to the other and repeats the action. "Gido. The Governor, His Grace, is here, correct?"

"He arrived last night. And yourself, Private Guard? If you could forgive me for asking?"

"This morning," Ilian lies, not wishing to admit his desire to be home stronger than his duty and responsibility to the Governor. Granted, every moment he finds the will to uphold his oath fading into the distance. His eyes fight not to give him away. "I need to speak with the Governor immediately. The-"

Guard Enamias holds up his hand to prevent Ilian from saying anymore. "It is not our need to know of your business with His Grace. And I cannot imagine he would decline counsel with his top Private Guard."

Ilian clenches his jaw, understanding his mistake and praying forgiveness from the gods. Revealing confidential information in any form may be viewed as treasonous, and these guards understand their positions to be below that of Ilian. Fear of betraying a higher rank guard may prove greater than loyalty to the Governor for many of the soldiers. Ilian discovers the trend not to be uncommon, especially after his run in with General Victorino. The guards separate and allow Ilian through.

Being within the palace, a divine spirit forces its presence through him, examining his sins and passing their judgment. A shiver courses through his body, as if reaching his very soul and shifting its position, reminding him of his own mortality. Ilian only hopes this spirit will not communicate his thoughts and actions with the Governor. A subtle roar echoes in his head, and he feels the predator's gaze penetrating him.

His boots click on the mosaic tile floor, glossed and cleaned, not a speck of dust or dirt on its surface. The Governor abhors the sight of a mess, believing it disrespect to the gods on such hallowed ground, as he claims the palace to be. Ilian remembers not more than two years ago dragging one of the cleaners to the prisons for spilling a bucket of dirty water on the floor. He had felt proud at the time, believing the act to be disgraceful and lacking the caution one should take in such a divine place. But he finds guilt creeping in as he recalls the events, the cries of the cleaner as her feet dragged behind them, unable to rise as he pulled her arm. Many bruises formed on her fragile body in later days. Caring for the tidiness of the palace had been her job for more than fifty years, age catching up to her. It was not the only incident, but the only which Ilian experienced firsthand. The soldier hopes, even after all these years, the gods will find it within their hearts to forgive him. However, with the transformation of the land, sea, and air due to the gods' wrath, begging the gods for forgiveness may not be his top priority. Rather than pray for forgiveness, he must prove that he has changed.

The thought clings to him, acting as if it passes but circling about him. To admit he's changed may be to admit he's lost faith. Alidora sees it as such, analyzing her brother and undoubtedly praying he will return to his old self. And a flicker in Ilian's eyes wishes the same. Ignorance is suffering's guise.

A plethora of memories attempt to capture Ilian in their wake. The palace offers its welcome in the form of intrusion, finding its way within the soldier. It crawls through the passages and doors of his mind, seeking answers. Investigating where and to whom his loyalty lies. The power strikes far greater than that which met him in the forest, home of the spirits and Mizochtal. A divine power reaching from the heavens, direct from the gods.

The echoes of the spirits dissolve into whispers of unseen phantoms. The energy emits a darker, colder sensation. An omen. No. A warning. The gods reach to him, in the divine palace, not to honor his return, but advising him to turn back.

He walks through the stone archway to the throne room. Empty. Doubt and fear fill him as he wonders why he chose to return so soon. *To ask the Governor for help.* The voice in his head answers, rational, reasonable. But his heart beats a different drum, its pace set with those in the worship site in the mountains. They beat fast. With force. Yet their tune is not one of the heavens. Like a battle set to commence. An echo similar to that weapon held by the general.

Pain grows within Ilian's head. As he brings his head to his hand, the sound of soft footsteps on tile reaches his ears. The Governor enters.

His long, sweeping robe flows across the ground, as his sandaled feet barely make a sound. Ilian bows to His Grace, but not before noticing the uniform Caseto wears beneath his cloak. One only worn in times of conflict. In times of war.

"You may rise," Governor Ralfonso Caseto orders, releasing his Private Guard from his bow.

Ilian rises and licks his lips. With a glance about the throne room, ensuring no others follow behind the Governor, Ilian waits. The silence fills the space, almost intoxicating to the soldier. He does not desire to be the first to speak, certainly not to admit to his own failure of the mission. But he also does not wish to keep the Governor waiting. Ilian knows all too well of his fiery impatience. The clock ticks. Time decays along with the world around them. Ilian wonders when it will catch up.

"Your Gra-"

"How did your mission go?" The Governor asks in an unwavering tone as he reaches for a grape from the glass bowl, sitting on a pedestal to the side of his throne. Ilian thinks of the pedestals for offerings to the gods. Was the Governor mocking the gods?

"Well, I-"

"You've come alone?"

The strength with which the question slips from his lips, despite the low volume he chooses, sends a vibration through Ilian's core. The drawl to follow his words constrict the soldier as an enchantment may, freezing him to his position despite the fear. In situations of flight or fight, Ilian was known to face the conflict head on. It was his moral obligation. His duty. But such events played out in his head did not involve the Governor as his opponent. As the Private Guard, he had no choice to surrender to the Governor's will.

"Yes."

The simple answer. No excuses. No room for interruption. Brief. Honest. And to Ilian's relief, the outcome of his mission. He would prefer Cordaya at his side, for the Governor's sake. Her words stick in his memory as if carved there by her glass sword. Relief fills him to know she is not here. The welcome may have been joined by quite a few more palace guards if that were the case.

Governor Caseto views his Private Guard through the slits his eyes form. His face reads displeasure. His silence reveals disappointment. Caseto folds his hands on his lap and issues a sigh. Exaggerated, perhaps. But Ilian knows of the Governor's mannerisms. A sigh of such degree could mean one of two things. The first that the Governor would be 'forced' to do something he'd rather not. Whether this meant torture or imprisonment could never be determined by the sigh, for there were no patterns for distinction. Another possibility for the sigh was that, though fortune had not fallen in his favor, he felt matters to be outside of his control. Ilian prays for the latter.

"It appears matters have slipped from our control."

Ilian closes his eyes and bows his head, partly for failing in his mission, partly to hide his relief. Caseto examines Ilian's crestfallen expression, the slits never changing size. Without peering at the Governor, Ilian senses his animosity. Predator staring at prey, waiting to pounce.

"How far did your travels take you?" Caseto interrogates, plucking a grape from the cluster and taking a bite.

"South, into the mountains," Ilian answers, checking his voice does not crack. He fights to swallow the saliva building up in his mouth. Tremors surge through his body as his nerves erupt, wondering where the questioning will lead. "Not far from the border with Niekalarah."

Caseto, who had been staring at the grape in his fingers, picking out the seeds so as to forego the need to spit them out later, perks his head. The slits return, a twitch crossing his right eye at the sound of the opposing nation.

"Niekalarah? How far from the border?"

"I'd say no more than forty kilometers. But that is by road, the curving about the mountains quite a hassle for travel and-"

"Are there Niekalarans working in these villages to the south?"

Ilian opens his mouth, ready to answer yet taken aback by the question.

"Umm, yes. Yes, I believe so."

"So, you did not see any Niekalarans but you believe them to be there? That is quite the assumption for one as observant as you, Private Guard Ilian."

The saliva builds up again, creating a constant block for Ilian's ability to answer with urgency. In most situations, the soldier stayed calm under pressure.

"I observed Niekalarans in these villages. Whether they perform work other than selling goods I cannot be certain."

"But they sell goods? To our nation? How do you know they are Niekalaran?"

Ilian remembers his run in with Julio Hernan, cousin to President Isara Hernan of Niekalarah. The laborers following behind the cart as they cultivate and farm lands for a foreign power. The images of the barbarians ascend into his thoughts, their blades marked with the alexandrite of the nation to the south. The words of General Victorino, the knowledge and inaction of him and his patrol an ever-lingering question in the back of Ilian's mind.

"Have you not questioned General Victorino of these matters? It is on his watch such vermin pass into Micacao, stealing, raping, razing, and killing our very own."

Ilian averts his eyes as he feels his throat burn from the fire in his words. It quickly extinguishes with his apprehensiveness.

Governor Caseto rises from his throne, pushing back his robes in a way to reveal the glint of his saber beneath. The Governor never treads without a weapon. His glare pierces Ilian. The Private Guard stares at the ground. Before his assignment to this mission, the Governor looked to him with utmost respect, trusted enough to seek counsel from him. Does the Governor sense the change within Ilian? Or have the gods communicated with the Governor of his guard's sins?

"Our conflicts with Niekalarah grow, as you may know. These past days, I've met with leaders of other neighboring nations, primarily those to the north. We do not wish to push for war, not of the physical variety. Trade. Denunciation. Plans are in the works."

"Excuse my assertiveness, Your Grace. But I did not exaggerate. War has begun. Barbarians are attacking the villages in the mountains."

"War is fought from two sides."

"What do you mean, Your Grace?" asks Ilian.

Confusion spreads across his face, disbelief as to the words to enter his ears. Blood spilled. Lives lost. Ilian believes he knows the concept, the definition of war. His responsibilities as Private Guard never took him to the front lines of a battle. Stories reached his ears. Scars shown to him by many a soldier. The physical and the psychological. If not war, what would the battles in the south be considered? A bloodbath?

"I mean as I say," the Governor states. He examines the large, jeweled rings on his hands with indifference in his tone and gaze. Caseto circles his Private Guard. "What occurs in the south, whether it occurs as we speak or not, is no war. Raids may happen. People may die. Is it a crime? Yes. Is it war? No, Private Guard Ilian."

"These people are Micacaoan. Citizens."

"War has not been declared and therefore these occurrences lie outside of this heavy word."

"Do you intend to demand Niekalarah and their President, Hernan, pay for these crimes? Or will they continue to go uncontested?"

Ilian's heart accelerates with every tick of the clock he hears. Every soft-soled footstep of the Governor draws near. The desire to run grows stronger, his heart threatening to do so if his feet refuse. Ilian gulps, not knowing if the sound he makes in nerves echoes through the room or only in his ears. Eyes gaze upon him from every angle. Caseto's silence constricts him.

"Your Grace, these are citizens of Micacao."

"And it costs our nation more to go to war than conserve any lives to be lost."

Ilian's mouth falls agape. The cold, chilling tone with which the Governor speaks sounds not as a god, but as a dictator. Perhaps his divinity allows him to view humans as lesser. Or arrogance shields his heart and mind from guilt and empathy. Ilian fights these conflicting thoughts, pushing back more so against the blasphemy than his intuition. The faces of Nelida, Ernesto, and Cordaya flash through his head. Imminent danger lurks near to him, to all of them. His heart does not falter. The Governor is Ilian's last chance to make everything right once more.

"More is at risk than the citizens to the south. Have the gods communicated with you as of late?"

Ilian frames his question as sincere. The voice of one with tremendous faith to the omniscient leader of the church, Ilian asks the Governor, the one with the greatest faith he knows. His heart calms as thoughts of the gods flow through him. Ilian always found comfort in his faith. Now it shakes under him, being the foundation on which he built his life. The tremors break the stone, rubble pieces falling into the void beneath him. Without looking down, he knows the colossal jaws of a lion open below. Should he fall, Ilian knows the end will not be met with his presence alone. The gods watch, meticulously, scrupulously, documenting his actions. Any missteps and the foundation will crumble, the omnipotent gods willing it to do so.

"Yes. Yes, they have, Private Guard Ilian. And I'm afraid they are angry. The word may sound tame but do not allow it to fool you. Subtle emotions for mortals, but for the gods these emotions are the reasons for the existence of mountains and volcanoes. Storms and twisters. A miniscule amount of discontent can bring war and famine. I do all I can to appease the gods. To reason with them. But this time it will take more than a little diplomacy."

The Governor huffs a puff of hot breath at the jewel of his ruby ring to clean in his cloak before gazing at the heavens. With a sigh, the Governor's eyes move to the mosaic floor and he begins his pacing once more. Tension builds in the room.

Ilian's mind wanders in panic as he deciphers the Governor's words. His Grace's voice, full of truth or conceit Ilian cannot determine, shares a taste of the ominous events and a fear for the future. Whether it be through premonition or no more than prediction, the soldier fails to conclude. And to appease a god where diplomacy no longer works, entails much more than Ilian wishes to believe.

"Appease the gods, Your Grace? How do you suppose we do that?"

"Why do you suppose no course of action is being taken in southern Micacao? This is our punishment. Our sacrifice."

Sacrifice. The word slips from the Governor's lips with ease. Yet the term suggests something of value given. A difficult and weighted decision with consequences to be taken. But a feigned care for the citizens of the mountains will not suffice. Caseto must believe he can convince the gods of such care, but the gods' wrath proves their omniscience, even in the presence of another divine. If anything, their anger magnifies with the lie, the diplomacy Ilian and Cordaya hoped to use may not be enough.

"Private Guard Ilian. Do you recall the scriptures? The letters from the third prophet to the divine leader of ancient Micacao, a civilization we've come to know as the Ilcaya. These letters come to us from the Enlightenment Period. Scripture reads 'The gods give and the gods take. There is a balance. As all in life, balance keeps the world in check.' A balance, Ilian. When we disrupt that balance, the world transforms. Life has been too easy for too long."

Tears form in Ilian's eyes as he bites his lips and shakes his head. Disbelief. He knows the scripture the Governor refers to. He often recited the passage whenever fortune did not seem to favor him. That the Governor would use such a time, and under such circumstances, to cite the scripture forces a chill up Ilian's spine. As if a privilege and ignorance before afforded to Ilian escapes him. A knowledge of more than the capital of Diodios, an empathy for others fills the gaps.

"You say life has been easy, but to whom do you refer? To us, here in the capital? Or to those to the south? Those whom your divine sacrifice punishes. Their life has never been easy, it is only after this mission do I truly see the economic inequalities we must address."

"In comparison to ours you make this statement, I presume. However, in comparison to those of the mountains in the past, their lives have improved in a number of ways. They do not know true suffering. Or, in the least, they didn't. The gods will rid these lands of the blasphemers and forgiveness will be upon the faithful."

Ilian opens his mouth to speak but no words find their way. The thoughts flying through his mind vanish. His heartbeat slows and the room spins about him. The cure, the panacea, to the plague and disasters spreading about the world involves ridding the lands and seas of those who do not believe. Specifically, those who do not believe in the right gods. The Governor's answer proves sound, for Ilian learned throughout childhood and well into adulthood the vengeance of the gods strikes with fury upon those who refuse to worship or give thanks. Ilian used his mission to spread his faith, to teach others of the right gods. His faith wavers. His fear grows.

"Private Guard Ilian. You have not reported the findings of your mission. I suspect you've collected more information than the knowledge of barbarians entering our territories. What of the warrior of the glass sword? Did you meet him?"

Ilian swallows his nerves. The image of Cordaya appears in his head, hoping it to be safe there. He no longer knows of the power of infiltration of the Governor, nor if his divine abilities will prove Ilian to be a traitor.

"I went from village to village. They have many tales of the warrior. Some say him to be the child of a god and human." Ilian speaks with bated breath, attempting to cover his lies in his confidence. He stares at the empty throne, not wishing to look the Governor in the eyes. The pounding of his heart against his chest may prove the second most difficult to hide. The first most difficult will be the thoughts, the knowledge of his lie and his control of doing so to His Grace. The gods will know. He simply hopes they will not tell.

"The child of a god? No more than myth that a child of a god would live among such brutes."

Caseto's voice responds in no more than a whisper, forcing Ilian to wonder if he was meant to hear. The harsh tone accompanied by raised eyebrows and frustrated amusement reveal a glint of the Governor Ilian had not yet seen. The change did not appear sudden, but growing for some time, nurtured with hate and prejudice.

Ignoring the Governor's words, Ilian continues.

"They say this warrior defends against the invading barbarians. Striking them down and protecting the citizens of the villages."

"Another lie," the Governor spits in a whisper, anger transforming his expression and hardening the lines on his aged face. "The child of a god would not protect against the wrath of the gods, rather help in their purpose. The ignorance is great among these uneducated peoples."

"Whether the child of a god or other supernatural foe I do not know," Ilian remarks. He needs the Governor to trust in him. His intuition tells him so, despite the ominous feeling that their fate intertwines for other purposes. "But they all speak of a crystal sword, transparent, unbreakable, forged by the gods and given as a gift to the warrior."

Ilian knows Cordaya would be quick to correct if she heard him refer to the sword as a gift. The disapproval on her face and in her tone proved evident the last time he did so. He begs the gods she may forgive him, for he has no intention of hiding the events and what had been said verbatim. That is, if the gods afford him the chance.

"It's the sound of a fallen angel. Thrown from heaven to live among scum as punishment."

Ilian's muscles tense as anger overcomes him. His fists clench but he forces silence. An ill glow emits over the form of the Governor, as if a shadow follows behind. Ilian wonders what his journey did to transform his mind. What spell enchants the soldier and raises his doubts and propels questions through his mind? A faith, one he believed unshakeable and impenetrable, turning to rubble in front of him. And the source. Mizochtal's words. Cordaya's action. Caseto's arrogance. Ilian's fingers twitch as they wish to reach for his saber, a defense mechanism when he feels unsafe.

"It's a wonder this demon still possesses his sword. I say we're facing a source of evil. He must be the cause of these disasters striking the world. Or the gods do so in an attempt to warn us, or protect us, from this monster. Scripture reads that a bloodthirsty, power-hungry demon will attempt to seize control of the nations, one at a time, after claiming dominion over the world and its creatures. We must destroy him."

"She is not the enemy," Ilian slips in Cordaya's defense before he realizes what he says. Shock overcomes him and his blood freezes in his veins. The Governor's eyes widen but as his mouth opens, they hear several sets of footsteps approaching.

Several women in soldiers' uniform enter the throne room. In V-formation, the women march toward the Governor, taking a knee as they stop in front of His Grace. Ilian recognizes the woman at the front of the formation. Long, sleek charcoal hair pulled into a ponytail flows from below her cap, which she removes in respect as she lowers herself. She wears several badges on her red jacket, many of honor and two of faith. However, he did not recall the eyepatch covering her left eye the last time they had met.

"Rise," the Governor commands of the women, his eyes slightly glancing at Ilian before returning their attention to the newcomers. "What news do you bring?"

"The new prototypes are ready for your blessing, Your Grace," Liza, the captain of an all-woman squadron responds as she rises.

A smirk spreads across the Governor's face. He folds his hands together and turns to Ilian.

"Private Guard Ilian, there is something I would like to show you. Liza, lead the way."

The group walk from the throne room, Ilian at the back. An ominous air fills his lungs. The worst is yet to come.

Chapter Twelve

Liza leads the group into the tunnels below the barracks. The damp stone creates a musty air which reaches Ilian's nose in an unwelcome whiff. Candles light the way as they reach depths the sun can no longer enter. Ilian had not marched these tunnels for several years, never having a reason. Perhaps more occurred in the lower chambers than he originally thought.

They pass many rooms to the women soldiers, hidden from daylight. Hidden from sight. Most citizens did not know of the women squadrons, believing these women to be serving in the piety of the Governor. In faith, not in battle.

The air grows foggy, and the smell of smoke consumes them with its presence. Ilian hears a strange metallic sound, a series of loud bangs, and hammer against stone. His eyes turn to slits the nearer they draw to an illuminated room at the end of the corridor. The Governor's cloak sweeps the ground in front of him, Ilian focusing on not stepping on the fabric while the distraction of his thoughts on what may lie ahead continue to spin in his mind.

Liza stops in the entrance and the other women disperse in the room, returning to their tasks of supervising the laborers. Every worker is either a woman, genderqueer, and or disabled. Ilian realizes this must be the way those discriminated against may honor the Governor without traditionalist backlash. This is a safe space for serving their nation and earning a wage.

But Ilian only recognizes this after shock sets in. The first object in the room to meet his eyes is the mysterious weapon held by

General Victorino and his men. That strange weapon that throws metal. Roars like thunder. Kills in an instant.

"Private Guard Ilian," Caseto expresses a wide smile as he turns around. His arm sweeps the room in pride as he showcases his excitement. "This is a weapon of the gods."

He walks forward and shows Ilian every step of the process, examining the workers' every movement, every action in forging these strange weapons. Simply peering at the object is enough to make Ilian's stomach churn as he thinks of the chaos an entire army with such power could be capable of. The image of Victorino and his pleasure to have such power in his grasp flashes through Ilian's mind. A maniacal authority given to those who cannot control their urge to exercise power.

It was a warning often preached by the pastors of the capital, even the Governor himself. Humility. Resist the thirst of such temptations for the one who falls victim will never be strong enough to sit among the gods. From the looks of it, the church's teachings were no more than an affront to prevent others from grasping power before the Governor. Caseto always enjoyed being multiple steps ahead. Ilian believes for this reason the relations with Niekalarah grow frail. Their president, Hernan, made great strides in improving the nation's economy and technology. Seen as a worldly superpower. His Grace, chosen by the divine, grew displeased.

As Ilian stares at the weapons, he cannot help but believe war and violence to be the only solution to their problems. Had Hernan started the battles in the south, Ilian could see no other option for the Governor. Caseto must protect his people. Yet, his words earlier in the throne room force questions into Ilian's mind, damming the flow of all reason. Of all he ever knew and believed. To think the meeting with Cordaya and Mizochtal would change him so. Humans were going outside of their bounds for no more than revenge and a thirst for power. No other reason stood proof for the need of such a weapon. Why should mortals have such power?

The Governor's eyes roam the room with the joy of a child in the serving line for milk cake. Victory appears close in his mind. The thought of diplomacy or an action of prayer asking the gods for their noble assistance lingers in the distance. Caseto envisions what Ilian can see flashing time and time again in his mind. A one-sided battle with assured victory.

"The idea came with knowledge sent down from the gods. Divine intelligence. This idea was gifted to our own Captain Liza. That is why I put her in charge of this project. The gods have touched her, Ilian. This gift was meant for Micacao and Micacao alone. I told you the gods were angry. And they've sent us a way to fix this."

"Are you not afraid of other nations getting ahold of this technology?"

Ilian watches as a man with no legs screws the long metal neck of the weapon into a tough wooden grasp. At the back of the metal neck, Ilian notices the flash of a small piece of flint. After completing his task, the man slides the weapon down a shoot to the next station.

A woman with shaved head picks up the weapon and continues the process. None of the laborers carry a hint of fear in their eyes, as if they do not understand the power they hold. Ilian wonders if they truly know. The sound the weapon makes as the metal ball leaves at lightning speeds. The damage the weapon causes when aimed at an object or worse, at a person. The sight of a body lying on the ground, blood pouring from no more than a single orifice, the size of a bean. An injury sufficient to kill.

"The gods will not allow for such passing of communication. And unless there be a traitor in our midst," the Governor pauses after speaking in a low, serious tone. A pressure pushes on Ilian's shoulder. "We do not need to worry."

"And this is our solution? To what exactly, Your Grace? I thought you said there is no war."

"Past. Present. Future. It will occur, as always in history. And we will be ready. This is a sign, Private Guard Ilian. The gods wish us to be prepared."

Ilian pictures General Victorino and his men with this weapon. War is not it's only use. It demonstrates power. Control. A scare tactic. They flash these weapons to the barbarians, allowing some to escape back to Niekalarah and reveal the truth. Instill fear. The uses for such a weapon are endless. And it appears they continue to upgrade the technology as they learn more about it. Several display stands with different versions of this weapon allow him this assumption. Not large changes, but small, subtle ones. Barely detectable if he had not been searching for them.

The Governor glides to the end of the assembly line to examine one of the finished products. He lifts the weapon with care, wary not to set it off. Comfort sets in and his fingers wrap about it in his thirst for power. Ilian turns to see Liza smiling.

"These newer versions have a shorter reload time and fire at much faster speeds. We tightened the spring to increase the force and... well, rather than tell you, let me show you."

Liza grabs one of the weapons and heads into another room, Governor Caseto and Ilian following behind. The laborers glance at the group, some eyes lingering longer on Ilian. An animosity seeps through otherwise empty eyes. The gods are not pleased with this invention.

The adjacent room proves larger than the previous. A training area of sorts for these outcasted military personnel. White chalk lines drawn on the ground indicate a position to stand. On the other side of the room, several straw men stick from the ground, propped into position with sticks, some with dried cornstalk poking through holes in the torn clothing. Practice. If it had been a person, Ilian is certain where the holes are located blood would be pouring out.

Liza takes her position behind the line. She fishes around in the pocket of her jacket and removes a small, metal piece and a sealed flask. Opening a compartment in the back of the weapon, Liza squints her uncovered eye as she pours powder from the flask. A dark, charcoal grey, the fine powder fills the compartment. The barrel of the weapon tilts toward the ceiling as she slides the metal piece in and it rolls toward the bottom of the tube. She lifts the weapon up, her good eye peeking over the long barrel. A finger on her right hand pulls back on the spring-loaded contraption with the bit of flint. Her left pointer finger finds the trigger located on the underside of the weapon. She pulls back and a loud boom echoes off the concrete walls of the bunker.

A surge of fear courses through Ilian. Hearing that sound, seeing that power, Ilian wonders if mortal man was meant to wield a weapon of this caliber. He could not think Mizochtal to be pleased to know of such a weapon. The echo of the boom continues to swirl in his head, dizziness overcomes him. He cannot shake the ringing in his ears, the pounding in his heart. He cannot forget the expression Caseto wears. Amusement. Hungry for more power. Though perhaps to some it would read as divine.

"Would you like to try, Private Guard Ilian?" Caseto asks with a smirk present. Ilian understands the Governor senses his uneasiness. His body tense and the words unable to find their way, Ilian feels himself give a subtle, obedient nod. Liza, glancing from Caseto to Ilian, knows she must oblige to the Governor's wishes.

She inspects the weapon in her hand, checking that the powder levels in the back compartment are sufficient for another shot. She holds out the weapon to him. Ilian reads the fire in her eyes. A protective, envious glare. He licks his lips in his hesitation. Steadying a hand, Ilian reaches for the weapon.

As his fingers close about the glossy hardwood back, a chill spreads throughout him. From the point of contact, the blood in his veins runs cold. The freezing aura rises up his arm and delivers the same sensation throughout the rest of his body. Ilian accepts the weapon and pulls it close it him, Liza reluctantly letting go. His other hand comes to meet the barrel. Cold, lifeless metal. Uncaring as to who it harms or kills. Uncaring as to its usage. Up to a mortal to control.

"You'll need this," Liza says with untrusting tone, shoving the metal pellet of ammunition towards Ilian. "You watched how I loaded it, right?"

Rather than use words, Ilian nods. He refuses to allow his shaky voice show weakness, especially in front of the Governor. His eyes, turned toward the ground, hide his trembling spirit. Not a spirit worthy to be named 'soldier.'

"Go on, Private Guard. Aim for the straw man and we'll see if you can hit." Caseto wears a challenging expression. As if Ilian's failure to hit would signify his unwillingness to serve the Governor and the gods. A revelation to all watching that he was not worthy.

Ilian swallows his fears and the saliva build up in his mouth. The weight of the small, metal pellet reveals its density, making it all the more believable that something so tiny could kill so easily. Inclining the barrel, Ilian slides the metal ammunition into position. He takes an opposite hand hold of Liza, himself being right-handed. His left hand creates the balance while his right hand slips its pointer finger where the trigger sits. Bringing the weapon level to his face, his eye lines up with the barrel. The dark cocoa iris reveals itself through no more than a slit, narrowed and focused on the target. Ilian sees the strawman opposite of him. Made of straw, not flesh. Not alive. Yet, Ilian twitches as he tries to overcome the malicious deed of firing the weapon.

"It's no more than straw," Ilian whispers to himself, staring down the practice dummy. "It's only straw. It's only straw. Shooting at straw is not a sin. May the gods forgive me."

As his pointer finger pulls the curved trigger towards his person, Ilian closes his eyes. The last fraction of the action proves harder than the first, waiting and not knowing at what point it will be set off. And then he feels it. The spring, once being tightly coiled now releases. A grand force pushes Ilian back. A loud roar fills the air. With wide eyes, Ilian searches the air for the small pellet, wondering if he can examine its flight. But it has already come and gone. The head of the strawman topples to the ground, the bullet hitting at just the right point in the neck.

Caseto's applause reminds Ilian he is not alone in this space. The booming sound of palm hitting palm echoes off the concrete walls of this underground arena. Liza stands in complete contrast, arms still at her side, unimpressed with Ilian's performance. His eyes find the residual hay dust clinging to the air where the head of the strawman used to be. They lower to observe the weapon in his hand, wishing to drop it, throw it, as the weight increases and the object sears his skin with immense heat. He wonders if it to be all in his head. Either way he offers the weapon back to Liza.

Unlike Cordaya's glass sword, this weapon does not possess a single ethereal quality. Unlike the glass sword, Ilian refuses to believe that it may be a gift from the gods. Or perhaps, as Cordaya suggests, both are curses. Both weapons prove a great responsibility necessary to wield. Yet, the sword only materializes for the warrior. This weapon, firing metal and bringing death to any in its path, has no restrictions. Liza and her team mass produce this weapon to please the Governor. Their duty. While His Grace suggests such knowledge from the gods to be favorable, Ilian sees the dark reality of a future where those with shaky or little faith take up such a weapon. Lack of guilt, foresight of consequences. Innocents will die, as they already have. The gods will grow angrier.

Ilian realizes he cannot make amends with the gods for such an invention. Passage of time results in greater knowledge. At some point in the future, Ilian thinks of the unimaginable being used as weapons. He cannot prevent mankind's thirst for power. But he may be able to convince the gods to weave this and future inventions into the fabric of fate so that when one has died the gods had willed it so. This insight will once again give them dominion over all mortals. No surprises.

Caseto drops his hands to his side as the last echo reverberates through the training grounds. His smirk elongates and his eyes narrow.

"What do you think of it, Private Guard Ilian? Is this not the weapon designed to win wars? Certainly it's better than alexandrite in every way. Would you not agree?"

The Governor presses Ilian with these questions. Ilian's mind spins as he searches for his response, one he wishes to not displease the gods with. For he feels them watching him. His every move. His every breath.

"I cannot think but of how these weapons prove superior to those of Niekalarah, and many other nations."

"Yes, I do agree. In this way we will have an advantage. Not only in Niekalarah, but the world."

Caseto's eyes glaze over as the dreams and aspirations leak into him. Focus leaves them as he stares at the wall with a vision. A vision of complete power. Of world dominion. Clearly a sin for mortal man. But nothing less than fate for the divine.

Ilian brainstorms the connections to what may be partly responsible for the anger of the gods. Surely not the mere invention of such a weapon would thrust the world into the throes of peril. But Mizochtal had said something. The gods anger for lack of faith. Lack of compassion. This lethal weapon does not align with the values of which the messenger advises.

"Your Grace," Ilian starts with eyes to the ground. His heart issues a prayer to the heavens. Caseto's eyes, filled with flame, find Ilian. With a gulp, the Private Guard pushes away any cowardice and continues. "Is this what will please the gods? Going to war? Is this how we prove our faith?"

Rather than an explosive wrath, Caseto's voice greets the air like a patient predator, not wishing to scare the prey.

"General Liza. Will you explain to the Private Guard what the gods revealed to you?"

Liza licks her lips and nods, a shaky breath escaping.

"In my dream, I heard booms of thunder. There was no rain or lightning. It was no storm that we know of. A chorus of the gods. Shouts and screams rang out. And then silence."

Liza stops and takes a deep breath. Her eye closes as she recalls the visions of that night. The sights and sounds scar her memory. She had been told of their divine origin, being promoted in the ranks for being the chosen one of the gods.

"They saw me. They glided down from the clouds and placed one of these," she says lifting the weapon, "into my hands. They told me I would need it. They told me to study it. I inspected every part, leaving no side unexamined. I awoke with new knowledge. In urgency, I sought counsel with His Grace that very day. He believed me, as the gods recounted to him as I had moments before. He provided me with the materials and labor to do so. In two days, we had our prototype. In four, we had a functioning handheld cannon."

Ilian stares in awe at the general. Nothing but divine knowledge could have led to such a breakthrough in such a short period. She had been blessed, and Caseto took the matter into his control immediately.

Ilian watches as his faith wobbles uncontrollably. The image of the talking, charcoal black mountain lion, messenger of the God of the Forest lingering in his head and heart at every moment. This weapon, created through knowledge gifted by the divine a heavy reminder of the gods he regretfully distances himself from. Separate faiths. Yet both govern such mortals with equally compelling miracles and equally threatening laws.

"You see, Private Guard Ilian," Caseto begins with his malicious smirk, the flames of power burn bright in his eyes. "It is the faith of the peoples of this nation that holds us together. It is a strong bond."

"Forgive me for asking, Your Grace. But is hiding this weapon from the citizens not dishonest? Do you think the average citizen would admire such an invention or grow to fear our military might?"

"Fear and respect are two birds of the same breed," Caseto responds, a chilling voice with the drawl of a snake's hiss issues forth. The Governor lifts a hand and plays with the minimal light bouncing from his jeweled fingers. "Let the people see what the gods have graced us with after they see the results. Many protested against the War of Dos Mares, but our great nation would have never reached Enlightenment without such a victory. The people were quick to change their minds when victory was within reach."

Ilian recalls studying the bloody battles of the war. Books called it a "war won by faith." Micacao's, or at the time the Planoro nation's, military might paled in comparison to the opposing country. A true miracle to claim victory ten years later. Caseto's great-great grandfather, the Lord Sovereign General of the war, ousted the king of Planoro and took his place on the throne, divinity in his blood and chosen by the gods to lead.

To be chosen by the gods is not a small task. But the undeniable pressure to appear flawless and divine never fazed these leaders who chose to wear such a mask. Ilian wonders if for fear of a revolution they wear a divine countenance or if the blood line had grown to believe it. Mizochtal stated Caseto was no greater than any other mortal man, insulted when Ilian insinuated the Governor to be divine. Ilian's head pounds as he attempts to differentiate the faith and beliefs he's held most of his life and that which shrouds him since his meeting at the World Tree.

"Private Guard Ilian," Caseto begins, pulling Ilian's mind into reality once more. "The gods do not always tell us which path to take. At times we face trials. We are presented many paths and we must choose. Through our knowledge and the readings of faith, we have the chance to make such informed decisions."

Caseto circles the room, inspecting the holes in the strawmen. His voice booms with tenderness, sound waves bouncing in all directions and attacking Ilian on all sides. The Private Guard gulps as fear creeps into him. An ominous sensation flows through his veins. Liza watches with an anxious expression. Her faith leads her to think most highly of the Governor, but his tone never met her with such sinister intent. The power in his words converts to a power-hungry longing, as if all Caseto possesses will never be sufficient.

"And the gods wish our nation to pass judgment then upon these other nations?"

"Private Guard Ilian," Caseto says with a sneer. As if an adult explaining to a curious child about matters that may not concern them. Never before had the Governor spoken to Ilian in such a way. Perhaps their communication had not been constant before, but His Grace often sought counsel with Ilian on the tough decisions, always discussing politics and growing tensions with other nations, and matters of divine communication never failed to enter conversations. But the sinister energy filling the training underground courtyard tugs at Ilian's heartstrings. "With this new technology, I may as well be the King of the gods. Will you choose to follow your king, Private Guard?"

Ilian freezes, hoping the skip in his heart's pace doesn't betray him. He swallows his fears, as per learning of his militaristic training. His mind whispers to him to escape, to slowly back away from the situation, no sudden movements, and, once out of sight, run and not look back. With a rapid glance in each direction, Ilian understands his imprisonment. There is no escape. How strange that his faith and mesmerization of the Governor quickly turned to fear, one which started as no more than a speck of doubt. Yet that speck became the clarity he needed. Ilian issues a silent prayer to the gods. For foolishness and for the move he was about to make.

"As your loyal Private Guard, I will follow Your Grace through all battles, to the world of the dead and back again. Protecting Your Grace and the honor of this nation is my duty and my pride."

Ilian takes a knee and bows his head to Caseto. A wide grin spreads across the Governor's face. He adjusts his rings as he approaches his Private Guard, his elegant strides taken with dignity, as if walking on the surface of the ocean. When the Governor's hand falls upon Ilian's shoulder, a shiver races down Ilian's spine. He does his best to calm his trembling, to ease his breathing, wishing nothing to give him away. But the deep growl in his right ear suggests something else to be there. Something else he should fear more than the Governor.

"And you should do well to never forget that. Private. Guard. Ilian."

Caseto exaggerates with his pauses in saying the soldier's name, the drawl in his voice leaving a sadistic scent in the air. As if the air itself thickens about Ilian, paralyzing him, constricting him. The pressure holds him down, though it could simply be the slight push of the Governor's hand on his shoulder.

Liza stares at the two, the interaction one of god bestowing honor onto mortal man. But the consistency of the air is different. The aura about the two should be a divine image, one great sculptors and artisans would mark into history. Her awe and admiration twists and contorts into a strange confusion as tension builds and strangles. Her faith trembles as the foundation quakes beneath her, as if a foreign thought crosses into her mind, breathing gone shallow.

Frozen to their positions, Liza and Ilian wait for Caseto to make the first move. The Governor shifts his eyes between both of Ilian's, the alert pupils fighting to cover his irises, threatening to give away his fear.

As Caseto's fingers curl, the gold and silver rings digging into Ilian's shoulder with increasing pressure, a distant horn sounds. Caseto's hand drops, and Ilian rises. Liza peers around with wide eyes, hand instinctively moving to her weapon. Any soldier would know the sound of such an alarm.

An attack on the city.

Chapter Thirteen

The women soldiers and laborers in the other room jump to action. They grab hold of the powerful weapons they constructed, tying to them pouches of the fine powder, and bolt for the upper turret. Liza glances at Governor Caseto, as if silently asking permission to leave his presence in this fight to protect. Caseto closes his eyes and takes in a large whiff of the damp, cellar air.

"Their blood shall spill and enrich our deprived fields. Come. Let us show Hernan we are no stranger to war," Caseto growls, eyes glowing in fury and hunger.

Caseto marches from the range and through the candle lit hallways leading to the courtyard. Ilian follows closely behind, hand on the hilt of his saber. Ilian's mind hardens and the Governor's Private Guard returns. The persona masked in duty and responsibility consumes him. Ilian forgets about what happened no more than five minutes before. He forgets about Hoja Rosa, the Morezes, the warrior of the glass sword. His mind centers on that which he spent his life training to do and to be. A protector. But not of the world. A protector of the throne.

A slim smirk covers Caseto's face, hidden from Ilian's view. He hears the sentient statue walk behind him, confident in his power and control. His hand does not even twitch to grasp his sword, knowing the strawman behind will sacrifice all so he would not have to do so.

As they enter the blinding light of the outside world, screams reach Ilian's ears. No matter the gap between the wealthy and impoverished, all screams sound the same in time of war. Every body becomes yet another to add to the trench. Every speck of blood unnamed, tattered garment unknown. Every shard of broken glass another hazard in the landscape. In the battlefield.

Ilian unsheathes his sword, exhilaration and purpose overflowing from his pores, mixing with his sweat in the moment. The drum beat of his heart matches the rhythm of his steps. His breathing attempts to mimic but to do so would deprive him of oxygen, as his breaths briskly leave after they shallowly enter.

Caseto and Ilian ascend the stairs to the tallest turret, stretching into the heavens and sufficient to see roads leading into the city on all sides. Caseto stands as a god viewing his world. Disgruntled. Disgusted. But not even a hint of intimidation meets his face. Ilian gazes upon the demigod, not feeling worthy to stand in his presence. A shadow passes behind them. Ilian turns with sword pointed at no more than the air.

"Your spirit is keen, Private Guard. That is how you sense that not only the armies of Niekalarah invade our city. Something more powerful lurks here."

Absorbing the Governor's words, Ilian squints at the battles below. Blood marks the streets and houses, dulling the glimmer of the all too familiar sliver of alexandrite. Marvelous weapons. Never do they grow blunt, and only with great force do they break. His eyes turn to slits as he examines a weapon designed to kill and kill and kill again. And then the thunder rings out. A lone enemy crossing the fields falls to the ground in pain. Struck by Caseto's secret. Alexandrite may be strong, but a long-range weapon gives his people the advantage.

Ilian's heart races. The intruders swiftly approach, as if granted speed by the gods, as if the gods assist them in their pursuits. Some of the townspeople run for their homes. Others grab their most precious belongings and attempt to flee the city. Little do they know their vanity to be the cost of their life. Inside the city proves to be the safest place. Ilian prays his family remain within their home. That they remain hidden.

Another cry of thunder fills the air. And then another. All sense of victory the army of Niekalarah may have had with their surprise attack fades. Faces turn a pale brown as the blood rushes from them. Some had heard rumors, but they did not expect to face the cruel, harsh reality of an army outside of their reach. Untouchable. Archers and lancers existed on a different level. The weapons of men were used in wars before. Now they fight with the weapons of gods.

Liza stands atop the roof, having climbed out the window of the central watch tower. She takes aim and another falls by her hand. The sound of the weapon is but the gods applauding her devotion. The dying enemy is her sacrifice unto them.

"You hear that, Private Guard?" Caseto asks in an insidious voice, filled with malicious delight. A flicker of the fire in his eyes gives away his excited disposition to war. "The gods cheer for us. These demons of Hernan will return to the icy flames of Inferno. Hmmph. Victory will be ours. And without some warrior of the glass sword."

An image of Cordaya flashes through Ilian's mind. When attacks happened on the towns of the mountains, she was their vision of hope. Utter devastation would not pass as long as she existed to protect them. Caseto played this role in the capital. Yet he wielded no sword. He did not strike down their foes. No more than his blessing from the gods inspired hope among all soldiers and townspeople. But was charisma a gift of the gods? More so than a crystal sword that only appeared in times of trouble? Were Caseto's abilities divine? Ilian glances at the Governor, attempting to catch a glimpse of heavenly powers. But only malevolence radiates from the man cloaked in extravagant delights. Clenched fist, slitted eyes, sly grin malevolence. Ilian's fingers twitch for his saber. He gulps.

Ilian takes shallow breaths. A low growl comes from behind his right shoulder. Ilian's eyes grow alert and turns to see an archer from atop the church's steeple aim in their direction. Aim for the Governor.

"Get down!"

Ilian throws his arms about Caseto and pushes him to the ground. The sound in his ear growls louder. Ilian unsheathes his blade and swings at the air, knocking the arrow to the ground. His eyes grow in shock, unable to believe himself capable of such precision. Ilian glances at his wielding hand then back to the archer. The thunder rings and the soldier with the bow tumbles from the steeple. Liza kneels down, raising a hand to the air then slightly pushing her lips to her fingers before placing them on the barrel of her weapon. Ilian offers a quick prayer of thanks before clutching onto the Governor's cloak. Ilian and Caseto meet eyes. Caseto holds an expression of amusement.

"Your Grace needs to get inside," Ilian instructs, panic leaking through his voice.

His eyes scan the surrounding area, wishing to see the next arrow or lance aimed to kill the one or both of them. Adrenaline courses through the Private Guard, or so he assumes to be the cause of the tremors he faces. But nerves sweep through him, as if in the blink of an eye Ilian realized what could be his fate. He never questioned his responsibility, his duty, unto the divine Governor. But, when he examined the arrow's trajectory, understanding the exact location it would hit, the Private Guard had flinched. Should he not have acted, the Governor would have fallen to the ground for another reason. Ilian hides his shame. But fear of divine judgment never escapes his heart. He analyzes Caseto's amused smile. Sacrifice for favor of this man is not his destiny.

With a shake of the head, Ilian clears his thoughts, but only for a moment.

"Your Grace must hide indoors. We could go to the tunnels. Flee through the hidden underground passage. Should this palace come under siege-"

"Private Guard, would you hide me from this beautiful, heavenly scenery?"

"Your Grace could be killed!"

"Let us see them try to kill a god!"

Caseto utilizes the stone brick wall to pull himself to his feet. Clutching cloak in one hand and wall with the other, the appearance of a feeble man enters Ilian's thoughts. This is not the image of a god. Caseto releases a suppressed cackle as he examines the fallen bodies in the fields not far. Like animals left by their hunters to rot in the sun. The paved street leading into the city glimmers with its puddles of red. Screams and cries sound as no more than a symphony, a fantastic orchestra. Ilian notes the madness in Caseto's eyes.

"Not even that warrior of the glass sword could strike me down! Let's see him try. These lowly scum of the pit, not even a cowering dog would bow to them! But all, even the strongest, wealthiest, and most powerful bow to me!"

The roars of thunderous booms fill the morning, drowning out any songs of the birds that may not have fled. To Ilian's ears, and perhaps his alone, the claps of the weapons transform from the gods' applause to their scorn. Angering, furious growls and shouts to the mortals below. So willing to take from another what is most precious to a mortal. Life. Perhaps the Governor is divine, for he does not seem to fear losing his.

"I beg of you, Your Grace." Ilian's voice trembles and he takes a knee, despite meant to have eyes on any possible enemy set to strike the Governor. "None are asking to test your divinity. For to doubt is but a sin larger than the rest. The miracles you have worked through Micacao, and the world as a whole, prove sufficient. And should be to all."

Ilian realizes through Caseto's unchanging expression that he may not be able to convince the Governor. An idea strikes him.

"What a jeer it would be to our foes to turn your back on this battle as if it no more than a mere quibble. The tiniest scratch on a stone pillar. Hernan's armies are nothing to fear. Your Grace will not quake at his threats. And neither will Micacao."

A grin, twisted and malevolent, sprawls across Caseto's face. He lets a snort leave before descending the stairs of the tower.

Ilian releases a breath of relief and glances in the direction of his home. His eyes move to the heavens, praying all to be well within. Should something come to pass, he could not imagine the grief. The pity he felt for those in the villages destroyed by the barbarian raids was not an event he ever thought would pass upon the holy capital. Ilian believed the gods shielded their followers from such heinous lawlessness. But even the gods will be challenged by demons. Even Caseto may fall one day. And perhaps he already had.

As Ilian's head lowers behind the brick wall as he descends, blocking his view from the battles below, he catches a last glimpse of Liza. She flips up her eyepatch to reveal a gruesome scar where her left eye used to be. The hardened warrior positions herself as a glass statue. In a state of peril but never flinching. Tears run down her cheek as another of her comrades falls. But the resolve in her face grows with every friend to return to the heavens. Her lips move in continuous prayer. Her concentration never falters.

The tower provides an echo chamber for the sounds of the weapon. The clashing of swords fail to overpower. Not even a scream can be heard at the moment of the sonorous boom. The image of the soldier in the field falling, seemingly hit by nothing, flashes through his head. The sensation of a thin needle piercing through skin, vein, muscle, tearing apart entire organs with such acute force. Pain and blood. And then nothing. The thunderous sound is but a taunt. An unreachable, unparalleled taunt to humiliate the enemy. Until they possess a weapon of the gods, Hernan stands no chance.

Caseto struts into the throne room, adjusting his rings and inspecting their glitter in the light to enter through the bubbled glass tile along the upper edge of the concrete walls. The room shines with brilliance in the day, as the rays hit the mosaic and with a haunting gleam in the moonlight as night passes through. The dynamic with which the lighting alone hit the throne room served as evidence to Ilian long ago that he sat in the presence of the divine. The ethereal way with which Caseto's cloak lays against him as he sits in his chair another example. But that image slowly starts to distort and dissolve as does the bubbling tortilla deflate as the comal cools. Ilian, in the face of a divine, experiences more fear than admiration. Or is it merely his guilt to blame?

His thoughts race when the growl of Caseto clearing his throat pulls his attention.

"Private Guard, tell me a story."

Caseto licks his lips, perhaps in anticipation, or perhaps tasting the fear emanating from Ilian. Swallowing the saliva to build up in his mouth, his fingers rubbing against themselves, Ilian's nerves grow. He knows of what Caseto wishes to hear. He desires a tale of the warrior of the glass sword. Caseto wishes to hear how much stronger, mightier, well-favored he is in comparison to the famed warrior.

All the while the battle continues outside. Screams and shots of that weapon muffle as they pass through the concrete and stone brick hallways. They produce an odd echo, mixing together as a haunting song. Almost as if returning to the worship site, the steady drums beating in the background. Granted, he may confuse drums for his heart.

"Private Guard." Caseto strokes his chin as a sly grin grows. "Tell me. Tell me of the events to pass on your mission. The people. The attacks. Tell me everything."

Ilian opens his mouth to speak but notices another shadow out of the corner of his eye. With a deep breath, and uncertainty weighing about in his head, he chooses what instinct, or the divine will, tells him.

"Your Grace. I humbly say to you as your guard and spiritual servant," Ilian pauses to absorb Caseto's inquisitive expression, "how grateful I am to you and the gods for this spiritual journey."

Caseto sits forward in his throne. Having expected no more than a journeyman's tales to pass the time, curiosity overcomes him. Ilian, always incredibly faithful in his conversations with the Governor, sees no fault in addressing him as so. Though perhaps the examination comes from Ilian's talk earlier. Ilian slipped in his words, some may even accuse him of having disrespected the Governor. Ilian could not deny his doubts in the Governor's true divine authority, especially with the eyes watching him from behind every corner and bend. The guard understands his place in the government, as a high ranking official in the social ladder. His beliefs may change but the circumstances have not. With a silent prayer, Ilian clears his throat.

"The events over the last couple of weeks have strengthened me not only as a soldier of Micacao and Private Guard to Your Grace, but also as a pious servant to the church. I have seen the heathens, those from Niekalarah, with their brutality and barbarism strike down innocents, children. I did my best to serve as a missionary on my quest, as the word of the gods is sacred and never falters to work nor play. I did as you had hoped."

"But I speak of the mission."

"A spiritual quest, indeed. For not only did it teach me of those less fortunate and educated than myself, a lesson in humility. But also-"

"Of the mission-"

"But also of how certain I am of my faith. A strong foundation that cannot be shaken-"

"The mission!"

Caseto slams his fists into the arms of his throne. The pound causes Ilian to jump and the echoes reverberate in tune with the shots of the weapons outside. With a gulp the Private Guard connects eyes with the Governor. Fire burns beyond. Caseto stands in his rage, curling his fingers inward and stalks toward Ilian. Ilian's fingers twitch for his saber, but he chooses not to move them. He places his trust in the gods.

Caseto grips a hold of Ilian's collar.

"You failed me and you failed the gods. You couldn't even bring me the warrior of the glass sword. No sword. No head. What use are you, Private-"

The floor trembles as several pellets from the weapons hit the outer wall of the throne room. Both of their eyes widen as they realize an enemy must have gotten past. Screams can be heard on the other side. Orders demanding surrender. The clanging of the sword as it's thrown to the stone slab ground. The voices die down.

Ilian and Caseto look to one another, one with fear, the other with ferocity, respectively. Caseto's lips curl and grip tightens.

The sound of an army of boots clicking on the mosaic approach the two. With a gulp, Ilian glances to the ground. Caseto drops his arms to his side. After a slight nod of his head, Ilian turns in a defensive stance, ready to protect the Governor in the face of the visitors. From around the corner of the wall appears Guard Enamias and four soldiers, two of which hold a bloodied man, the other two with sabers pointed at his back.

Caseto squints, the whites of his eyes no longer visible. He analyzes the enemy with a lick of the lips. Ilian, unable to glance at the bloodied man for more than a second, focuses on the wall behind them, flinching with every drop of blood to splash on the mosaic tile.

Wearing an olive green uniform and jaguar crest on his jacket, the Niekalaran releases fragile breaths as his life slips from his grasp.

The metal pellet from the weapon remains lodged in his arm, blood cascading from the hole in his body, staining the last coat he will ever wear.

The sight does not baffle nor offend the Governor. Rather he chuckles in amusement. Only an itch of anger courses through him at the burgundy liquid dirtying his floor. Impure. Unfit to be sacrificial. Yet the divine Governor thirsts for more. With another lick of the lips, Caseto tilts his head.

His men stop in front of him and bow, their hands forcing the enemy to do the same. The bloodied form winces in pain at the vehement blow. He glances at Ilian, whose eyes fixate on the wall beyond.

"It is no more than a strawman..." Ilian attempts to convince himself. Flashbacks spring to life within his mind, to the children and women of the villages facing barbarian raids. The glares of those fiery, focused eyes return to him. The gods watch.

"Rise. Rise," the Governor commands, a slight grin revealing its cruel self. His fingers tap the arms of his throne, anticipation leaking through his cold exterior. The Governor's manner reads stoic and stolid, but his eyes betray his excitement.

"Forgive us, Your Grace. The enemy attempted to sneak into the holy palace. Claims to be a messenger of the corrupt President Hernan," Enamias states, no emotion visible on his face. The war veteran, accustomed to seeing such sights on the battlefields of his youth, does not flinch as blood splashes on the floor behind his boot.

"And you allowed entrance?"

"Your-"

Caseto lifts a hand to silence the guard. Enamias bites his lip to stop his speech. A steady glare falls upon the man with shallow breaths, muffled chokes full of liquid. Ilian gulps, swallowing a strange guilt as compassion courses through his veins. He would have never thought to feel empathy for the enemy before. Any danger to the Governor deserves whatever merciless end they receive.

"It's no more than a strawman. An enemy strawman..."

Caseto glances at his Private Guard. Ilian's anticipation and twitches prove his gained weakness, a curse placed upon him by those heathens of the village. Ilian grimaces at his transformation as well, understanding he would have never acted in turn before his mission. The lines of his mission, of his life's duty, blur. A budding empathy and desire for change swell in the Private Guard's heart. The gods anger more with every drop of blood, and not for its unfit value as sacrificial.

"Was he armed?"

"No, Your Grace."

"Does he bare a scroll?"

"Unfortunately, it was lost in our attempt to detain him. We do not know where it could have gone."

Enamias's eyes shift to look at Ilian. Their eyes connect and a fear transmits between the two of them. Enamias's fingers fumble slightly at his sides, a nervous shake. Ilian understands, the unspoken language between comrades, between friends, underestimated by many a ruler throughout history. A prayer issues from Ilian's mind, a distraction to the red river forming on the tile. A strange comfort finds Ilian for this treasonous action of his comrade, as if appeasing the gods. More war in such times would only work to spark greater fury. However, a messenger with the ability to speak does not need a scroll.

The other soldiers bow their heads in embarrassment of losing the scroll. Their shame exudes through their tightening fingers, covered in blood due to their urgency to bring the enemy before the throne. Hopes and prayers called that the Governor may force the message from the Niekalaran before taking his final breath. Enamias could not persuade the men to wait any longer, to convince them to search for the scroll already turned to ash. His own actions may have led him to his death as well.

"What say you messenger? What news do you bring from the inept Hernan?"

Rather than look to the bleeding man, Caseto analyzes the rings on his fingers, wiping away any stray dust particles settling on top of the jewels. Enamias steps to the side, wishing to glance at the messenger. The enemy chokes up more blood, gritting teeth to not scream in pain. After a few shaky breaths, he opens his mouth to speak.

"The great President Hernan... sends me," he says with shaky voice. He attempts to stand tall in pride and patriotism of his nation, but the pain from his many wounds prevents him from doing so.

"He sends his best, I presume? Tell me, what news do you bring, Niekalaran crustacean?"

Caseto taps the pointed tip of his sandal on the tile, the click a threat should the messenger rely on dishonesty.

The guards forcefully adjust the messenger's posture. The grunts of pain to issue result in a delay in his speech. Caseto scowls. The guards step back and peer at the ground.

The messenger puffs his chest despite his shattered form. Pride swells within him.

"The time... has... come."

The messenger bends over into a coughing fit. More red specks join the others on his faded canvas sandals and matting what little facial hair had grown on his journey. A mix of phlegm and blood hits the tile.

"What time would that be?"

Caseto speaks in a monotone as if the situation be a jest. As if mocking the messenger, Caseto. The Private Guard takes a defensive stance, the Governor demonstrating vulnerability as an insult the more reason to remain on high alert.

"War... destruction. Not only... Niekalarah... but from... your own."

"Is that so?"

Crossing one leg over the other, Caseto leans back with eyes closed.

"Your President is brave, indeed. Sending his own on this suicide trek to deliver words which the gods have already echoed in my ears. To think he so clever as to attempt to infiltrate the ranks... I have eyes and ears everywhere, scroll mule. The gods are on my side. How will Niekalarah stand to the divine?"

"With a weapon... of greater... holy strength."

The messenger cripples beneath his weight, his legs numb as the last of his energy seeps from him.

Caseto rises and glides to the messenger. His towering form casts a shadow over the man kneeling on his tiles. Pulling back his cloak, Caseto unsheathes a jewel encrusted dagger, its blade like that of a kris with jagged edges.

"What holy weapon would surpass my own?"

The messenger gazes up at the Governor and opens his mouth to speak. Hollow breaths are all he can manage. His head bobbles and body sways, no doubt vision blackened. He is lost to this world.

"Speak!" Caseto roars. His command reaches into the depths of the man's mind, prying the information free of the blood filling his throat.

A gag imitating a chuckle issues from the messenger. The ability to anger the enemy, one of such stature as the Governor with he himself having been no more than a stable hand before the President sought his assistance, truly an honor. A badge he shall wear to the grave and into the endless ocean of the afterlife. His people will never know, his story never added to the history books. But his ancestors have seen and will reward him justly. They will know and their pride will be all consuming, all other sins erased with this one act. Not every legend has their passage. Not every legend fits the definition by their life's end. But legends are for mortals, and he will exist beyond from this point forward.

"Glass sword."

The words leave in a whisper. Caseto prepares the dagger in his hand for the strike, but the messenger collapses before his opportunity to be executioner. No further sounds leave, the only movements those of a body in the final throes of life. The soul and spirit have departed. A physical body, a shell with no host, remains.

"Dispose of this wretched servant at once. Cover the face, let none know his appearance. He no longer exists in our world. His words nor life will leave no print on this event. A stain to my reputation should any know he had been brought before my presence. Incinerate the clothes, the bones. Leave no evidence this person ever arrived at my palace. Let Hernan believe their attack to be no more than a fruit fly at our table. Go now."

The two guards take up the body, one grabbing the hands, the other the feet. Blood drips from the corpse as they sidestep to the door. Caseto exhales in agitation and turns from the sight.

Ilian gazes upon Enamias who returns it with weary eyes and a gulp.

The Governor circles the room, examining every speck on the tile floor. Grimacing at the dust particles floating in the sunlight streams not yet settled from the movement of the those in the palace due to the attack. Eyeing the blood pool laden on the floor, an outer ring drying as the time passes. The Governor smirks as not one maiden of the palace has attempted to enter to clean the mess. They must be in hiding, as all in the city did upon the first clashing of swords. Upon hearing the screams of those around. A battle so close to home had not happened in centuries for those in the capital. A surprise attack indeed.

"But why?" Caseto mumbles to himself. Again and again as he paces around his chair. The stalking movement transforms into an aging trudge. Ilian senses the Governor's confusion. And he knows that the people, living in the protection of their faith will not understand the true cause.

"The gods are angry, Your Grace."

Caseto and Enamias turn to Ilian. His words strike a fear into their core that not even the Niekalaran attack could have. That is because the words were not superstitious. They were not delivered as a threat. A truth laces the voice of the Private Guard, a vulnerability nonexistent in the guard before his mission.

"You have been humbled," Caseto states, voicing his stream of thought. "Never have I seen such a fear in your eyes. Your resolve had always been clear to me. Your loyalty unto the nation, unto me, never wavered no matter the assassination attempts nor the thought of war. You stayed near to me, more so than any other private guard within the palace. They were always intimidated by you. Your faith... your faith has shattered and been reforged. And not to my liking."

Ilian prevents himself from gasping. He wonders how long the Governor had known. Doubts circle his head. Ilian no longer feels safe. As if the predator lures him in, a cow letting the butcher tie him to a tree.

"Tell me, Private Guard. Tell me that answer to my question that the gods have interrupted so many times before. What happened on our mission?"

Ilian glances at Enamias who stares at the mosaic. A rage exists within the soldier's eyes. As if Ilian's betrayal is more cause for punishment than his own. Or perhaps his own guilt for his betrayal proves far greater than that which he feels the Private Guard deserves. The Private Guard, with greater status within the nation for protecting a divine leader, holds to a higher standard than his lowly position. But at what cost to the Private Guard, his friend?

"Do not worry for Guard Enamias. He will be my witness. A witness to the testimony of a traitor. That is if your words prove outside of my liking. It would be shameful to lose someone as fit, strong of mind and body and spirit. But the gods will offer me another in time. No one is holy within these lands but me. You, Private Guard, are a mortal. With imperfections and all. Do not think you cannot be replaced. Arrogance is a sin."

Ilian swallows the saliva build up in his mouth. The growl behind him comes at the comment the Governor makes. In its low, deep voice, Ilian hears the word hypocrite. Realizing he had no escape, nowhere to run, Ilian sighs.

"Your Grace, I have not turned from you. My faith in your rule has never been greater. My loyalty to you goes unchallenged."

A thunderous boom occurs outside, shaking the walls. But it was no sound of war. Rather of unexplained origin, as the thunder booms with the sun ever shining.

"Prove it, Private Guard. Though it may sound blasphemous, as faith must exist without need for evidence, I as a divine wish to test you. Not for my sake, but for your own. Prove to me that your loyalty unto me has not declined."

"I did as you told me. My mission was to go in search of the warrior of the glass sword and bring them to you. I assumed the task simple, for my own belief in your might and divinity. Little did I know of the tests to exist beyond the capital. Not all worship the same gods. Not all worship you, Your Grace. This came as a surprise. Though I'd been told of such heathens, I had yet to interact with any outside of those criminals attempting to do you harm. Little did I know the influence of evil carried such power."

"Your words are empty, Private Guard."

"I met her."

Enamias turns to Ilian with wide eyes.

"And what did this warrior of legend say to you?"

Ilian's eyes scan the walls of the chamber, searching for answers. Their conversations amounted to much more than Ilian could repeat in a single sentence, a brief answer being what the Governor asks.

"She told me of their faith and their work in the mountains."

The Governor scoffs.

"This is how I know she is not divine. A god would not stoop so low as to do manual labor. There is no need."

Ilian's body temperature rises. His fingernails dig into his palm.

"I talked with many who clearly look to her as their hope."

"It is unfortunate that their hope has been stripped away by the measly forces of Hernan."

A shaky breath leaves Ilian.

"Her faith is strong as a mountain, its rooted deep into the fabric of the earth."

"Easy for brutes to believe lies told to them by the witches of the woods, their worship leaders. They are not asked to prove much."

"The strength of her faith shook my own."

Caseto stops his pacing. The glow of wrath in his eyes meets his Private Guard. What once impressed and inspired Ilian as divine powers, emotion ranging outside of mortals turns to scorn for a man who fails to understand the most basic essence of humans. Military might and fortified lies lay far outside of the realms of faith of the humbled and honest. Ilian remembers Mizochtal's words. And then it hits Ilian. How much will Caseto expect? How much can Ilian get away with not telling?

"The ability to believe and continue believing in such hardships as war and poverty to hit their villages proves just how far their own faith has come. It is easy to believe when life gives no more than privilege with little hardship. But these people, they believe despite all their hardships, and-"

"And they fail where it really counts."

Caseto rubs the back of his chair, as if soothing an animal before killing it. The fluidity that moves in his fingers differs greatly from the rigidity of his body. His stoic form, chest puffed, and chin tilted at an incline, demonstrates his belief of how a god should look and act. Regal. Majestic. One to be looked upon for greatness and flawlessness. Only one with such quality should have the right to be praised by others.

"Private Guard, if they do not worship our gods and respect me as their divine leader, they have already been thrown outside of the lines of what can be deemed faithful servants. Or have you forgotten as much?"

"No, Your Grace. I have not forgotten."

Ilian bites his lip. His mission remains the same as that first day. Find the warrior of the glass sword. Being in the hands of the enemy proves a greater risk to Cordaya's life than facing small tribes of barbarians before. Yet, what does it matter if time runs out? The gods are watching and waiting. Their fury growing with every passing minute.

"Good. So, tell me. If your explanation had been the same as mine to you, why did the warrior of the glass sword not come with you to meet with me? Surely, she," the Governor pauses and takes a deep breath, "she should have understood your reasoning and what a great honor it would bring upon her and her family. In fact, her very presence could have proved a saving grace to her village. We could have helped them, Ilian. Poverty is their choice."

"You're right," Ilian says, puffing his own chest and choosing a different tone. "The economic inequalities they face, such as the time and energy they put into their work to receive little profit, have absolutely nothing to do with their poverty."

"You mock me?" Caseto says with raised eyebrows.

He steps around his chair and takes a seat. Ilian grits his teeth at the Governor's confidence. Sitting, a vulnerable position, serves as no more than bullying the Private Guard. The only person in the room to protect the Governor should Ilian snap would be Enamias. Ilian looks to the soldier. He senses no desire in Enamias to stop whatever move his comrade makes.

Caseto absorbs the tension and issues a deep chuckle.

"The gods are angry, Private Guard. And you turning on your divine leader is the only proof I need to validate my premonitions. You are weak. The moment you stepped outside of your comfort, your foundation cracked due to fragile faith. You have failed your test. This is why your mission could have been none other than a failure. I put my own faith in you. I trusted in your abilities. But-"

"Your Grace, please. Ilian is strong. A dark force must have-" Enamias speaks up, his head shaking from the words of the Governor. Every soldier knows and respects Private Guard Ilian for his hard work and loyalty, putting the Governor before all else. People would talk of how Ilian was born with a sole purpose, to protect the Governor.

"But," Caseto holds up a hand to silence Enamias, who does so in an instant. "I will offer a second chance to redeem yourself, Private Guard. The battle here has ended, but a new one will begin. Enamias, send for Liza. Have her gather her forces and those of your own. We will keep the group small but strong. Ilian. We will find the warrior of the glass sword. As my meeting with her is the only way to appease the gods. You are correct. They grow furious as the time for this prophesied meeting draws near with no assurance it will happen. And you must help me strike a bargain with Hernan. This will be a test of your faith. An opportunity for forgiveness."

Ilian thinks of Cordaya. This could be his chance to save her. Enamias glances at his friend before bowing to the Governor and turning to leave. His march shows hesitation and nerves. Like a drum hit out of rhythm. Despite the doubts, despite his growing scorn for the Governor, Ilian nods.

"I will truly and graciously accept this second chance. An opportunity to redeem myself. And should I fail this time, I shall pay with my life."

"As you should."

The venomous tone cuts at Ilian's spirit. He feels a snake wrap about his legs constricting him, a threat, to follow Caseto. The presence of the being that had been growling behind him vanishes. Yet those eyes, far away and penetrating eyes continue to watch. This is a test. Whether set by Caseto or by the gods themselves, Ilian knows he must not fail. Not only will his own life and possibly Cordaya's be at risk, but the rest of the world as well. Ilian thinks of his family, of the Morezes. Failure is not an option. Not now.

Caseto stands and leads the way from the chamber. He climbs the tower, Ilian following closely behind. They observe the city from their pinnacle between the heavens and the mortal world.

"How beautiful is my city. Strong and resistant."

Caseto glares at Ilian, as the Private Guard turns to his house to ensure no damage has occurred. Broken glass can be seen from fallen streetlamps and damaged windows. Nurses and doctors find assistance from nearby soldiers in bringing bodies to their hospitals. Many of the bodies they carry are Niekalarans, or as the messenger suggests ex-citizens. Ilian knows they will not live long. Caseto does not believe in helping the enemy. Any such acts are blasphemous and will be met with extreme punishment upon a person's death. Therefore, the nurses and doctors administer poison to such cases, disposing of the bodies quickly afterward to not contaminate their rooms with any demons that may try to escape and find a new host.

Ominous, charcoal colored clouds make their way for the capital. A faint glow illuminates the sinister backdrop, a slim strike touching down. The low rumbles meet Ilian's ears as growls. An omen to what lurks ahead.

"Your Grace, do you believe it best for you to partake in this mission? What if harm were to come to you?"

"I am a God, Private Guard. I will not part from this planet until my choosing. My faith gives me confidence and my divinity shields me."

"And you believe them to be holding the legendary warrior hostage in Niekalarah?"

"Hmm..." Caseto examines his ruby ring, twisting it into proper position on his finger. He wipes a speck of dust from his cloak and clears his throat. "It is possible they have not yet left. Though I do wonder in what company they hold her."

Silence overtakes them. The rumbles of thunder grow louder.

"Well. We shall leave upon first light. After all, I still have duties to attend to after such an exciting day. Our casualties were few, but a service is in need for a blessing upon our city. Come Private Guard, we must gather and send out the message."

Ilian nods and they descend the tower.

Chapter Fourteen

Ilian stands at the Governor's side, hands behind back and stern expression, his usual stance when guarding, as the priests and high-ranking officials collect their duties from the Governor concerning the night's activities. Ilian stands guard and listens, not a word to escape his lips. His offering to the Governor. Silence.

"Why of course, Grand Brother. Also, we will need Don Isafel's wife's ripest chrysanthemums and marigolds. I expect you and the committee can make this happen tonight so the spirits of those taken from us may not wander far from their path to the heavens."

The Grand Brother bows and exits the chamber. The next to enter is the Governor's personal messenger.

"Send word of tonight's services to the townspeople. Remind them to bring their offerings to the dead."

The messenger bows and leaves. Ilian glances at Caseto and notices a malicious smile spread on the Governor's face. The Private Guard feels a nauseous twirl in his stomach.

"I will retire to my chambers in preparation for the service. I suspect you need to do as much," Caseto states, eyeing Ilian up and down.

"And your protection?"

"My guard is more for your status than for your own. Remember, Private Guard. I am a god."

"Yes, Your Grace."

Ilian bows his head, a cramp in his neck forcing him to stay down longer than he normally would. When he rises, his eyes meet Caseto's.

"I suggest you change to your ceremonial saber for tonight's guard. I would not wish to disrespect the dead. You never know what curse may follow us on our quest should we not test caution."

"Yes, Your Grace."

Ilian exits the chamber and heads for his home.

Specks of blood litter the streets every now and again. Streaks where bodies had been dragged. Every step he takes, the stone trembles beneath him. Tremors created by the messenger of the God of the Earth, sending a message to the Private Guard. All the gods' messengers seem to be communicating with Ilian the chosen. The thunder, the growls, the tremors. All serve to be a constant reminder to Ilian's true quest.

Eyes watch him pass through the streets. None approach. None speak a word. Ilian believes even if they had, he may have ignored it. His eyelids droop over his eyes, the light of the afternoon blinding as the sun fights to escape coverage by the storm clouds.

He draws near to his house when he hears metal bouncing on the stone. Having not noticed, the Private Guard kicks at the metal pellet. Ilian bends down to pick up the smooth, semi-chipped sphere. He rolls it around in his fingers, its cold metal sending a chill down his spine.

"Thank the gods you're okay."

Ilian rotates to see Alidora jogging to him. He straightens up in time to receive her hug. Warm. Familiar. Full of love and compassion. Tears form in his eyes to think of all that could be lost should he fail. With every ounce of willpower he can conjure, Ilian holds back the flow of sadness.

"I saw a man charging for the palace. I had no idea what plan they had. Possibly an assassination attempt. I was terrified."

"You do not have to worry, sister. Our Governor is divine. No attempt would occur unless it be the will of the gods."

"Right," Alidora says, scanning the emotion in Ilian's eyes. She strokes his arm and slightly shakes her head. "I'm just glad you're okay."

Ilian releases a shaky breath and turns his head away, tucking the metal pellet into the pocket of his pants.

"Is everyone safe? Where's ma? Your son?"

"Il, calm down. They're fine. By the grace of the gods, we are okay."

An outburst of crying occurs in the house to the right of their own. The woman of the household, a sweet, wrinkled lady who always handed out ice creams in the hot summers of Ilian's childhood, opens the door wide as her sons and sons-in-law carry out the body of an older man. Her husband bleeds from a hole in his neck. His body lies limp in their arms as they rush him to the nearest hospital. Ilian closes his eyes and offers a prayer, the widow in need of every blessing the gods may offer. Upon opening his eyes, he turns his head to the window of their home and sees the point of entry. A small, circular hole lie in the glass. The metal sphere in his pocket grows hot as he imagines the stray pellet striking the man, in his fear and vulnerability, in the place he believed he would be most safe. The probability of it all shocks the Private Guard. Even more so when he realizes it could have been one of his own family.

Ilian glances at Alidora, whose eyes follow the family down the road, pity and sympathy filling them.

"Let's go inside, shall we?"

Alidora nods and they enter the home.

As Ilian steps through the entrance, a force tries to take him down. His mother, rushing to embrace her son.

"Oh, by the god's grace you are safe! Thank you, my gods. Praise to you, my gods."

Her tears hit the shoulder of his jacket, absorbing in the material of the arm. Her arms tighten about him as she gasps to find air through her crying. Ilian says nothing. No words to make her feel safe. No prayer to calm his mother. For he struggles to keep his own emotions within. He fights back the tears, building up the dam to prevent the passage.

She pulls away and wipes the streams from her face, but the glitter in the lamplight remains.

"My dear son, by the grace of the gods, my son."

Ilian's mother examines his form, meticulously searching for any scratches or stains to prove he's been wounded. With no immediate notice of physical injury, his mother folds her hands into one another and looks to the heavens, whispering a grateful prayer.

"Mother, sister. You must ready yourselves. There is to be a service held tonight for those lost. The Governor does not wish their wandering souls to travel far."

Ilian turns his head to the floor and marches to his room. Alidora opens her mouth to call out to him, but quickly shuts it.

The Private Guard closes the red cedar door, creating a division between himself and the world. Ilian examines what he often deemed to be his humble abode. A fine, mahogany bed with feather filled mattress and pillows and a set of pure cotton sheets gifted by the Governor, a canvas painting of a foreign landscape, and religious glass ornaments decorate the room. His mother never threatened nor acted in remodeling his room or repurposing the space for herself or others, despite his neglect in visiting his family while in service to the Governor.

Guilt eats away when he thinks of how Alidora must care for his mother and her own family. Ilian, with no children or spouse of his own, believes it his duty to care for his mother, yet continues to put nation before blood.

His sister's image projects in his head. Not those with her smiling face and caring embraces. Nor of her soft, strong voice singing in the choir of their church. None of these memories of the joyous occasions meet him. Her tears. Distressed wrinkles and unkempt hair, panic-stricken expression and lightning-fast heartbeat. Ilian clenches his fists and sits on the floor, leaning against his bed.

Guilt was a parasite riding his shadow. Always there. Always chipping away at him. Dissolving his person in the mold. Forming. Shaping him. That word. Humble. A compliment. The greatest trait of the faithful. Humble and loyal, words always arriving at the same time. Yet these guests do not find Ilian, even after the nation's victory from an attacking force of those with nothing to gain, prepared to lose it all.

With steady fingers, Ilian removes his belt, laying his saber atop the bedding. Wrath and fury fight to break through, but he resists. Ilian bites his lip and shakes in place as he imagines the devastation to come. Surely whatever the gods would conjure exists far outside the realm of his own beliefs. He recalls the stories of the Tome Sanctus. The accounts of punishment. For sin always came with consequence. Whether immediate or delayed, it would find a person. Ilian believes his sins may have caught up to him.

He rises to sit on his bed, soft and adjusting to his weight to ease the pressure of his heavy form. Nothing like the bed offered to him by the Morezes. Like an imprint on his mind, on his heart, the memories of his time in Hoja Rosa continue to affect him.

With a sigh, Ilian walks to his wardrobe and refines himself for the services of the evening. After polishing his ceremonial saber, the Private Guard heads to the palace to act as the escort to the Governor.

Eyes meet him the moment he exits his home.

"Shame I left Pinto at the palace..." he thinks as he marches on his way.

Ilian taps the archway to the Governor's dressing quarters, a coded series of taps to let him and the current guard on duty know he, a non-hostile visitor, has arrived.

The other guard bows to the Governor and heads on his way to dress into his ceremonial suit. The Governor stands in the middle of a semicircle of mirrors, examining himself. Surrounding the Governor, an air of elegance for his flowing, velvet burgundy cloak. The rubies and emeralds shine upon his fingers. A smoked quartz charm hangs to the height of his ribs from a gold chain around his neck. The stone symbolizes death and new life. The Governor and his father before him wore this charm to all such services of the church. It was a part of their tradition. A part of their divinity.

"It is a pity we must see one another again in this garish garb. I must say the style is quite pompous for my simple taste," the Governor laughs and licks his lips. His eyes look through the reflection of the glass and into Ilian. The Private Guard holds a straight expression, standing tall with his hands stiff at his sides, acting as though his duty is not one of conversation with the Governor. His duty entails protection.

The Governor squints.

"But as is tradition and a responsibility of our faith, we must carry out such tasks to the expectations of the gods above, or risk losing those poor souls trapped below. Wouldn't want a dear friend's soul to be lost, wandering forever, due to a simple missed button. Am I not correct, Private Guard?"

"Yes, Your Grace."

As stolid as he is stubborn, Ilian denies the emotion to show itself.

The Governor rotates to look Ilian directly in the eye.

"I am pleased to know we are on the same page, Private Guard."

Caseto's eyes move down to Ilian's sleeve.

"Button up."

A gust of wind fights to knock Ilian down as Caseto struts past him. The Governor's meticulous eye would have impressed Ilian before, drowning out any doubt in the Governor's divinity. But admiration transforms into intimidation as the Governor's taunts find him as the target.

The Governor boards into his horse drawn chariot, Ilian following behind atop Pinto, and the two, with much applause and prayer to meet them, make their way to the church.

Grand turrets spring from the entrance, elaborate designs carved out of the stone with which the building was built. The flight of stairs to reach the sanctuary, carved perfectly from rock, used to tire Ilian in his younger days. In comparison to the mountains in Hoja Rosa, these stairs prove no difficult task.

The Governor ascends, a chosen disciple of the church lifting the cloak of the Governor behind so it does not dirty. When he reaches the top, the Governor turns to examine his city. Though rising to a higher elevation than the palace, the Governor refuses to allow his home seconded to the marvel that is the church. For this reason, generations of governors have refused to expand the church. The people of the capital wait below, knowing they can only seek entrance to the church once the Governor permits it.

The Governor, with glowing eyes and brimming smile, chuckles. The malevolence hits Ilian. His attempt to ignore it is met by a growl in his ear. He turns his head to see no sign of the origin of such a sound.

As they enter, the other disciples and the Grand Brother bow to the Governor. Ilian notes the anxious expressions on their faces. His mind wonders what may be the cause when he gazes upon a vase of dead flowers in the hands of one of the disciples.

"What are those?" the Governor asks, a hissing sound leaving his tongue.

"Those, umm," the Grand Brother shakes his head as he glances at the Governor. His prayer hoping the Governor would not notice went unheard, unfortunate for him. "You see. Dona Grazia graciously offered an entire week of cuttings to the church for tonight's service. We placed them upon the altar. But upon our return, one of the disciples found the flowers had all died. Dried up in less than ten minutes."

"Who entered upon that time? What blasphemy to enter the church to vandalize those offerings of our brethren?"

"No one entered, Your Grace. Cousin Aldo stood outside the entrance to notify us of your coming. No one entered."

"Then it was one already within these walls-"

"I don't believe-"

"Bring me their name."

"Yes, Your Grace."

The Grand Brother closes his eyes and forces a bow. With hurried pace, the faithful servant takes off on his mission.

Ilian parts the right side of the majestic double doors, placing his back against to face Caseto as he passes through. The Governor inhales profoundly, shoulders rising and diaphragm inflating. With a great exhale, Caseto adjusts his robes.

The Governor strides to the middle of the gargantuan sanctuary. Velvet banners with silk tassels, colored with pinks and indigos of distant nations, hang from the walls. Brilliant lanterns dangle from chains in the ramparts for evening and midnight services. A doubled curtain hides the carnation stained-glass ceiling, that which provides light for morning services.

Fingers clasped atop his abdomen, Caseto pauses at the stairs to the center pillar, a stage for those most faithful. A stunning silence shatters any attempt for a footfall or other activity. The church hands wait with hushed tones in the stairwells in the corners of the sanctuary, their tasks not yet complete but knowing not to interrupt the divine in his entrance. Permission will be granted for further movement. Superstition was not to be toyed with.

An altar emptied of flowers but littered with dried petals causes a groan from Caseto. Licking his lips, his fingers release from their position as one hand rests upon the rail. He climbs the stairs, passing the stage in the center of the pillar and rising to the one at the top. A stage no other can set foot on. Only the most faithful of servants may clean the area and only after hours of prayer beforehand to cleanse them of any and all evils that may taint the divine pinnacle.

Ilian allows the door to close as the Governor takes a seat on a small, cushioned stool. From that position, the Governor could see all members of the church. The only faithful servants out of his sight are that of the Grand Council and the chorus on the mid and bottom stage of the pillar. But that was why Ilian's position as the Private Guard was on the ground. The Governor's right hand would need to betray those underneath the pillar of the divine who deviated from the most faithful of practices. And at one time, Ilian would not have hesitated to do so.

He worried that he was no longer the same. Inside the sanctuary walls, the eye of the gods would see him, not only physically but spiritually. The gods would betray his thoughts to the Governor, but the odds were, they already had.

Caseto waves a hand and the servants of the church continue their tasks, with more urgency and care than before due to being in the eye of the divine. Should they be judged, it should be for their best. No mistakes.

Ilian stands at his post, poised and stoic, the expression of a hardened soldier crosses his face. A threat to any who dare break the rules. Unfortunately, the guise often wavers. Flinching at every sound, fingertips digging into palms as an imaginary clock ticks. Nerves fight like a tremor attempting to escape the ground. Seats filled with naught but ghosts haunt the sanctuary. Another bouquet of flowers is brought then discarded. More than simply the faithful and the Governor were in attendance.

A thunderous bang fills the sky outside. A panicked screech of the birds fleeing their roosts high atop the church's parapets follows. Ilian chuckles.

They've already integrated that dreaded weapon into ceremony. They have truly made it a device of the gods and not handheld death.

The youngest church hands pull the doors back and tie the lassos about the handles to the pillars to keep them in place. They quickly take their place at the bottommost stage of the pillar.

Elderly couples in garments worn to many a mourning enter first, taking their seats at the innermost rows, splitting their ways to keep to tradition. A mix of younger families and young adults enter, their clothing pristine and some never worn prior. The only constant among all the faithful are wooden bangles etched with a prayer. Each prayer was different, assigned by the token Grand Council member to perform their first cleansing. Ilian had not worn his in years, the Governor burning it in ritual flames as a part of his entering the Private Guard. The only prayer that mattered to him were those words muttered by the Governor that day.

"Should your health be maintained and your faith move mountains, so long as your soul be devoted to mine."

Dried streams of tears, some still moist upon the cheeks, line many of the citizens' faces. The air of sorrow to enter with the crowd fills the sanctuary. The weight of others' emotions alone could crush the Private Guard. His eyes find those of his mother, her emotions always much stronger when entering the sanctuary and peering upon the fine Governor.

Another bang of that weapon sounds. The faithful servants close the doors. Caseto stands.

"Welcome, my daughters, sons, my children of new and old. This is a gathering of mourning. A requiem to be made for our dead. We lift high this orison to our gods. Save them!" A boisterous call to the heavens. "And save this beautiful city built by my ancestors and by me, thanks to the plentiful restoration projects I have funded."

Ilian rolls his eyes. Listening to the words of the Governor before felt like what it may feel like to hear a god speak. After having been in the presence of the messenger, the lion spirit, Ilian hears no more than a man with an audience to bolster his pride.

"My people, my faithful servants. The gods are testing us. They test your faith. They test your devotion to them. To me. They have observed weakness. For that they were able to subterfuge their attack. The divine eye lost its full power due to lack of prayer. Lack of offerings.

"In my absence from this town in days prior, the gods came to me. They told me of lawlessness. Of sinful acts and betrayal of vows committed by our very own. I do not need names. I know their names. The gods wanted a cleansing.

"The attack may have resolved our issues," a hiss sounds as his tone grows venomous. "However, I can never be so sure others have not been tainted, enchanted into ways that defy our gods. Defy me.

"Let us hear the first hymn of mourning and a scripture from our servants."

Caseto takes a seat.

Many stringed instruments, from harpsichord to basses, players of woodwinds, and a piano start up a melancholy tune. The singers in the chorus stand in a ring facing the members who lower from their seats and bow to the pillar.

Ilian notes Alidora as she sings the somber tune. Her eyes meet his and words slip on a lyric. Fists clench and she regains her composure. Her eyes turn away.

The Private Guard bites his bottom lip and peers up to the Governor. Caseto closes his eyes and sways his head to the music. The tune holds no sadness for him. It fuels him. As the peoples' emotions drain from them, he understands his hold over them.

The control he wields evident in every arched back from an elderly person in need of assistance to rise. The control over the young adult who understands their freedoms to be heavily tied to religious laws. The control over the nation, for anything that happens can find blame in another and never him. He holds no responsibility for the misfortunes, for the disasters to pass. He will always be divine. Fortune his doing wherever and whenever it may be. But misfortune, that is his punishment, proof that his divinity should never be in question.

Any questions should be evidence of a lack of faith. And the gods find ways to punish those who are weak.

A chill courses through Ilian. He no longer fears Caseto the god. He fears Caseto the man.

Chapter Fifteen

I lian takes up his corner position in the eating hall. A grand table stands in the center, a velvet table runner with intricate stitching runs down the middle. Burgundy and gold, the metallic thread dazzling in the light from the candelabra. Many chairs line the table on all sides, only one of the chairs occupied in this moment.

"What did you think of the services, Private Guard?"

Caseto addresses Ilian. Changed from his ceremonial robes, Caseto tucks a cloth napkin into his woven cotton chemise, with ruffled sleeves and an embroidered geometric pattern on the sleeves. The smell of food arrives from all corners as the servers to the cooks deliver trays of food to the Governor. Ilian salivates.

"The services went well, Your Grace."

A bowl of pork and broccoli cream soup lands to the upper corner of the Governor's seated position. Fresh grapes and watermelon cubes find the table next to the ceramic plate with fried cheese quesadillas with cream and chopped scallions atop. The final offering, from one of the ranch hands, a charred flank steak, smothered in a fresh seasoning of parsley and thyme and salts from the mountains finds a place in front of the Governor. He licks his lips.

"Yes, yes. The services went exceptionally well, I would say."

A young woman leaves a chalice of wine in front of the Governor, bows, and exits. The others bow from the doorway and exit behind her.

The Governor slices at the beef, producing satisfied moans as the juice seeps from between his knife and the cut. Ilian stares at the feast and can't help but draw a comparison to the Morez's table. Not only theirs, but the many families who may not see a meal. Ilian hears a growl and mistakes it for no more than his stomach.

"And why did the services go so well, you may ask? I will give you one word. Fear."

Caseto plops a grape into his mouth and squeezes his jaw shut, a spritz of the juice leaving between his lips. He moves a quesadilla to his plate and pauses. With a profound inhale of the aromas to fill the space, Caseto releases a sly grin.

"Fear is powerful. It's intoxicating."

Ilian gulps and adjusts his posture.

A strange glow overcomes Caseto, the candlelight accentuating an aged face. Wrinkles, not from days working in the sun or stress from financial paranoia or in anticipation of another attack from Niekalaran mercenaries, sink into his forehead, the shadows making mountains of hilly plains.

"Invoking fear, giving fear the principal position on the pedestal, it is what gives these services power, Private Guard. It is what keeps the people faithful."

Another slice of steak makes it to the Governor's mouth.

Ilian bites his tongue and looks to the floor. *Fear.* To use fear as an artifice did not serve to guarantee those of faith. It was no more than a term synonymous with controlled.

Caseto slides the bowl of soup to him and bends over to scoop the spoon into his mouth. He swirls the spoon about the bowl in admiration as he savors every flavor of the bite. Once he swallows, he continues.

"The gods did try. They did, never doubt, never doubt. The gods attempted to keep the people faithful by no more than trust. Trust that worship and offering would continue if they provided all the people needed. Answering every prayer swiftly, leaving no individual without. All in good health, all in good company.

"But, when all is good, the people turn away."

Caseto examines the spoon as he pulls it upright from the creamy broth. No bit of pork nor stem nor floret of broccoli sticks. The cream takes with it all parts and returns them back to the bowl. Ilian observes.

"When the people have all they need in amenities, they do not need the divine. They do not seek the divine."

The Governor takes a spoonful of the soup and scoops it into his mouth. A stream of the broth slides from the corner, but his tongue quickly finds it. He brings the quesadilla to his lips and bites down with a crunch. As he pulls away, the cheese stretches until it rips from a distance. Caseto picks up the hanging strand with his finger and deposits it in his mouth.

Ilian ponders the Governor's words. Words that were not contrived of the teachings of the Tome Sanctus. These were words passed down by his ancestors, generation after generation. Words ingrained into the brains of the young diplomats in order to maintain power.

"Of course, fear is not the only way to achieve such rank, such levels of loyalty. However, it is the most efficient."

Ilian glances up at the ceiling above. The smokiness lifting from the foods shrouds the ceiling with a spiraling mist. The room will carry the scent for many weeks to come as the aromas seep into the wooden supports, the heat from the day opening their pores, the coolness of the night not having closed them quite fully.

"Tell me, Private Guard. What do you fear?"

Ilian feels an itch at his nose but refuses to react. A low rumbling growl echoes in his ears.

"I fear a day will come when I fail to fulfill my oath. When my failure will permeate and besmear the honor of my family."

Caseto scratches at his cheek and takes another grape in his fingers. He rolls the red fruit from side to side, examining the flawless skin and perfectly spherical shape.

"Failure of breaking an oath is not something to fear. Death of the punishment is what should be feared."

Caseto smirks and places the grape in his mouth. Ilian shivers.

"I do not fear anything. Do you know why, Private Guard? Because fear is a weakness, and the gods are not weak. Those impoverished to the south, their weakness is a belief in the nonexistent. Their supposed chosen is a poor farmer wielding a sword. There is no being I should fear for all should fear me."

Caseto lifts his chalice.

"A toast. To the gods and to finding the poor man's legend. Salud!"

Caseto imagines clinking the chalice and takes a hearty gulp. Ilian reveals a closed lip grin and nods his head to the Governor.

Returning his eyes to his steak, the Governor ignores Ilian's presence.

A knock at the door interrupts the silence. Ilian licks his lips, with a gentle glance at the Governor before moving for the door. He opens it to find Liza standing beyond, head bowed and hand to her chest.

Ilian turns to see the Governor, one hand with spoon to mouth, the other already beckoning her in. With a nod and a gesture, Ilian permits Liza entrance to the hall.

"Your Grace, apologies for interrupting your dinner. I came the moment your summons arrived to my ears. I had not realized-"

"Come, come. Sit, General Liza. Your presence is of no consequence, for my hunger will soon be satiated, both of body and mind."

Liza glances at Ilian and finds her way to a seat, leaving one empty between herself and the Governor. Caseto notices, his eyes transforming to no more than slits. He clears his throat.

"Tell me, General. Are the newer prototypes ready? If you recall, I set the deadline and expect it to be met."

"We are working steadfastly to make the adjustments you requested. We have found it a bit difficult, but believe-"

"So, they are not ready? Yes or no."

"No, but-"

Caseto clicks his tongue. He grabs the chalice and swirls about its contents.

"That is disappointing."

Liza turns her head to the table and gulps.

The Governor stands, crumbs falling from the fabric wrinkles of his clothes as he does so. Caseto pays them no mind. Ilian pulls back his chair to allow the Governor space to pass through.

"Our mission is set. We leave tomorrow. Gather your team and advise Enamias to do the same."

"Yes, Your Grace."

"I hope you can place something of worth in my hands tomorrow upon our departure. It would be a shame to know the gods had left you already."

Liza shakes her head, hands trembling slightly, only to be seen by those looking for it.

"Private Guard, General, stay and eat what you will. You both will need every ounce of energy you can muster before our journey tomorrow. May the gods be with us. All of us."

Ilian and Liza, who is now standing, bow as the Governor exits to his resting chambers. Ilian glances to the table and licks his lips, grateful of the offerings of the Governor no matter how suspicious the circumstance. He takes a seat across from Liza and avoids eye contact. She, however, stares at him.

Ilian slides the unfinished plate of flank steak in front of him and starts to cut the meat. It was no longer steaming hot, but the lukewarm juices still flowed as the knife cut through. Ilian struggles to swallow the saliva buildup in his throat.

After a moment of dreaded silence and inability to pick up any of the pieces for consumption, Ilian sighs and places his fork and knife on the plate. His eyes meet Liza.

"You have come far, General. You have been blessed with a gift, one that can truly help the Governor." Ilian speaks with sincerity, attempting to break down the tension building around them. His attempt is met with a glare.

"You have come far, as well, Private Guard. Though I would say in quite the opposite direction. Your mind seems distracted. Pulled quite far from the palace and His Grace."

"Do you accuse me of lack of duty?"

"I accuse you of lacking the ability to perform your duties as you once had."

"My travels took me far beyond any lands you may have met in your missions. Fatigue has still not completely left me."

"Pardon my accusation."

Liza slides the bowl of fruit in her direction and separates the grapes from the watermelon within. She eats only the cubes of watermelon, leaving the grapes behind.

Ilian, at long last, takes a bite of steak. The flavors awaken his taste buds in a way food had not for weeks. The people of the villages did not use spices, their cooking quite simple. Ernesto Morez would no doubt take in Ilian as a son should he bring a steak of such caliber to their table.

Ilian searches the table, a plate of tamalitos, such as those he would eat during a long day of harvesting coffee, would be the perfect companion to the steak. The masa would perfectly pick up any juices on the plate and cleanse his palate for the next delicious bite. Nelida would laugh, as she always referred to a tamalito as the poor man's food.

Memories of his time in the village seem to hit him harder than any he could recall before his journey. Perhaps Liza was correct. His mind wanders and his thoughts continuously transport him to the village. From their joyous religious worship to their celebration of the dead. Their sense of community and welcoming of a stranger. Emotions tug at Ilian in a way he had not been prepared. The hardened guard feels his stone foundation crack, and Liza predicted he would crumble.

"I respect you, General. And though perhaps I question more than I once had, I feel it is maturity of the senses. Willed by the gods."

Ilian does not look up but plays with the last slice of steak on the plate. He swirls the piece in its juices, a faint, bloody color painting pictures on his plate that he only ever envisioned in his nightmares.

"What are you saying, Private Guard?"

"My senses tell me the Governor should not assist us in our mission."

"Instinct or prayer led you to this thought?"

Ilian pauses and sets down his utensils. His eyes catch that of Liza and he sighs.

"A feeling so strong it must be a divine message."

Liza tears off a piece of queso from the quesadilla and sticks it in her mouth, gently chewing while pondering.

"Do you believe it is wise to allow the Governor to join us on our quest, General?"

"We cannot deny him that which the gods have instructed."

"And if awful events were to transpire? Would we not be at fault in the eyes of the gods?"

"That which transpires will be the will of the gods."

Ilian licks his lips and blinks in confusion. Faith conflicts with duty in his eyes. His sole role is to protect the Governor. His role to eliminate any and all dangers present in the path of His Grace. On such a journey, through flatlands, mountains, and jungles to the border of enemy territory, the role would prove impossible. Too many factors. Too many possibilities.

Yet, Liza does not face the same conundrum. Her faith is as great as her oath. They intertwine. Her duty is bound by faith just as her faith is dependent on the fulfillment of her oath. They support each other as two falling pillars wedged against the other. They depend on one another to remain standing. They cannot stand alone. But fragile justification would easily crack at the pillars if doubt were to ever enter. But she does not doubt. She never questions. She trusts in faith and believes in words written on the pages of an ancient tome. If she ever saw what Ilian had seen, she would surely waver more rapidly than he had.

"The will of the gods..." Ilian repeats her words as he too ponders. "The attack by the Niekalarans on this capital. Did we intercept the will of the gods? Did they intend this capital to fall?"

Liza furrows her brow as she gazes upon him in disgust.

"The gods expected us to fight to prove our worth. Prove that we had listened, that I had listened. The dream was not only a warning but their instructions. Should we follow, all will be well. Should we ignore, destruction and devastation will meet us, just as it has done for those to the south."

Ilian flinches, an anger toward one of his own, one who swore a similar oath to himself and whose faith not only moves mountains but shakes the sky. Wrath, not unwarranted but unlike the guard taught to hold his composure. His fists clench.

"So, you know? You know of the attacks going on to the south?"

Liza licks her lips and folds her hands on the table.

Ilian shakes his head.

"One would assume all to swear the oath to act in such good faith. Unfortunately, your assumption is wrong. Extermination of the problem includes silencing any who may malign the solution."

Liza sighs.

"If it is the will of the gods-"

Ilian drops his fist on the table, trembling at her nonchalance. His tone resembles a shout while his volume takes on a whisper.

"Why should the Governor wish to see this chaos unfold? What mission do we have that will solve any problems which our nation now faces? Why should you deny that this weapon you have crafted is not a gift but a curse?"

Liza stands, retaliation evident in her stance but a conflict of authority restraining her.

"I once respected you above all others with the exception of the divine Governor. Your faith and commitment to duty inspired and motivated me to be a better person in my faith and in my oath. I feel conflicted that you would believe the gods to have sent a curse to our lands through my hands."

A tear slides down her cheek and her breathing grows erratic. Her chest trembles as she attempts to control her emotions. Shame and embarrassment shine through her expression.

"Should I now question all I have believed? All I have been taught? I thought to never doubt, the Governor chose you. I trusted in his words, in the gods' will. But should their will have you corrupted? Are you the sacrifice to our party? The betrayal and false prophet acting to split our loyalty, rob our trust in our Governor?"

"Our mission will reveal many truths, Liza," Ilian speaks to her soul, not one of rank or duty to the Governor but of blood of the earth. "And fate may have plans the ancient texts have not prophesied. The gods may have intentions that once contradicted all we have learned. When the time comes, I hope you understand this is not your fault."

Liza opens her mouth as if to speak, but words fail to form. Anger dissipates to puzzlement and confusion. Her eye finds the table runner, tracing it from candelabra to cascading off the end of the table.

"I believe the Governor issued instruction. You must go, inform General Enamias and your troops of the plan. I hope the prototype to be ready for the Governor by morning, for your own sake more than mine."

General Liza thinks to bow but, glancing about to see that no other is present, she decides to go against the urge. She will pray later for forgiveness. As she exits, she turns time and again to observe the Private Guard, ensure it is him and not another in his place. A doppelgänger come to assassinate the Governor, take rule of the nation, bring destruction and further devastation. But if it comes to pass, surely it will have been of the gods' will.

Ilian releases a profound exhale as the door closes behind the general. Surely this would be the interaction Alidora has warned about. A conversation that would lead the once honored Private Guard to be disparaged by the entire nation. Honor to be expunged for generations, his family cast out of the church. A thought and fear that once shook Ilian to his core. Yet, in this moment, it fails to conjure a tremble or the slightest acceleration of his heartbeat. Disappointment in the faces of his sister and mother would surely crumble him, but to know his prayer and devotion would no longer be dedicated to the Governor did not strike an unpleasant chord. And should his own family expel him from their presence, Ilian knew of another who would gladly take him in, even if he could no longer afford their rent in terms of gold pieces. Payment in labor and company. His heart warms.

Ilian rubs at his chin and wonders the purpose of the mission. Would they really face Hernan, bargain through diplomacy? Would war be waged in front of his eyes? Or did Caseto seek something else? Did his pride want no more than to capture the warrior of the glass sword for himself, barter for her release? What would he give?

In his peripheral vision, Ilian catches the glimpse of movement. A shadow in the candlelight perhaps. However, he knew better than to rationalize a divine message. A reminder. The time was drawing near.

Either the issues would be resolved, and the World Tree would heal.

Or evil would spread, and all life would rot due to the toxicity of such a plague.

Caseto would worry neither way. Fear would always be present.

But Cordaya would settle for none less than saving that which is most precious. She was not fear. She was hope.

Chapter Sixteen

Caseto leads the way on a majestic obsidian black mare, Ilian trailing close behind. Ilian turns back to see the capital falling out of view. Guards atop the wall appear as no more than fire ants on the edge of a doorstep, scouting the area, searching for prey. Smoke rises from the backdrop, the scent of blood carried by the wind. Ilian's heart beats to the tune of a sorrowful funeral drum, a death march. The ominous forest looms ahead. Its whispers crawl into their ears, its breath caresses their necks. The soldiers grow anxious. Their hands rush to their hilts in moments of paranoia. Their minds play tricks on them. Or perhaps the supernatural beings deceive the soldiers... noting their every move, demanding their attention and its presence.

Caseto's stern and stoic expression never wavers. He stares ahead with determination and confidence. Ilian reflects on the idea that the Governor may be a god, or in the least divine in some way. The inability to fear is a characteristic of heavenly origin. With the thought, a pit falls into Ilian's stomach. The shadows in the forest ahead grow darker. He gulps down the saliva buildup in his throat. A tremble courses through Pinto.

"Shhhh," Ilian whispers, as he strokes her neck. He envisions Cordaya, who may have been afraid but would hide it well. Honor and faith before fear. Courage, a quality Ilian wishes to possess, even if never before in his life, to acquire in this moment.

The road transforms from pavement to dirt underneath them. Travel turns from smooth to bumpy as the horses gallop forward, stepping into the divots in the earth. The heavy weapon hanging from Ilian's back bounces against him.

Gravity suddenly increases as the pressure of his thoughts grows. A residual bang echoes in his ears. Memories soaked in screams and blood rain down his skin. He loathes the weight of the weapon and the responsibility to accompany it. The weight only increases as the gods watch.

His eyes turn to the heavens. From over the roof of the forest, a dense, black cloud races west. But the movement does not occur smoothly. As if dust flying up after throwing a sack of rice to the ground, the sporadic movement of the cloud causes many to pause. The soldiers behind mumble in their curiosity and uncertainty of the cloud. A low rumbling and ticking sound meets their ears.

Caseto chuckles.

"Oh, yes. They know we're coming."

Ilian's eyes grow wide. A swarm of flying termites.

Swords swish from their hilts, the soldiers hastily preparing for battle. Caseto bellows as his horse trots on. No hesitation. No fear of confrontation.

The cloud of swarming insects grows larger as more termites fly through the canopy of the forest to join the forces of nature. The thunder of beating wings deafens the soldiers. They break ranks as they freeze to stare at the spectacle.

Ilian's heart pounds as if in a hollow cell, his breath short and rapid. An unknown force pulls his eyes from the swarms and to the shadows of the forest. A pair of glowing eyes stares back.

Before he can react, the swarm descends on the soldiers. Screams muffle against the sound of wings and dropping swords. Some soldiers abandon their weapons to fight with their hands, swatting at the insects circling their heads. Rather than fight, some shield their ears and squeeze shut their eyes and mouths. Unfortunately, two hands are too few.

The termites land on the shoulders and uniforms of the soldiers, shed their wings, and crawl across their skin, biting as they go. Those who tried to force their mouths shut no longer can resist the urge to scream at the pain of the nibbling insects. At the chance, the termites dive into a soldier's mouth. He chokes and falls to the ground, the first death.

Those around grow petrified at the prospect of dying to the swarm. A woman wields her sword, slashing through the air in an attempt to strike down the insects. Another woman crosses the path of her blade, a cut to the back. She collapses to the ground, the termites moving like sharks to the pool of blood.

Ilian flicks off every bug to land on him, swiping with quick speed any to land on Pinto. The wings stick to his uniform, breaking apart like dried leaves with the slightest wrinkle of the coarse fabric. He unties the scarf from about his belt and wraps it about his head to prevent the termites from tunneling into his ears. Ilian hears the shrieks behind but refuses to turn to the devastation.

No termites fly near Caseto, a shield of light radiating from his spirit, protecting him from the swarm. Ilian panics as one after another dart toward his face. Curses slip through his clenched teeth. A prayer issues from his heart, one for forgiveness, another for protection. Three multiplied to three hundred as he pleads from the bottom of his soul with the gods. His prayer not delivered to Caseto nor the church the Governor serves. The plea searches for the God of the Skies. The God of the Seas. The God of the Earth. The God of the Forest.

The screams dissipate. The beating wings calm. The fragile, paper wings of the termites litter the dirt road. The insects crawl along the earth, retreating from the scene.

Ilian turns his head to look behind. Several soldiers, most of the lower rank, lay on the ground. The woman who was slashed lay in a pool of blood, swirls of dirt and wings floating atop. Another soldier lay with bite marks covering his face, the blemishes red with specks of blood in close proximity. On one unfortunate soldier, several female termites decide to nest, squirming in and out of the dead soldier's ears and nose. Ilian trembles at the sight.

"Private Guard Ilian," says Caseto with a jovial ring to his voice. "Send a projectile flying. General Olivio will understand the signal and send scouts. We do not stop to clean or weep. We ride on."

Ilian nods. Or so he believes, perhaps the head bob no more than his numb body reacting to the bumpy road. With a swift gulp and a false hope that another termite swarm may come to kill him before the chance arrives, Ilian reaches behind him to slide the weapon near. He releases the knot of the sash binding it to his body. Trembling hands fumble for a metal pellet within a casing on his belt. The cold, smooth sphere brushes against his fingertips. He bites his lip as he withdraws it. He slides the pellet into the weapon and pulls back on the spring-loaded lever. His finger wraps about the lever and tightens it back.

The force pushes him back, dropping one hand from the weapon to clutch to Pinto's raiment. The bang rings in Ilian's ears, Pinto halting with an alert stance. Ilian places a palm on her neck to calm her. Liza, also on horseback, smirks as she joins at Ilian's side.

"You'll get used to it. She will, too."

Liza nods at Pinto. She rubs the neck of her black and white steed and whispers words into its ears. Ilian cannot make out what she says, but the horse's eyes alight like a gas lantern in the night. Orange and burning.

Ilian knots the sash about his back, swinging the weapon behind him, and continues on. They break the threshold to the forest. The canopy blocks the sun, the shadows dancing about in the distance, peeking about the trees to observe the damaged unit.

Caseto only ever looks forward. His posture remains unchanged, his expression one of amusement. Excitement. The Governor challenges the gods with his demeanor and poise. The challenges only serve to prove his divinity. No human could compete with a god. However, another god may stand a chance.

Every few steps, the sun's streams through the canopy causes a glare in Ilian's vision. Ilian forces himself to blink away the black dots. In these moments, the shadows make hurried and erratic movements before all returns to normal. Ilian examines the surroundings, knowing it not to be a slip of his sight and thought.

Light bounces from puddles on the ground left by the storms the day before. It reflects off the mirrored lenses of the small creatures hiding in the shrubbery. The humidity rises with the sun, hot days turning to stormy nights as the wet season begins. Sweat drips from Ilian's brow. The marching transforms into a tired, paranoid trudging.

A shadow whirs by Ilian's feet. A gentle breeze sweeps the back of his neck with a seductive caress. An omen.

A low rumble sounds from a hierbimora bush to the east. Ilian stares at the spot, hoping for the creature to reveal itself, rid itself of the shadows surrounding it. A scurrying of dried leaves occurs accompanied by the passing of an indistinct mass. The blur appears as if viewed from his peripheral vision, but he stares directly at the being.

A grunt thunders as the feral boar kicks from the ground and jumps at Caseto and his mare. Ilian's jaw drops to yell in warning but the thin saber of the Governor slices through the neck of the creature in a swift cut.

With the boar skewered on his blade, Caseto uses his force and leverage to throw the creature from the path. A paralyzing cry bursts forth from the boar upon being impaled, an echo reverberating through the forest even after it collided with the earth upon its death.

A low hum, forceful enough to cause vibration, rings throughout the land. Red, glimmering sets of eyes run toward them from all directions. Ilian withdraws his sword without hesitation and rides to the Governor's side. His life for the Governor's, the moral code of the Ilian he used to know. A part of him remained buried inside, forcing his way out. Will he die for this man? Or will he sacrifice himself for a god?

The grunts of the creatures draw near as their dead kin relinquished its form to the God of the Forest. Liza withdraws her weapon. A shot into the shadows. A cry and stumble. Ilian's eyes grow wide as he remembers the weapon slung round his back. He fumbles for the weapon, terrified to wield it but fearing more the beasts stampeding in their direction.

A herd of boars, the skin tone blushing fuchsia in what appears an unquenchable rage, charge at the soldiers. Their glowing, scarlet eyes sear through Ilian as if the gods watch through the boar's perspectives. As if the gods manipulate the will of the beasts, possessing them as if demons.

Grotesque, ivory fangs hang from their slightly parted mouths, salivating at what they believe to be a meal. Another bang rings out and the soldiers' battle cry answers the call. The bludgeoning of dull swords hitting tough flesh fills the forest. Ilian's attempt to drop a pellet into his weapon ends when a boar leaps through the air at his leg. The metal pellet drops to the ground.

Ilian lunges forward on Pinto, wrapping his arms about her neck so he does not fall from her back. He kicks at the boar with fury and fear, both consuming him. He withdraws his saber once more, its grip laying more comfortably in his hand than the handheld cannon. Resuming his posture as a royal guard, fear turns to courage and courage to overconfidence as he swings at the beasts at his ankles. Ilian turns around. Something did not feel right. The tremble of the earth suggests more than the few attacking boars present.

The low rumble begins once more. A second wave. Boars the size of their horses emerge from the dense forest, ravaging the land by tearing apart the shrubs and vines, trampling the smaller trees and wildflowers. A self-mutilating god, tearing apart its creation for untainted revenge.

A boar with four sets of monstrous fangs emerges with eyes locked on the Governor.

"My lord!" Liza screams in warning, wishing to race to his aid but for the boars pouncing at her from all sides. She stands on the back of her horse with great balance, not swaying nor tempted to stumble despite her slaughtering of the beasts.

Ilian knows he will have to make a choice. With saber drawn, he leaps to the ground and slashes through the prey. The boars jump back as his divine pulses emit from where he steps. Their eyes switch between red and black, fury and fear. Just as the soldiers who fight for their lives, the creatures of the forest do the same.

Time seems to slow. Ilian sees it on their backs, under their snouts, growing from their stomachs. Violet, luminescent spores, similar to those from the World Tree. It was not the gods possessing these beasts. It was the evil threatening to overtake the world. An evil the gods permitted to do as it pleased.

Ilian bursts for the opposite side of the Governor, throwing himself between the gargantuan boar and Caseto. The Governor does no more than laugh as he sits with arms crossed, no boar having approached him since the first. Ilian breathes heavily, unsure of why his instinct led him to his current position, doubting in his ability to protect the Governor from such a monster.

A low grunt and a sliding hoof threaten to charge at Ilian. Ilian gulps. Aware that a collision could end him, he weighs his options. The weapon hangs at his back, burning at his skin as if a reminder to its presence. His palms sweat as they grasp his saber, using it more as a shield than a weapon in this moment. Close combat would be no more than suicide should he attempt it. His sword is incapable of divine acts. He is not the Governor. He is not Cordaya.

Sweat drips from Ilian's creased brow, his worries no doubt bound to add wrinkles to his youthful face.

Before the charge, the boar's ears perk up. Ilian stares at the beast but tries to listen past the pounding of his heart. A low rumble, the ground pulsing, leaves and blades of grass swaying, and not due to the wind. Pebbles clatter as they roll downhill toward the group. Commotion dies and a new fear rises. What started as a rumble turns to thunder. One or two pebbles transform into hundreds, then thousands.

A rockslide.

"Get to high ground!" Liza screams as she jumps from her horse's back to grab onto an overhanging tree branch. With her fantastic upper body strength, she pulls herself up to sit in the tree branch, her hand as a visor to the sun as she looks to the oncoming terror.

The attacking boars flee down the mountainside. The gargantuan beast glares at Ilian and releases a steamed breath of irritation. It slowly backs into the shadows of the forest before misting into them. As if no more than melting into the surrounding air, it disappears.

Larger rocks spiral down the mountain with a collection of branches and small trees that have been broken and uprooted due to the force of the slide. The soldiers panic. Some climb the nearest trees, pulling at the uniforms of those climbing too slowly in front of them. Others run down the slope, hoping their speed will exceed that of the racing rocks. Soldiers who had been injured badly by the boars, yell from the ground for help, clawing their way to safety or wriggling in panic. Screaming prayers, the bleeding soldiers cling to the little hope they have left.

Pinto rears back, whinnying in fear. Ilian calls to her and they meet in the middle, directly behind Caseto and his mare. Ilian grabs a hold of her reins and swings himself onto her back. He rubs and pats her neck, leaning close to whisper in her ear.

"It's going to be okay. Everything's going to be okay. Dear God, my God. Look after us. Love us. Lead us. Guide us in your steps. Bathe us in your eternal light. Grant us mercy for the sins and atrocities we've-"

A cackle. Deep. Sonorous. A gust of wind and a chill sweep up and strangle Ilian. In hesitation, he opens his eyes. The rocks and boulders stream past them. Diverging no more than a meter in front of Caseto's mare and merging once more about a meter after Pinto's whipping tail. The violent sounds of the slide fade and Caseto's laugh echoes through the forest.

A low hum erupts into a growl, sending Caseto's fit of laughter into the realm of maniacal. The ground beneath them shakes, the boulders bouncing as they roll. Ilian fails to determine the source.

Does the ground quake of natural causes? Does Caseto's laugh hold influence of the earth? Do the gods anger? But why do they avoid Caseto? Do the gods only wish to threaten? Or does his divinity protect him?

The growl increases in volume. A branch flies from the rockslide and swipes at Caseto's cheek. Blood trickles from the perfectly straight line carved into his skin. The beautiful crimson paints its river as it drops to the ground.

In that moment, the stones cease. The ground stills. The air shifts.

Silence consumes them as they examine the renewed environment. The soldiers, embarrassed by their own cowardice, fearful of the punishment for their disloyalty, climb down from the trees. Those who had run away do not return, their fate unknown.

Liza jumps from the tree limb, adjusting her eyepatch once she hits the ground. While all others stand in awe of the events to transpire, gawking at the divinity and omnipotence of their God, Liza's expression reveals a different realization. Her right eye glances to Ilian, who looks away in a fluster. She squints behind with hopes of seeing her horse but notices no movement down the trail. Liza sighs.

Without word or direction, the Governor leads his horse forward, stepping through the rubble and continuing up the mountainside. Ilian commands Pinto forward. The other soldiers march behind, stumbling over the rocks, refusing to glance at the groaning figures beneath.

Liza examines her weapon for damage and uses a bristled stick to clean out any residue left behind in the barrel. During the fight against the boars, several of the metal pellets found their resting place in the bone of the enemy. The tip of her tongue finds the lower part of her top lip, tasting the blood building up and forming a hardened shell. Bitter and metallic. She cautiously steps through the pile of rocks. Even on flat earth, she limps as she walks.

"Captain Liza, if you would like-"

"I'm fine."

"It is a long journey. Switch my place and Pinto will carry you."

"I trust my God will watch over me. Should it be his will that I sacrifice myself to save him, it will have made my life meaningful and bring great honor to my bloodline. I trust in my God. Do you, Private Guard?"

Ilian gulps and nods. His eyes meet her, her menacing stare burning through his thoughts. Searching. Scavenging. Rampaging.

"I'm certain your faith could move mountains, Captain Liza."

Her glare sends a chill up his spine. Other soldiers view their interaction with wide eyes and raised eyebrows. Caseto takes no notice. At least none that his facial expressions deceive. His eyes focus onward, his stoic form showing no tension yet no relaxation. His narcissism blesses him with the ability to feel no fear.

As they march on, every cracking twig, every rustling leaf, causes the soldiers to jump. Ilian imagines the forest spirits watching them from the shadows, running about to get a look before delivering their message to Mizochtal. The sleek, black fur seems to take form in the darkness before dissipating once more.

Ilian scans the forest. A clearing opens ahead as they reach a road curving about the mountain, one side no more than a steep drop over the cliff. He turns behind to see the capital, the palace and church the only distinguishable building as their parapets tower over the walls. Ilian wishes to do as they do. Reach for the heavens. Relinquish himself to their mercy. Granted, if the boars and the swarms were their will, mercy may be far away.

They arrive to the first fork in the road. Ilian recognizes the path.

"Which way, Private Guard?" the Governor questions.

"Umm," Ilian hums. They head to Niekalarah. To reason with the President? That's what Ilian believed when they first set out. But why do the gods fight against them?

Peering overhead, storm clouds whirl in one direction while in the other chutes of grey smoke issue into the sky. Those wisps did not rise from the fire under concrete stoves or outdoor bread ovens. Surely they would do best to avoid the battles ongoing. Ilian had no doubt that Caseto would force these men and women to watch the devastation and razing as a lesson to return with to their families. He would not allow them to intervene. He would not be the savior to the innocent citizens struck down in front of their homes. If they did not believe him a god, there would be no salvation.

Ilian pointed to the path leading toward gloomy weather, sprinkles of rainwater hitting their cheeks and foreheads better than the stench of burning skin. Caseto lifts one side of his mouth and chuckles.

"A wise choice," he mutters, whether understanding or not that this path would extend their journey to Niekalarah.

Ilian swipes a hand across his brow as they march on. The others did not know that which he and Caseto sensed. And despite avoiding the alexandrite swords of the ruthless mercenaries, danger did not stray far in this direction either. Should the sunny portion of the day bring swarms and stampedes, the stormy evening may prove all the more disastrous to their troops.

Ilian gulps as they climb the mountain path. The trees sway to a ghostly breeze as he feels nothing upon his cheeks. The birds squawk and scream but no sound of wings taking flight nor the volume distancing surfaces. The insects make hesitant chirps, other ants and beetles forming lines as they head in the opposite direction the troops walk. All is different than the first time he walked this path with Cordaya. The sensation of imagined panic, the worries of a hypochondriac, fill him. None other slump as the pressure builds on their shoulders. Ilian fights the toggle of gravity, but the weight grows too much to bear. He falls from Pinto's back.

Ilian hits the ground with a thud. The soldiers behind, though exhausted and confused, rush to the Private Guard's aid. Caseto turns to look into the treeline. A rustle occurs somewhere just beyond their vision. Liza does not pay attention to Ilian nor the beings moving in the distance. Rather she stares at a single point on the trunk of a tree nearby.

"I'm fine. I'm fine now. Thank you," Ilian whispers to General Enamias and several of his soldiers as he stands and brushes the dirt from his uniform. His eyes follow Liza's and he sees it. Embedded in the bark of the tree is a shard of glass.

"Cor-"

"Why did you fall before it struck you?" Liza's tone is one of irritation.

"What do you mean?"

"Private Guard," Caseto says, a deep chuckle interrupting his thought. He shakes his head and brings a hand to his mouth in an attempt to control his malevolent laughter. After calming himself,

Caseto clears his throat. "Is this a message they believe you to understand and no one else?"

They?

Ilian scans the glass shard, wondering if there is more to the phenomenon that shot him to the ground. No inscription. No prior warnings or calls. Nothing but the glass shard and the paranoia that others watch from beyond.

They... The gods.

Chapter Seventeen

The group follow the flashing of the firefly lights into the forest, dense and dark as day passes to evening. Ilian freezes midstride. His jaw drops and his fingers twitch for his saber. The trees and bushes, once filled with the ripest and juiciest of fruits, the vines with their marvelous bunch of vegetables, are all bare. Liquid, its color the darkest shade of purple and substance unidentifiable, drip from the leaves while the bark and stalks glisten with any bit of light to touch them. No one seems to notice or appear concerned. The land is foreign to them. They would not know the normal from the irregular. Ignorance is bliss.

Caseto's eyes do not gaze at any space but straight ahead. The World Tree.

Liza, suspicious of all to happen thus far, checks her steps. She listens closely for any unexplained sounds. For lack of vision, her senses are sharp.

The Governor steps in front of the pedestal and slides from his horse's back. The mare darts in a panic down the forest path. Some soldiers attempt to restrain the horse, but as Caseto expresses no concern, they allow the horse to escape.

Rustling and metallic slides occur from all sides. Ilian reaches for his saber when he feels the prick to his neck and freezes.

"You make any moves and it will be your last, Private Guard," the snakelike voice hisses. Ilian never heard this man speak in such a tone for, when near Cordaya, he always attempted to sound charming.

Ilian gulps and moves no more than his eyes. Several soldiers panic, swords drawn, tip to tip with blades carved so smooth, appearing like ripples in the water with three thin strips of alexandrite.

"It seems you've upgraded your weapons," Liza says with a hesitant edge. Her pride swells, "Well so have we."

She whips about her handheld cannon and reaches for a pellet. Before the Niekalaran militia can react, Caseto raises a hand.

"No need for battle on holy grounds," says Caseto, his speech like a hum.

"And what do you desire from these lands, Governor Caseto?"

"What is rightfully mine, Hernan. You are a Hernan after all, correct? Fighting your President's wars. Leading his men. Military and farmers alike. Bribing my own men on the border." Ilian's eyes widen as he thinks of General Victorino. "No worries, Private Guard. Your warnings led me to send their reward. An eternal reward. A swift execution.

"As for you, Hernan. It seems your own family has gifted to you the sour bushel of berries. They reap the benefits and you exhaust yourself in the sun."

"My God prizes humility more than wealth."

"Yet you have neither?"

"Why have you come here?"

"I wish you to answer first."

"As you wish."

Julio Hernan inhales sharply, his sword wavering from the nape of Ilian's neck to his upperback. Despite being the enemy, Ilian marvels at the control of Julio's fears. He could never speak to the Governor as so.

"Unfortunately, a series of supernatural events led us off course. Mudslides, field fires, the unusual stampeding of bulls without a master nor mutt to quell their rage. None too odd on their own, but all within the time experienced quite a series of misfortune. Our scout located traces of your troops and we followed at a distance."

Caseto chuckles. His gaze returns to the Tree. The glimmer in his eyes reflects his marvel of the dying monument.

"You say supernatural. I will say divine events have led us here."

Ilian's heart pounds in his ears. The silence of those around consumes him as he's unaware if time has frozen. The haunting sound of the silent group with their screaming thoughts. Distrustful of the enemy, of their allies, and whatever mystical beings lie beyond the shadows. Full of fear and questions. The unknown. The next movement. The next word. The next breath. All is no more than a precisely placed piston in the divine machine.

"Where is the warrior?" Caseto asks in a forceful whisper, attempting to mask his bloodlust. His hatred.

Julio scoffs, as if now understanding the true meaning behind their journey.

"So that is how it is? This is not a diplomatic mission. This is a hunting party."

Ilian looks to Caseto with begging eyes, hoping it not to be true.

"Where. Is. The. Warrior!"

Caseto's scream echoes throughout the forest, not even the dense canopy able to suppress the vibrations. The trees act more as hollow posts as the words bounce off each and return with every heartbeat.

"She is within our custody," Hernan states, his voice calm.

Ilian releases the breath he was holding. Cordaya lives, the thought enough to give him hope. His muscles relax as he thinks of ways to negotiate from their current defensive position. His eyes meet Liza, whose subtle squint tells him she's thinking the same. Ilian controls his breathing and counts down to his spin to knock Julio Hernan away, giving him the time necessary to unsheathe his saber.

Three.

Two.

Ilian twitches, doubting his timing. Striking too soon could lead his comrades to injury. Striking too late would mean they're all dead. The clock ticks in the background.

One.

As Ilian places pressure on the balls of his feet, he notices movement in his peripheral vision. The shape is not human.

A blackberry bush not far from them rustles. All turn to face it, wishing to give face to the new threat. Soldiers grow confused as to where they should point their swords. A knock on the trunk of a tree occurs to the other side of the group. They are surrounded.

"You sent for more troops?" Hernan questions, trying not to sound panicked. He releases a nervous snicker. "The coward Caseto, afraid his men cannot hold their own."

"They are not mine and your deceit does not fool me. Bringing backup shows distrust and lack of confidence."

"Your lies do not convince me. If they are not yours nor mine, to whom do they belong?"

"They belong to none but the gods," her stern tone forces even Caseto to drop his jaw and turn in awe. Cordaya marches around the World Tree, Liza flinching as Cordaya passes by her. She does not observe the others, not even a gentle smile in Ilian's direction. Cordaya glares at Caseto, her only focus.

"You."

No more than this word leaves Caseto's lips as if floating on his breath. But the scorn to issue with such a curt breath... The wrath radiates from him.

"Liza! Restrain her!"

Liza glances at Cordaya then back to the Governor. She hesitates to approach the warrior, trying to get a peek at where she hides the glass sword. With no vision of her mystical weapon, Liza aims the unloaded weapon at Cordaya's head. The prick returns to Ilian's neck as he lifts a foot from the ground.

Cordaya does not fight Liza's grip about her arm. She could pull away easily should she please, but the warrior stands unmoving.

"Governor. Don't tread where you dare not suffer the consequences. She is our prisoner of war and I will be taking her with me."

"And what are your plans with this divine being? Execute her? Have you ever tried to kill a god?"

His mocking tone transforms into an intimidating chuckle. Cordaya expresses no fear, resolve alight in her eyes. Ilian, paralyzed between the two men of power, breathes in the thick air, riddled with tension and the smell of a bitter vapor. His eyes move to the World Tree, the purple liquid bubbling profusely.

"Death is no doorway for a goddess."

Julio drops his sword to his side as he stares at Cordaya. Her obsidian hair has grown frizzy from the humidity and her tattered clothes prove the struggle she's faced since Ilian last saw her. Her feet and the bottom of her skirt are covered in dried mud. The rope sheath hangs at her side, frayed and worn, and home to no object. Despite her outward appearance, exhaustion nor surrender can be found in her eyes. Nothing proves to cut down her spirit or faith.

"We shall return to Niekalarah and I will make her my wife," Julio states, revealing truths in a haunting, melodic tone as if a serum forced his honesty. "We should cast the President aside as the people's respect for us should surpass his. We'll be a nation with the gods on our side."

"What say you to that, warrior?"

"I commit myself to none but the gods."

"So you say."

Caseto taps his foot. All wait, knowing none other than him should break the silence. The rustling of the bushes and cracking of the twigs disappears as the tension grows between the two groups and the warrior of the glass sword. Ilian wishes to say he is on her side, but he feels no more than a pathetic bystander. His death would erase their chance for succeeding in the mission given to them by Mizochtal. But where is the Messenger of the Gods? Does it not listen? Does it not understand?

"When I first heard there was a great warrior of legend in the countryside, I did not believe it. Why would the gods sculpt their warrior in an area of so little nourishment? Would a farmer plant their seeds in a desert? Would a fisherman cast his rod in a well? The gods are omnipotent, omniscient, yet tricksters in their ways. I should know, for I am one."

Cordaya flinches forward with fists clenched. A sparkle glimmers at her hip as an object begins to take form. Liza reaches for a pellet when a bang fills the forest. Cordaya stops in her tracks, shock covering her face. Caseto points his weapon in their direction, the tiniest sliver of smoke slipping from the barrel.

Liza gasps and drops to the ground, one hand breaking her fall, the other pushing at the soft spot between her ribcage. Horror fills the soldiers, Niekalaran and Micacaoan alike. And the same terror holds them in place, not wishing the same fate should they move.

Caseto removes a metal bristled brush from an inside pocket of his jacket and cleans out the barrel. He thumbs around for another pellet and slides it in.

"Oh, General Liza. Amusing discovery I have made for such a weapon. I find if you load after the shot, and not before, you'll be better prepared for an attack."

Ilian gazes in their direction, no longer certain if what he sees exists or if he is merely hallucinating. He gazes upon the dying Liza, losing consciousness with every slight movement to send a jolt of pain throughout her body. A prayer will not save her. An answer to a prayer might.

A drop of blood hits the ground where Liza lay. An outline of stiff lines and bulbous eyes manifests to more than a drawing in the air. The spirit takes form. First one, then several.

The soldiers, still in shock from Caseto's betrayal of his general, direct their weapons to the forest spirits. Caseto squints at the wooden bodies of the beings, as if not believing the truth to stand in front of him.

"So, this is a god?" he mumbles, unable to comprehend that which occurs.

The forest spirits conjure bands of a divine material from the earth under them. They remove Liza's hand from her wound. One spirit, with several flexible twigs as fingers, caresses her injury. The metal pellet dislodges from her organs and falls to the ground. All around stare in awe as the spirits plaster the band to her.

"These... they are gods?"

"No," Cordaya answers, a tear falling down her cheek as she marvels at their compassion. "They're the laborers of the God of the Forest. Sent from above and bound to the earth and the trees."

The glimmer that once shone from her hip no longer exists. Ilian stares at Liza, who now sleeps on the ground, blood no longer leaving her wound. He finds comfort in knowing she will heal, so long as they can make it out of the forest. His eyes shift from Caseto to Cordaya. Their words and actions will dictate what happens next.

The forest spirits slowly fade to dust, swept away by a gentle breeze that did not exist prior. Their work is complete for now. But their presence transcends the tangible form they take. Eyes watch them. A low growl rumbles.

"So, Cordaya, is that correct? This is the name of a legend? Private Guard, am I pronouncing it correctly?" Caseto raises his eyebrows and turns to Ilian. A malevolent smirk shines at him. "Private Guard, is this the legend you would have brought to me?"

Ilian trembles, unable to catch his breath, to form a word. Yet, he cannot determine which word to be best. Yes? Yes, this is the legend you sent me for, Your Grace. Or no? No, she is not who we search for, it is no more than a trick by Hernan. Let her go... Ilian wishes to find an answer, any answer, to free Cordaya from Caseto's wrath. But she is stubborn. If Ilian does not answer with honesty, Cordaya will. And then they will both be targets for the Governor's rage.

"Yes," Ilian mumbles, searching for more words but finding none. Caseto scoffs.

"What an insult."

The Governor points his weapon at Ilian, one finger tempting the trigger. Ilian freezes with jaw agape. A prayer issues from what little sense he manages to make of the situation. Their mission will never see completion. For he will meet with Death.

Cordaya lunges for the Governor, her glass sword manifesting at her side and swinging to her grip. The other soldiers take the opportunity to attack the enemy. Swords clash, sparks flying where alexandrite hits steel. Caseto's reaction proves that of the divine. He pivots and in a moment locks onto Cordaya as his target. A resounding boom shakes the earth underneath them.

Ilian stares in horror. He breaks from the trance of his paralysis and darts to Cordaya's aid. She managed to deflect the pellet with the glass sword, the force of the strike sending her flying toward the World Tree. When she hits the bubbling bark, it sizzles where the violet liquid meets skin. The sword slips from her grip and lands a few meters away. She falls to the dirt, on hands and knees, gasping for breath. Ilian arrives in time to see the violet marking seared onto her back, the sap-like substance burning through her clothes.

"Cordaya, are you-"

"Tsk, tsk, tsk."

Caseto clicks his tongue as he cleans the barrel of the weapon, blowing a puff of air at the rim for added effect. He fiddles for a pellet and slides it into the barrel of the handheld cannon. He directs the shot at Ilian's forehead.

"You've always been a flea in my hair, Private Guard. Your morals exceed your loyalty. I'm afraid I'm no longer in need of your services."

As the pellet flies, Cordaya jumps in its path. The metal piece lodges itself in her forearm. Cordaya bites her bottom lip, holding back the scream, while her eyes start to water.

"Damned girl!" Caseto yells. He unsheathes his saber. "Greedy god! You should not take that which is not meant for you, and as so you receive your divine punishment."

Ilian unsheathes his saber and rises to his feet, placing himself between Cordaya and Caseto.

The Governor raises his eyebrows and licks his bared teeth.

"Dear boy, what have you become?"

"I am no longer a servant lost to the dark. The light has been revealed to me."

"You would place the life of this fraudulent deity before your own?"

"It is my duty to protect. I swore an oath. My duty is to the citizens of Micacao."

"Your allegiance is to me."

"Was. I believe that contract was broken when you aimed that dreaded weapon at me. Twice."

Caseto chuckles. He rolls his head back, no fear present in his posture. They look around, soldier after soldier falls to the Niekalarans, their combat methods much better trained. The vines of the forest creep over their forms, the soil acting as quick sand to consume them. Yet the forest accepting these sacrifices fails to be the reason of pause in Hernan. Rather, Julio Hernan gazes past Ilian. Shock fills his expression as he yearns to assist Cordaya while knowing his place. Julio does not fear Caseto but rather the World Tree beyond.

"I must apologize, Private Guard."

Caseto resheathes his saber as he stares at the magnificence of the World Tree. Tall and elegant it stands before them, roots stretch throughout the entirety of the world. A ruler of every land.

"I believed sending you away would allow me the time to lay out the strategy, communicate with the generals on all borders and bring to them the prototypes of our new weapon. Allowing passage to barbarians is not a plan you would have agreed to, and unfortunately your faith would tether me.

"Whether a god exists in this countryside or not, I hoped the barbarians would raze it and all within these lands would either be forced to migrate or perish with their belongings. Niekalarah makes far more wealth from these lands than Micacao. Why should I waste my precious resources in dealing with a war that would cost a fortune and see no significant profits even with a victory?

"Why should I, God of the Human Realm, divine leader of Micacao, bow to a peasant from the South?" Caseto harrumphs.

His hands reach for the collar of his velvet cloak, adjusting the fabric to bring attention to his stately presence. As he sweats, the pale foundation on his face drips. Caseto licks his salty lips. They come together to form a twisted, malevolent grin. Similar to a child in a cheated victory, watching as the competitors fall behind, the proud expression worn by Caseto ignites wrath within the Private Guard.

From within his cloak, Caseto withdraws a different weapon. A shinier, modified model of the hand cannon created by Liza. Ilian had not thought anything of the weight sagging at the Governor's cloak until his eyes fell upon the sight. Ilian gulps. With a steady shot, the weapon would kill on the first attempt.

"Private Guard. Though I am unaware what occurs beyond life for these peasants, I can assure you one thing. Death is not an escape from me nor the god that chose me. Eternal punishment shall be your prize. Your faith may move mountains, but mine will tear them down."

The Governor aims the barrel at the Private Guard. Frozen to place, Ilian offers what he believes to be his final prayers. He closes his eyes, not wishing to see the end. Not wishing to see what will become of Cordaya when he can no longer protect her. Silly of him to believe he could protect anyone...

A voluminous roar fills the lands. It shakes the earth underneath them, traveling up the trees to their uppermost branches. All fighting stops in an instant. Wide eyes stare into the shadows and fear unknown to any man meets them in the instant. The Niekalarans race from the forest, their duty to their mission far less than their duty to preserve their own lives. Hernan gulps as he finds himself alone. He licks his lips, fiery eyes searing through Ilian, and pursues the men who betrayed their nation. Those injured on the ground scatter to the fringes of the forest, no longer worried that the Niekalarans may attack but experiencing greater distress for whatever natural power they have angered. Even Enamias, despite hesitation from the shackles of loyalty and duty, finds his exit from the raging aura that permeates the lands around.

The lion manifests from the shadows themselves, black with a violet glimmer as the freshly hardened obsidian of a volcanic bank. The colossal threat sent by the divine. The Messenger of the God of the Forest.

Ilian gazes in wonder upon the lion, questioning as to the summoning of the faithful messenger. The Private Guard turns to Cordaya. Blood runs down her arm and into the font. The crimson glitters pure and deep in color. A testament to her faith, she makes the sacrifice to call upon the Gods' assistance. Their necessity overcoming her pride.

Mizochtal's gaze meets Ilian with an intense fire. The Messenger's head twitches as the scent of blood filling the land sends a lust to its eyes. Ribs press against skin in a hungry inhale of battlefield scents, wrath causing a pounding heart to blur vision of rationality. Ilian begs in expression that Mizochtal stays still. Caseto will show no mercy. Caseto does not believe in the strength of gods outside himself. And his inability to identify his weaknesses creates a more dangerous monster than one may first assume.

"How dare you and your filth desecrate sacred ground," Mizochtal roars, an aftershock following the previous quakes shaking all around.

Caseto chuckles and turns his aim to the lion. Mizochtal raises an eyebrow, as expressively as a creature may, and bares its fangs to the Governor. Glaring through no more than slits, the lion begs Caseto to try any move.

"This land is of Micacao and therefore mine," Caseto announces to the forest and all within. An arrogant smirk falls upon his face. "These are my lands. My citizens lie within these god decreed lines. Lines bound by law. My law. God's law. And those who don't obey the law face punishment." Caseto's finger caresses the trigger. "And I, holy mountain lion, just so happen to be the judge."

Ilian leaps from his position as Caseto sends a pellet flying. The metal sphere penetrates Mizochtal's hip, forcing the great creature to the ground. With a lunge toward the Governor, Ilian aims to tackle him, offset his center of gravity. Caseto pivots and pushes Ilian past him. Ilian rolls on the ground as Caseto reloads the hand cannon. With a determined lunge, knowing time to be the only factor on his side, for his power and speed cannot surpass the metal sphere, Ilian pushes from the ground in a way only muscles formed from hiking up a mountain with lumber upon his back may, wraps his arms about Caseto, and pushes with all his strength, hoping to force the Governor to the earth. Caseto stumbles back and back, maintaining posture yet unable to stop Ilian's momentum. A sudden stop sounds with the sizzle of the sap burning through the Governor's cloak as Ilian realizes his effort led them both to the trunk of the tree.

Purple sap oozes and drips, moving as if sentient about the Governor. Constricting and absorbing, the goo corrodes the jewelry about his fingers and neck, connecting like leeches to his face and skin exposed by clothing burnt through. An obsidian glow enters his eyes.

The awakened, toxic miasma oozes from the tree, racing to the body of Mizochtal. In a flurry of bright darkness, the smog consumes the lion. Obsidian fur turns to coal fire as the malevolent parasite takes over. A low, rumbling growl vibrates the throat of the beast. The sentient creature turned monster by a ravenous disease.

Caseto thrusts Ilian from him with a single, forceful shove. Ilian falls to the ground with a grunt but bites his lip to prevent any other sound from leaving. Caseto brushes dried specks of the purple amber from his clothing and peers at the beast.

"Now is the time I send you to the grave. You and any memory of your gods will perish. May they save you while they still can."

An explosion sounds as the pellet leaves the barrel. The pellet hits the fur of the lion with a burst of soot. The splatter dissipates to reveal no wound.

"Dreaded beast of a calamitous forum. I shall banish you and any tale or deed of your dreaded existence from this land. Your only lot, death!" Caseto exclaims, a slight trill ringing through his voice. Another pellet fires.

An eruption of smoke covers the beast's face. The pellet struck an eye. As if an eruption from a volcano, a crack of thunder from the roar of the lion causes the forest to tremble.

"Damned, cursed creature."

Caseto fumbles with another metal pellet. Despite his haste to clear debris from the barrel, he loses precious time.

The creature that was once Mizochtal stares down the Governor. Caseto's power over the land and its people appeared miniscule in the shadow of strength and stature of the Messenger of the God of the Forest.

Caseto takes aim at the jet fur of the mountain lion's chest, purple pustules oozing with toxic streams. Corrupted flesh meets tormented eyes, on two accounts.

The explosion of pressure rockets through the air. Caseto holds his breath, bloodshot eyes burning from his inability to blink. He mustn't miss the legend waiting to be written. To witness the godly creature's last breath. A divine end that he caused. Arrogance, excitement, and fear dance within him.

The pellet pierces the wall of fur. With not even a flinch, tentacle-like hair halts the metal sphere and consumes it. The corrupted beast, one which had never appeared quite mortal or the other, shines with a stature of invincibility.

Time freezes about them.

Caseto and the beast that was once Mizochtal hold gaze, one upon the other.

Before another toxic drop could drip from a wilting leaf of the World Tree and to the earth, the mountain lion pounces at the Governor. Every future venture vanishes as the fangs close about his face. Screams are muffled by the sizzling of fabric and skin encountering the acrid, acidic ooze. Globules of slime consume the Governor like a shroud, eliminating any ability to identify who the being is. Flesh melts away. If godly powers were ever to have been present, Ilian believes this would be the God King's moment to use them.

But there is no spectacular explosion of light.

No heavenly entities float down to offer their wards of protection and healing.

There is no evidence reincarnation or salvation will ever take place.

Immortality is not a power the supposed God King possesses.

Caseto will no longer draw breath from the air they breathe.

Ilian's instinct to protect the Governor at all costs subsides as the weight lifts from his shoulders. Guilt finds no company in him.

As the form sinks into the ground, the lion moves its gaze to Ilian. Barred fangs beg the soldier to make the first move. No god could help him now.

A glimmer enters Ilian's peripheral vision.

The sword.

Ilian pushes off into a sprint. He trusted his speed against other men, but doubts emerge with outrunning a wild beast.

The demonic form of Mizochtal pounces. Ilian dives and tucks into a roll, the lion's outstretched claws arching to scrape his jacket as it flies over. Ilian catches himself and lunges forward.

The beast twists its body and snarls.

Sliding across the earth, Ilian's fingers wrap about the grip of the sword. A glow illuminates like a bolt of lightning lives within the crystal blade. With a forceful grunt, Ilian pierces through the chest of the beast.

The lifeless carcass falls on Ilian's outstretched feet, a weight crushing his ankles and shins sufficient to bruise for weeks to come. He wiggles his feet from beneath the body and shoves the beast to his side and exhales in relief. A prayer thinks to form, but he knows not whom to thank. Which god will listen? Which god exists to do so? And which god will care?

The being that was once Mizochtal disintegrates into a million cockroaches running across the soil until disappearing into the forest. At the core of the being, a black lion cub lays curled into a ball.

Ilian reaches for the creature.

Light reflects from its eyes as the first sign of life enters it. The lion stumbles into a run toward the font at the base of the tree.

As it hits an invisible wall, its body evaporates into dust, which settles into the soil, unrecognizable from the dirt and sediment present.

As he stands from the ground, his gaze passes the mutilated face of the Governor. He doubts a fairer fate had been granted to many.

"Is it over?" Ilian questions.

"Not yet."

Cordaya eyes the World Tree. Pustules continue to pop, and wisps of toxic fumes float into the canopy. She hovers her hand above the corrupted bark and winces at the burning sensation to caress her palm.

Ilian peers at the tree then turns his attention to its reflection in the blade of the sword. His eyes meet hers.

He tosses her the sword which truly belonged to her all along. Mere contact with her skin causes a shimmer which turns to perpetual glow.

Cordaya raises the sword with one hand, her other arm also extended toward the heavens.

"God of the Skies, grant to me your swiftness. God of the Seas, grant to me your strength. God of the Earth, grant to me your steadfastness."

Cordaya bit her lip in the brief silence to pass.

"Oh God, my God of the Forest. Grant to me your forgiveness. As a sprout plucked from the dying bush, you will be revitalized. May your roots, that go deeper and spread farther than any evil, provide.

And for your forgiveness, I grant you this promise. May I be your servant as long as life shall lend me the ability.

Hear my prayer."

A whirring hum resonates through the forest. Unseen eyes of a million creatures watch on, or so Ilian feels of their presences.

Cordaya draws the sword behind her. With a quaking inhale, she swings at the trunk of the tree. Ilian expects many problems but none of which come to pass.

As if slicing through with no friction, the sword passes through a third of the trunk. A guttural wail resounds. Liquid particles take flight and slither away upon landing.

Cordaya withdraws the sword and slashes again.

The sword arrives a little ways past midpoint.

Tentacles shoot forth in an attempt to loose the sword from Cordaya's grip. She swats at them with her free hand. As she places a foot on the trunk for leverage in removing the sword, a thorny vine wraps about her ankle.

Ilian's eyes grow wide.

He attempts to move to help her, but his ankles are fixed to the earth as his feet sink into the mud that had not been there previous. It holds him like quicksand. He struggles to find his balance from the attempt and falls forward.

Cordaya fights the vine, wincing as the thorns prick her skin. Warm, crimson blood runs from the wounds and drips to the ground.

The twig beings that roam these lands peek their heads from the bushes and move toward Cordaya. Glowing eyes examine the vines, moving toward the tree with caution. The first forest spirit to reach the vine opens a chasm simulating a mouth and gnaws away. The other spirits follow suit.

Each vine constricting Cordaya goes limp and falls away as their life source is cut off. The spirits step back. Glowing eyes grow dim and their bodies dissolve away. They make no sound nor express emotion. The spirits vanish.

Cordaya collects her breath, grips tight to the sword, and swings the fatal blow to the trunk of the tree.

As the sword passes through the other end of the trunk, it turns to dust before their eyes. Cordaya peers at her empty hands, hoping the God of the Forest will forgive.

Ilian examines the trajectory of the falling tree and gasps. He digs his elbows into the dirt and manages to crawl himself to freedom. Kicking off the ground to a standing sprint, he wraps his arms about Cordaya and tackles her to the ground.

The tree accelerating toward her bursts into a million pieces. Shock and awe cover their faces. The golden leaves that had been losing life transform into yellow butterflies. The extravagant maze of branches turns to the tails of the quetzals that take flight. Violet bubbles that had escaped the trunk to spread their corruption swiftly transfigure into hummingbirds.

A tear streaks down Ilian's cheek.

His own tear.

He never imagined crying in astonishment of the glory of a God's beauty. The other soldiers would have bullied him had they seen it. But many of them were now lost to the forest.

The creatures take off in all directions, called to the wind and skies above. In rainbows shooting through the canopy. Good, uncorrupted, simple good and beauty absorb any negative energy or tension the air once held. In its release, fresh gusts of wind assist the wings and allow a rainfall of petals from adjacent fruit trees. The rotten fruit falls, fertilizer for the earth. Perfume from new flower blooms and fresh growth rush to their noses in a pleasant whir of tranquility. Then calm.

A silent calm that arrives after the storm. When the clouds open to reveal the sun's rays. Moisture that once accumulated on the ground dissipates. Doors and windows open. Birds take flight and insects sing their songs. But it comes in silence. A drowned out silence that slowly adjusts to normalcy. The pounding of the rain and the thunder the only comparison in that moment. The transition jolts, an odd sensation courses through. But calm nonetheless.

"Now it's over," Cordaya states.

She crawls to the stump of the World Tree and places her hand upon its bark. Her eyes close and she issues a prayer, one between no more than herself and the gods. Ilian observes the speed at which her lips move. It is no prayer, carefully crafted, no fear of misinterpretation or poor word choice. She speaks from the heart, from the soul. And the gods surely listen to every syllable.

Ilian scans the forest floor and spots Liza. She stirs from her deep sleep and sits up. After a few deep breaths, she raises her eyepatch, wipes her face with her sleeve, and focuses on breathing. Ilian walks to meet her.

"How are you?"

"I've been better."

Ilian kneels down and plays with the blades of grass near his feet. He finds a metal pellet, semi buried in the soil. Displacing the dirt with his fingers, Ilian retrieves the sphere. He offers it to Liza. She releases an audible exhale.

"I don't believe I want to see one of those ever again."

She grabs the pellet and rolls it around in her hand. Her eye finds Cordaya and the stump. Memory strikes. With a jump, Liza looks about her, trying to identify any further presences. She touches where her wound once was, no blood nor pain emanate from the spot.

"I thought," Liza pauses. She shakes her head and looks to the grey clouds forming overhead. "I feel owed an explanation."

"We'll have plenty of time for that."

Water droplets find their way through the canopy.

Cordaya approaches the two and avoids eye contact.

"We should leave. We have overstayed our welcome."

Without questioning the decision, the small group walk the path of the forest back to the road. Cordaya leads the way, followed by Liza then Ilian. The shadows do not move nor do they watch. All is quiet but from the rain hitting the leaves and the ground. Ilian turns behind for a moment and catches the glance of a glimmer. As if sun catching glass. But there is no light present to make it possible.

Ilian smiles.

He will never doubt the possibilities again.

Chapter Eighteen

The drizzle sprinkles the dirt road, puddles with slick mud forming under their feet. Liza rides on Pinto, exhausted and holding her arms as she shivers. Cordaya and Ilian trudge alongside. Silence fills their journey. None have anything left to say. Not even the creatures of the forest speak.

They arrive at the metal door, the bougainvillea petals stuck to the concrete step as the wind has previously whisked the blossoms from the stem. Water flattens them to the ground, a carpet of celebratory confetti for the group, their parade to the door anything but joyous.

Cordaya knocks, feeling a stranger to the place she once called home. Ilian pleads that the Morezes are unharmed. He wishes to see them, to know the chance for normalcy still exists.

Nelida and Ernesto Morez open the door and beckon the group inside. Nelida removes her shawl and covers Liza as she enters, leading the bloodied warrior to the table. Ilian takes a seat, the same seat he took for meals and conversations many a time before. It feels different now.

Cordaya stares at the Morezes for a moment, her eyes glistening but her expression revealing no emotion. She exits the kitchen.

The savory aromas of refried beans and freshly heated tortillas greet him as Nelida increases the heat of the stove. He had never been so grateful for sense of smell, the comfort brought by the foods one so welcomed to the once Private Guard.

Cordaya returns with wool blankets, designs of flowers in flight woven through the fabric. Without making eye contact, she hands one to Ilian. He accepts with a grin, forced yet sincere. His quaking muscles struggle to separate the folds of the blanket and drape it over his knees. Damp clothes press against him. He removes his jacket and hangs it from the back of the chair.

Nelida sets down a plate of beans in front of him. Then she places an equally sized portion in front of Liza. She returns to the heated metal stovetop and flips the tortillas, taking care to swiftly grasp them with the tips of her fingers before briskly flipping. She places the baked and browning tortillas into a cloth laden basket and sets it on the table.

Liza peers at the food in front of her then glances at Nelida. Her lip quivers. She brings her hand up to adjust her eye patch, her arm blocking most of her face in the process. Ilian's lip raises to a half grin.

Nelida's smile grows, forcing her to squint. She grabs two glasses and dips them into a tall pot of water near the stove. Once full, she places the cups near the two soldiers and steps back.

The rain picks up outside, constant pounding on the laminate roof drowning out any opportunity for conversation. Thunder rumbles, singing its own chorus with the rain as its music. A cool breeze blows through the metal bars of the door. Warmth of the fire finds them. Comfort of silent company hold them in place. Empty plates mean nothing but satisfied hunger. There is no urgency, no rush to return. The gods would pause time for them if it was their will. But stealing moments of silence was no crime. And rest would quickly find them when they were ready.

That which occurred after their meal was like no more than a dream as Ilian awakes the next morning. The calls of the roosters as the sun rises over the mountains to shine into the valley fill Ilian with a nostalgia that felt years old. Sore and tense, Ilian rises from his bed to wash his face.

As he enters the kitchen, a smile spreads.

"Good morning. Come, I've prepared some fried eggs."

"Have any others eaten?"

"Cordaya and Ernesto both headed out already." Nelida catches Ilian's concerned expression. "Ernesto is helping his brother, Cordaya simply went for a morning stroll, I believe. And your friend has not come out from her room yet."

Ilian relaxes. He takes a seat and picks at the eggs with his fingers, drizzling salsa atop them with a spoon once he realizes the dish sits near. The tortillas are warm to the touch as he takes one in his hands. Rolling it up with his fingers, he takes a hearty bite. His entire body heats with the comfort and warmth of the kitchen and Nelida's cooking. Ilian sighs.

"You have my deepest gratitude for all the kindness and hospitality you have shown to a person like me."

Nelida shakes her head.

"You're spouting nonsense. You need more rest surely."

"I see now what my fellow comrades have done. I understand why any distrust of myself or any other government official or affiliate of the capital, was not unwarranted. My eyes have opened."

"And that is your doing. We have done as our gods have instructed, to try to lead a life of humility and love."

"And I have felt it. You are my family as you took me in no different than a son returning after a long journey. Though I was a stranger, unrecognizable and a world away in belief. Ignorance diluted my compassion and-"

"I would not hesitate to call you my son."

Ilian smiles, not knowing how he longed to hear pride in her speech of him. He so longed for the approval of others, the ones he sought to see him as faithful and dutiful. The approval of the Governor the greatest prize he had won, that which earned him honor and privileges afforded to none other. And despite this respect, the privileges afforded, he was never any more than a pawn. And pawns do not hold authority over any. One pawn does not move farther than another. Caseto saw him as a tool to be used when needed. He found Ilian's purpose, that which best suited what the Governor needed. But all pawns were no more than pieces to be discarded when no longer needed. Caseto made that very clear before his end.

To hear Nelida's approval, that of a proud mother, brings a tear to his eye. Ilian peers at Nelida to see if she notices, and as their eyes meet, a tear slides down Nelida's cheek.

Silence fills the space. Nelida brings a cup of coffee to Ilian along with a basket of sweet breads. Ilian shakes his head in disbelief of his luck after the tumultuous events of the past few days. His heart warms with the sip of coffee, knowing no other comfort in his life may ever compare.

"To know I must return to the capital grieves me more than I would ever expect."

"You have your family."

"Yes, but blood can only transcend so many layers before it becomes indistinguishable on the fabric. With these new thoughts, this new vision of mine, those I believed I once knew appear much different now."

"People will change. It is inevitable. But love and acceptance will always fill the space left by the growing distance."

Ilian chuckles and takes another sip.

"It is my duty to return. My oath to the people of Micacao. An election for a new governor must take place, and I should not seek to run from my post now." Ilian gazes about the kitchen, trying to memorize every pot, pan, sack, every tiny detail so he can easily recall it in his meditations, or as he sleeps at night. "If I cannot secure a place in the coming guard, I would need to seek employment elsewhere." Ilian offers a breathy laugh and shakes his head. "It's odd.

Not knowing where tomorrow may take me. At one time, I would have been anxious, hesitant to make any sudden moves. But now... now I feel as though I am not alone. The gods will lead me."

"You must give yourself some credit. The gods open multiple doors, but you must choose which to walk through."

For a long time, he had questioned whether his thoughts mattered. Whether every fear, every action, every decision was foretold, long written into the fabric of the universe. If the gods had their plans, what kind of meaningful existence could one hope to live? The gods had decided their apostles, their prophets, long before life was conceived. A breath, a skipped heartbeat, a false prayer, these were all decided before the person committed to that path.

Nelida's words coursed through the soldier, offering a breath of fresh life to every organ, every bone, flowing through every vein and interacting with every cell. A servant he had been born, bound to duty and no more than a vessel to enact the gods' will. But when the doubts arose, he knew it was not of their doing.

"Aye!" Nelida exclaims, searching a small cabinet within the kitchen. She kneels down, a hand offering stability as she lowers. Moving packets, jars, and boxes about in that small space, Nelida fails to find what she searches.

"I hate to be a bother. Would you mind one last walk up to the town to fetch me some groceries?"

A large smile crosses Ilian's face and he nods without hesitation.

Ilian fights a jogging pace as he descends the hill from the town center above, bags in hand of what Nelida needed along with a few parting gifts of food as well as his own stores for the road. He sweats as the heat of the day picks up, wondering why he never leaves his uniform jacket behind when fully aware of the weather patterns of the mountains. The chill of night dissipates quickly when the sun wanders over the peaks.

A lone wolf lay resting in the sun at the edge of the road, paying no attention to any that passed. Ilian realizes the stray packs were fewer and far between since his return. Perhaps the chaos and attacks had scared the wolves to new territories. Or perhaps their own lands were suitable for life once more.

The air on the breeze arrives with a fresh scent of blossoms and pollen from the harvests. A sweet smell of the bougainvillea reaches his nose as he nears the Morez's residence. Liza sits on the concrete step outside, wearing her uniform pants and loose black undershirt, dried from a night by the fire. She caresses a flower petal in her palm as her eye scans the road. The thoughts and questions swirl about in her head, her face reads tired and confused.

"How are you feeling, General?"

Liza gazes up at him and shrugs.

"Better."

A few seconds pass and Ilian realizes those may be the only words he gets out of her. Not wishing to press further, he steps toward the kitchen door. Her words stop him in his tracks.

"I apologize for my judgement, Private Guard. I hope you can find it in you to forgive me."

She does not look at him but at the pink petal in her hand. A finger follows the veins throughout, a maze of complexities within the tiny piece of life.

"I cannot accept that which is not due. Would it have been any other, I would have passed the same judgement upon them. You were performing your duty, both to the nation and the gods."

"I fear my doubts expanded more than yours ever did. I could not imagine returning to the capital, presenting myself in the eyes of the divine, with the images replaying in my head without stop. The gods would quickly deduce my lack of faith."

"Do not assume I did not carry the same fear. Especially being in the presence of one as faithful as yourself."

Liza drops the petal between her fingers and clasps her hands together. She releases a swift exhale, uncertainty and fear still present.

Ilian drops the bags on the other side of the metal door and joins her on the step. He watches a bee buzz from one flower to another, performing its responsibilities to not let down the hive. Its duty to provide food for the queen its sole mission, focused on the task and not hesitating despite any dangers that may be near.

"We owe it to the people of Micacao to return and assist in the election of the new governor. It is with our new knowledge, that which inhabits our minds and has been delivered specially to us by the messengers of the gods, that we will see a new Micacao rise. A new era."

"But what needs to change? What could possibly change to ensure nothing comparable happens once more?"

"Faith cannot exist without empathy. Without hope. We must erase the fear. Erase the thought of blasphemous doubt and distrust. Compassion must be our stronghold. Compassion must be that which unites not only the people of this great nation and world but create a connection to all other life within it as well."

"How can we establish such a precedent? Our minds have been melded from seeing that which the gods give. Our vision a witness and our words the only testament. How do our positions give us such authority?"

"We cannot force respect and trust. The gods will open the doors for many minds, but those individuals must choose whether they wish to enter."

Liza sighs and accepts the inadequate response of allowing the people their choice, unknowing if the people would be willing to bend to a new generation of thought. Abandoning an oath, one which devoted her to only one reasoning of thought and enforcing only that which she had sworn to, causes her to tremble.

"They have allowed me to see them, healing me, reviving me from a dying state. I should think to do no other than devote my life to them."

As they sit in silence, Cordaya rounds the bend further downhill and ascends toward them. Her eyes avoid Ilian's as she passes the Morez's and continues uphill. Ilian jumps up and jogs to catch up with her.

"How are you doing?"

"Well."

Ilian grins and shakes his head. The desire to work consumes her. A long morning full of harvest reveals itself through the dried mud on her sandals, dirt stained on her white, long-sleeved, cotton shirt and sky blue skirt with a pattern of monstera leaves embroidered with green thread into it. Her hair hangs out of the string she uses to tie the longer strands back, not having the time nor desire to fix it in between jobs.

"Where are you off to now?"

"Dona Kristal has asked me to buy flowers for the grave of her recently deceased son. Her fragility no longer grants her the ability to travel to the town center. I promised to drop them at the site as well."

"May I join you?"

Cordaya exhales, agitation not as apparent as confusion.

"Your governor is dead. It is no longer your mission to lead me from this place."

"I understand. But my oath is to assisting the people. If I can help in any way possible, I feel, in the least, it is my responsibility to offer."

"Fine."

Cordaya's response rings with humor rather than irritation.

After arriving at the cemetery, Cordaya walks among the stones until she finds the one.

"This is him."

She places the flowers, three stems of cartuchos, that which the woman could afford, on the stone. Ilian kneels at the grave marker and places the thin paper which he purchased as his own gift, atop. He works to rip the paper into strands and ties them together as Nelida once taught him. When finished, he hangs the paper garland, with bright blues, greens, and pinks, about the stone.

He smiles at the beauty of celebrating life in death, proud of his work and hoping any to lay eyes upon it will remember the woman's son with the joy he may have brought to the village. As his eyes lift from the sight, he notices Cordaya stares at him with soft expression.

"Well," Ilian starts with a laugh and gesture at his work. He wipes the sweat from his brow, the sun now at its highest point in the sky. "I'd say we work well as a team."

"You're returning to the capital?"

Ilian licks his lip and sighs. He takes a seat at the front of the stone, a downslope that overlooks much of the village below. The town center reveals itself as a mass of houses and many people walk around its cobbled streets. His eyes move to the Morez's residence and the other houses scattered further into the valley.

"Yes. Liza and I will leave tomorrow morning at first light. It is our duty to be there when discussion for the next governor convenes."

"And what will you say? Will you tell them how the governor died?"

"Perhaps. I don't wish to tell a story that would raise him to a position of greater worship, place him as a deity killed by an equal of power and divinity. History will know him by name and deed, that which will not be hidden any longer."

Cordaya nods and throws her gaze to the town. Smoke from sugar farms rises in the valleys of the mountain, clouds racing overhead as another storm threatens their evening. The wind whips Cordaya's hair about. Rays of sun break through a space in the clouds and find her. Her hand rests on her lip. At one time, she wore a leather belt with sheath of equal material. It was nowhere to be seen on this day.

"Did we do it? Will the world heal now?"

"Your guess is as good as mine."

"And what do the gods tell you?"

Cordaya glances at him then back to the sky. Birds fly overhead, the call of a toucan arriving from the mountain peaks behind them. Chickens cluck and caw as they march about the roads in search of insects and feed. Commotion of people going about their day's work echoes through the valley.

"A deed from one day will not repair generations of devastation. The gift was not rebirth, another chance. The gift is the knowledge, that which needs spread. Minds that need watered with information, grown in nutrition of that which is right. And when the gods choose, they will harvest that which has fully developed, that with no growth left."

She places a hand on the cold stone of the grave, issuing a silent prayer of safe passage.

"When you return, you must teach them. Teach your people that which is right. That which is just. The true gift is that which already lives around us. That which we make with our hands can assist or destroy. It is up to us to make that choice."

Ilian nods and stands.

They say their goodbyes to those who walk with the gods, with the messengers, as the spirits of the world. Hate, fear, malintent will never fail to enter a human heart. But hope, love, compassion will cure. Harvest the good, destroy the evil. Treasure the land and all its life.

A new day will bring a new governor, and with a new governor will arise a new chance.

Ilian finds himself alone on the concrete step when they arrive at the Morez's. His foot plays with a pebble and realizes a metal pellet to be on the ground nearby. Liza must have dropped it from her pocket, whether intentionally or not.

He picks up the sphere and rolls it around in his fingers. A curse, a blight. They cannot forget that which their hands have made. But now they have the responsibility to do better, to use it for better.

The sweet smell of rice pudding with cinnamon reaches his nose. The scent lifts him to his feet and guides him to the door.

The next day he would return to his family, but he did not needlessly allow that future to disrupt his present.

For he knew the bronze sun would rise another day, by the grace of the gods.

Author's Notes:

Hello, everyone! You've made it to the end. Thanks again for supporting me and the work I pour myself into. Check out my other speculative fiction under the name M. A. Morales. If you're into contemporary romance, you can check out my other works under the name of Elle Oaks.

Read on to get some Q&A about **A Garden of Glass Blades**, the inspiration for it, and what I hope you can get from it, even if nothing else sticks.

Please check out our socials and our website. Please also rate if you read all the way through. For an independent author, reviews are a great way to show support. But again, just reading is very appreciated!

Author Question and Answer:

Question 1: What was your inspiration for A Garden of Glass Blades?

My inspiration for **A Garden of Glass Blades** came from the period my husband and I lived in Mexico. For some background, we met in the United States but he is an immigrant from Mexico. After we got married and he received his residency, we made the choice to live for a short period in his home village in Chiapas, Mexico so I could meet his family and better understand his childhood and culture.

From the mountainous landscapes to the vast forests, there was beauty to be had. But I also saw the hardships of those living in these regions. Poverty was rampant. Wages were scarce. The sense of community and family were strong and those bonds were vital to the society all partook in. As so, religion was a large aspect of every individual's routine. I wanted to draw of that aspect of faith being so personal to the people.

As for Cordaya. The inspiration for her character came from the many women I met. From my mother-in-law to my sisters-in-law, I met so many independent, strong women while living there. When we went to harvest coffee or carry lumber, they would go with babies strapped to their backs. When it was time for our break from the harvest, they would still be working as they prepared the food for all. After returning from a long day of work, again they would prepare meals. The young women learn from a young age all these responsibilities, from raising their siblings and cousins to washing dishes and clothes by hand. On top of it all, the women were incredibly faithful and played large roles in contributing to society by running small shops out of their houses. Cordaya is an embodiment of the strength, the determination, and the faithfulness of these amazing women.

I'll get into the themes of the story in more detail below. I do feel it necessary to say clearly and with conviction that **A Garden of Glass Blades** was inspired by a need and desire for all to do better in this world. Our world. Caring for the environment and all creatures and beings that rely on clean water and air to live (yes, that includes us). Dismantling systems that aim to cement stereotypes and eliminate critical thinking by forcing us to question that which is taught to us and find our own paths toward a greater knowledge. Showing compassion and teaching and learning empathy. Understanding that so often we see violence as a means to an end, failing ourselves and the society we live in by refusing diplomacy and compromise. I will go more in depth below but I want to make it abundantly clear what I stand for and what **A Garden of Glass Blades** should convey to its audience.

QUESTION 2: YOU TYPICALLY write women as the leads in your stories. Why did you choose Ilian as your Main Character?

I do typically write women leads because I relate more with the feminine perspective. I also enjoy centering stories around women. So why Ilian for **A Garden of Glass Blades**? I could have gone with Cordaya, putting the most interesting character in the middle of the narrative. But I could not do so.

A common piece of writing advice is "Write what you know." While I know there is a lot wrong with this statement, I felt the truth when exploring my outlines of this story. I knew very early on in the process that Cordaya could not be the main character. It took me a while to determine who the lead would be. I chose Ilian for multiple reasons. The greatest reason of all was that Ilian had the most to learn. He was me and I was him.

We both traveled to places very unknown to us, that of which we'd been told stories and tales that seem to come from no more than hearsay. It wasn't a lack of empathy that failed us to create a connection from a distance. It was the distance itself. Imagination is a powerful tool. Experience creates a lasting impact. His character is quite a hyperbole to my own thoughts. Even though I listened and believed my husband with all he told me, the distance from that reality stripped away the emotional connection that I needed to truly empathize. Ilian had been fed stereotypes and fully bought into them. Only through experience was he able to understand that everything he had learned he needed to start to question.

I could not have done Cordaya justice. She is a character that I love, as I said, an embodiment of all those traits I admire. But the distance between her lived experience and my own was too great to justify writing her perspective. She deserves more than that.

Ilian felt like a more personal perspective. One of understanding. One of wanting to be the best person one can be and realizing just how much he had been screwing up as he experienced life in a way different than he is accustomed to. The doubt. The fears of disappointing others. The emptiness when the truth of reality hits in an unexpected way. These were all things I also felt. I connected with him. I understood him. And I wanted to see him grow.

QUESTION 3: IF THE readers take anything from A Garden of Glass Blades, what should it be?

This is a loaded question. I already laid out some of the inspiration for **A Garden of Glass Blades** above, so now I'll dig deeper.

First, this is a story about preserving that which we have been granted. The forests, the rivers, the creatures, all things living and not. Creation does not owe us anything. Yet, as humans we take and take without care. We owe nature, the world, for our continued existence. But we don't stop to take care of that which takes care of us. Entitlement? Maybe. I know we can't change the past. Just as the World Tree needed cut to sprout new life, humans must get rid of that which poisons. We must do better. It's not a do-over. It's a second chance. We can't erase what's been done so we need to do better going forward. It's hard. It will take society as a collective to want and execute this change.

Second, I tried to establish a dichotomy between Cordaya and Caseto. Both are powerful figures for their people. But while one represents fear, the other represents hope. If it was not obvious, leading through fear is what I would consider malevolent. Twisting peoples' emotions to ensure one can bend them to their will, even if that means leading them against their own better interests, is not only corrupt but disgusting as one should feel so entitled to a position of power to be willing to do so.

This can easily be seen in how each view their positions and the power they've been granted. Cordaya continues to work to help those around. Caseto places the blame on others, avoiding responsibility of his own. Cordaya considers herself a servant of the gods. Caseto considers himself a god. And the greatest difference is the source of their power. Cordaya has a glass sword which grants her the abilities of a renowned warrior. She considers it a curse. She believes abandoning diplomacy and using violence as a means to resolve issues is disgusting and immoral. Caseto and his people are gifted with the knowledge to build a handheld cannon. If it wasn't obvious, this is a gun... Caseto considers this weapon a gift. He believes that the ability to win wars and therefore impose their dominion and power over others works far better than diplomacy. Draw what conclusions you will about my stance on other issues, but obviously I prefer Cordaya's desire to help others and gain their respect as opposed to Caseto's entitlement and show of violence to keep power.

The biggest point that I hope to get across in this book is empathy. Empathy is the ability to feel for others and their situations and therefore create an emotional and fully human bond in doing so. Empathy is learned. To learn, it needs to be taught. Learning requires active listening. Teaching requires research and understanding. Compassion is also important, but more superficial. Compassion is the feeling. Empathy is the understanding.

Ilian starts this tale with a head full of beliefs that he believed to be concrete. His first mistake. He also buys into the stereotypes of civilizations and peoples of different regions. His second mistake. I did not like using the terms 'barbarian' for it seemed rather insensitive. The connotation that derives from the word is primarily negative. Barbarians are warriors, typically uncivilized brutes with no more in their head than a thirst for blood. Cordaya mentions that they may also have families and may also be fighting on behalf of one they believe to be right. She calls them 'mercenaries' (much different connotation). That is just one example of many of Ilian seeing others as less civilized, less human than himself.

But we also see him grow. Ilian's mind changes with the exposure to knew experiences and a different way to live. It took getting to know people and literally, not figuratively, walking several miles in their shoes. But it took him going there, living and experiencing life, to finally connect. To empathize with their struggles and come to understand them. It's not that Ilian didn't care before. He has a big heart, he was always compassionate to their suffering. But he failed to truly connect with their experiences until given the chance to do so.

So, what does that mean for us?

Experience as much of the world as you can. Read about other cultures and other peoples' stories. Research living conditions and possible socioeconomic inequalities in regions throughout the world, historic events that may have led an area to waste and poverty. Don't just listen, ask questions.

My husband told me many stories about his youth. I thought I could empathize with him through no more than hearing his story. But, when I traveled with him to his hometown, I realized how wrong I was. Tears filled my eyes on several occasions as I experienced that which he had told me. Guilt filled me to believe that his defense mechanism to such suffering was to joke about the hardships. It may have helped him cope, but it also prevented me from a truer understanding. That teaching was not his burden to bear. He had already lived it. It was my responsibility to dive into it and experience it for myself.

Do not place the burden to teach empathy on those who have been shown so little. Take it upon yourself to learn about the suffering and hardships of your fellow humans. One can ask questions, but not all individuals are looking to unload what they deem a burden or to relive those experiences.

Empathy is vital to the human race, to our continued existence. If you take nothing else from **A Garden of Glass Blades** please, please, please, stop to consider any biases, prejudices, and stereotypes you've been taught and fight against them.

Together we can make the world a better, happier, and safer place for everyone. We just have to want that for everyone.

THANK YOU AGAIN FOR reading **A Garden of Glass Blades**

Check out elleoaks.com for our other titles and get the links to all places they are being distributed.